P

"Alice Hoffm... ...s and lets us see and fe...

—AMY TAN

"Hoffman seems certain to join such writers as Anne Tyler and Mary Gordon . . . A major novelist."

—NEWSWEEK

"One of the brightest and most imaginative of contemporary writers."

—SACRAMENTO BEE

"Her touch is so light, her writing so luminous."

—ORLANDO SENTINEL

"Her novels are as fluid and graceful as dreams."

—SAN DIEGO UNION-TRIBUNE

"Showing the magic that lies below the surface of everyday life is just what we hope for in a satisfying novel, and that's what Ms. Hoffman gives us every time."

—BALTIMORE SUN

"A reader is in good hands with Alice Hoffman, able to count on many pleasures. She is one of our quirkiest and most interesting novelists."

—JANE SMILEY, USA TODAY

"With her glorious prose and extraordinary eye . . . Alice Hoffman seems to know what it means to be a human being."

—SUSAN ISAACS, NEWSDAY

continued on next page

...and her other bestselling novels

HERE ON EARTH

"Dark and wonderful ... Hoffman's most powerful and moving novel to date."
—*WASHINGTON POST BOOK WORLD*

"*Here on Earth* is Hoffman's 12th novel, and the spell she casts is stronger than ever."
—*ORLANDO SENTINEL*

"A sound addition to an impressive body of work."
—*BOSTON GLOBE*

"Sumptuous prose ... a way with words that can leave readers breathless."
—*DENVER POST*

"Hoffman conveys the mesmerizing lure of a lost love with haunting sensuality ... high drama ... assured and lyrical prose."
—*PUBLISHERS WEEKLY*

"Her books unfold artfully without feeling fussed over or writing-workshopped to death; her characters are idiosyncratic but emotionally immediate; her use of language is never fetishistic, just effortlessly right ... [In] *Here on Earth*, she plumbs the interior lives of, among others, a drunken recluse, a heartsick teenage boy, an angry daughter, a near madman, a cuckolded husband, and three wounded women, with such modesty and skill that she seems to witness rather than invent their lives."
—*ENTERTAINMENT WEEKLY*

"It's always a pleasure to read Hoffman's lyrical, luminous writing."
—*SAN FRANCISCO CHRONICLE BOOK REVIEW*

"A *Wuthering Heights* for the '90s . . . profound."
—*THE NEW YORK TIMES BOOK REVIEW*

"Hoffman's is a gentle kind of magic that exists quietly on the edge of our vision, changing and reordering small town and suburban lives . . . one of her most disturbing works . . . *Here on Earth* will disappoint none of her fans, and proves again that to read Hoffman is to have one's life enriched immeasurably."
—*ROCKY MOUNTAIN NEWS*

"Hoffman takes great care here to examine the many facets of love and relationships, turning them like a prism to reflect on March and Hollis. [Her] evocative language and her lyrical descriptions of place contrast sharply with the emotional scars that her characters must uncover and bear . . . Highly recommended."
—*LIBRARY JOURNAL*

SECOND NATURE

"Magical and daring . . . very possibly her best."
—*THE NEW YORK TIMES BOOK REVIEW*

"Suspenseful . . . a dark, romantic meditation on what it means to be human."
—*THE NEW YORKER*

"Hoffman tells a great story. Expect to finish this one in a single, guilty sitting."
—*MIRABELLA*

continued on next page

"Splendid . . . *Practical Magic* is one of her best novels, showing on every page her gift for touching ordinary life as if with a wand, to reveal how extraordinary life really is."

—*NEWSWEEK*

"One of her most lyrical works . . . Hoffman is at her best."

—*SAN FRANCISCO CHRONICLE BOOK REVIEW*

"Charmingly told, and a good deal of fun."

—*THE NEW YORK TIMES BOOK REVIEW*

"Written with a light hand and perfect rhythm . . . *Practical Magic* has the pace of a fairy tale but the impact of accomplished fiction."

—*PEOPLE*

"A sweet, sweet story that, like the best fairy tales, says more than at first it seems to."

—*NEW YORK DAILY NEWS*

"[Hoffman] has proved once again her potency as a storyteller, combining the mundane with the fantastic in a totally engaging way."

—*BOSTON SUNDAY HERALD*

"[A] delicious fantasy of witchcraft and love in a world where gardens smell of lemon verbena and happy endings are possible."

—*COSMOPOLITAN*

"Hoffman's best . . . readers will relish this magical tale."

—*PUBLISHERS WEEKLY*

Also by Alice Hoffman

PROPERTY OF

THE DROWNING SEASON

WHITE HORSES

FORTUNE'S DAUGHTER

ILLUMINATION NIGHT

AT RISK

SEVENTH HEAVEN

TURTLE MOON

SECOND NATURE

PRACTICAL MAGIC

HERE ON EARTH

ANGEL LANDING

Alice Hoffman

BERKLEY BOOKS, NEW YORK

ANGEL LANDING

A Berkley Book / published by arrangement with
G. P. Putnam's Sons

PRINTING HISTORY
Berkley mass market edition / October 1993
Berkley trade paperback edition / February 1999

The Penguin Putnam Inc. World Wide Web site address is
http://www.penguinputnam.com

ISBN: 0-425-16684-8

BERKLEY®
Berkley Books are published by The Berkley Publishing Group,
a member of Penguin Putnam Inc.,
375 Hudson Street, New York, New York 10014.
BERKLEY and the "B" design
are trademarks belonging to Berkley Publishing Corporation.

PRINTED IN THE UNITED STATES OF AMERICA

10 9 8 7 6 5 4 3 2 1

For Tom Martin

ANGEL
LANDING

Alice Hoffman

OUT OF THIN AIR

ONE

ONE AFTERNOON, IN EARLY November, the sky slowly began to change color. Although daylight saving had ended a week before, I was still not used to coming home from work in the dark. Now I sat in the parlor of my aunt's house, waiting for the phone to ring. I looked out the window, through the lace curtains, but I wasn't really watching the harbor or the horizon. I was imagining Fishers Cove as it was that first year my parents and I drove out from Manhattan. That summer was so hot that the pavements buckled beneath the tires of our old car. Twenty years ago the harbor was clean, we could see all the way to Connecticut even on hazy days, as we sat on the porch of Aunt Minnie's boarding house surrounded by the odor of sea lavender and clams.

In those days the house was full of boarders every summer. All of them bore the name Lansky, and no two of them looked alike. There were blond Lanskys and brunette ones; Lanskys who had known Aunt Minnie as a girl in Russia and those who had never met her until they stepped off the boat in New York, even though their passage had been paid for by Minnie alone. Some of the Lanskys were directly related to Minnie; others were related to her husband, Alex, himself a Lansky, a cousin twice removed through divorce and death. Even then I was not quite convinced that Minnie and I were kin—I was the only relative who refused to eat the vegetarian meals Minnie cooked for all the summer Lanskys; I was the one who refused to be a part of the Lansky chain letters—letters petitioning congressmen and governors to vote her way on certain propositions and laws. Still, I had spent as much time as any Lansky in Minnie's house, watching the August constellations through Uncle Alex's telescope set up on the wooden porch; Fishers Cove meant summer and long evenings, squash cooked with wild mushrooms, arguments, chess games, and beaches lined with green rocks.

But now Fishers Cove had been deserted by the summer people; they had begun to move farther east—to Orient Point, to the Hamptons and Montauk. If Fishers Cove had remained the same, Minnie might not have responded so quickly to my letter requesting a room, no matter how difficult it was for her to resist a correspondence. In other years there had never been a problem finding boarders, even in winter. The wooden floor at Minnie's glowed, the tea brewed at breakfast was a Russian blend sweetened with cinnamon and honey, there was a harbor view from every bedroom window. There had always been nurses from the Veterans Hospital or divorcées in need of temporary lodgings, there had even been an artist from Manhattan who returned for the deep sunsets in October and May.

When I arrived at Minnie's I found just Beaumont was left. Her sole boarder was the thin old man who had come to Minnie's after his stay at the V.A. Hospital in 1956. Beaumont had refused a bedroom with a harbor view and had moved into the basement, where he collected pots and pans and matchbook covers sent to him by all of the Lanskys who fondly remembered him, the boarder who came out only at night.

No one came to Fishers Cove anymore, not even the Lanskys; even they could afford summer places at Montauk or the Jersey Shore. And just as the town was forgotten by some, it was discovered by others. A series of builders had circled the area; the original port town had been surrounded by housing developments. There were two Fishers Coves now—the lower section near the harbor was ringed with the same huge Victorians that rested in the sun like colored lizards; but up above there was Harbor Heights, a line of tract houses which had replaced the marshes and fields. And on Angel Landing, the point jutting out from the far side of the harbor, where there had once been thousands of shells called false angel wings, a nuclear power plant was being built. The metal scales of Angel Landing III now rose into the sky with the terrible force of centuries.

The power plant was the reason I had returned after so many years—I had accepted a job at Outreach, a counseling center in town, and rented a room at Minnie's. But if not for that plant on the tip of Angel Landing, I would never have come back. I was here because Carter Sugarland followed nuclear power just as a dove follows olives, and I, in ardor and in haste, had followed Carter. Of course Carter could not make a commitment to me; he had told me that five years before in the hallway outside our seminar in group psychology; he was already committed—to Social Change, to peace, to the earth itself. Still, when I wanted to follow him to Fishers Cove, Carter did not argue. I moved into Minnie's house, and Carter found a place in town. He dragged a mattress up to the apartment, which had become the only regional office of Carter's antinuclear group, Soft Skies. There we would meet weekends and Wednesdays for lovemaking, marijuana, and endless games of hearts.

It was a Wednesday night—our night—and like the woman in love I considered myself to be, I waited for his call. My aunt walked into the parlor, and set her cup of tea down on the mahogany table. At seventy-four, Minnie seemed much the same as the first day I met her, nearly twenty years before. She had always worn her fine, long hair wrapped in a bun, and she was still impressively large, five-foot-eleven, tall enough to make heads turn on the street when she walked home from the market with bundles of wheat germ and radishes. Unlike most people, Minnie was not shrinking with age; instead she seemed to be growing, right before my eyes—in the morning, when I walked past her room, I could see Minnie's long feet hanging over the edge of the bed. Now, my aunt straightened her back and sat in the easy chair near the wood-burning stove.

"Tea?" Minnie asked me.

I shook my head. She had once tricked me into trying a cup of golden seal tea; the taste had been foreign, so strong it had stayed with me for days. "Not just now," I said.

Minnie sighed and lifted her teacup. "You're impossible."

"Not everyone likes golden seal," I said. "It's a matter of taste."

"I'm not talking about tea, Natalie," Minnie answered. "I'm talking about you. Everything about you. For instance, the telephone. The telephone was made to be used, it was invented to be used. You have to dial."

"I'm waiting for Carter to call," I informed my aunt.

"Aren't you always," Minnie smiled.

"What is that supposed to mean?" I asked. "Exactly what?"

"Why don't you pick it up? Why don't you call him for once?"

"What goes on between Carter and me is private."

"Women don't sit around waiting for men to call. Nobody does that anymore. Believe me."

"Carter's busy," I said. "He has a difficult schedule and his phone can't be tied up."

"Carter." Minnie nodded.

"Oh just admit it," I said in a flurry of anger. "You don't like him. You decided to dislike him the first time you met him."

"Well, well," Minnie said, raising an eyebrow.

"You never did," I said. "From the first time you saw him."

"Wrong," Minnie said. "Absolutely wrong. Of course there are things I don't like about him. I was never crazy about blond men."

"Well, I'm crazy about him," I said.

"But I do like Carter," Minnie went on. "Sometimes I even respect him. Though frankly, I, personally, would have never chosen him as a lover."

"Minnie!" I said.

Now I wondered: Had she heard us? The walls of the house were thin, the floorboards creaked, and twice I had persuaded Carter to spend the night, assuring him that Minnie could not possibly hear us from her bedroom down the hall. She couldn't possibly have known that sometimes, when we were through making love, and Carter fell asleep or left the bed to telephone Soft Skies organizers in New Hampshire or Cambridge, I turned my face to the pillow and wondered what it was that felt like a sob caught somewhere inside.

"You're afraid of honesty," Minnie told me now. "I've seen that fear in the people at Mercy, but in someone as young as you. . . . Face the facts—Carter isn't your type."

"I see," I said. "Working at that home has given you the background to make an in-depth psychological diagnosis of my relationship with Carter."

"Did I say that?" Minnie said. "All I said was he isn't your type. Love affairs are like shoes—they get so comfortable you don't want to throw them away. Throw them away, throw them away; why are you holding on to an old pair of shoes?"

"That's all very interesting," I said. "Not at all true, but interesting."

"Listen," Minnie said confidentially. "Do you want my opinion?"

"I'm sorry," I said hastily, "but I really am waiting for an important call."

"Wake up!" Minnie cried. She placed her cup and saucer on the table with enough emphasis to spill tea on the mahogany. "One day you'll wake up and you'll be sixty. Sixty-five. Seventy."

"Age does happen to everyone," I agreed.

"It happens faster than you think," Minnie told me.

"How about dinner?" I said, realizing that Carter's call would be late. "I could fix something for us."

"Not in my kitchen," Minnie shook her head.

"I don't see why you won't allow anyone else to cook," I said. "Not all vegetarians are as obsessive as you. Some of them will actually eat a meal cooked by someone else."

Minnie refused to answer; she waved her hand in the air and ignored me, just as she had ignored the facts she didn't care for all throughout her life. The Lanskys had all told different stories as they sat on the porch drinking lemonade. But they all agreed on one thing: Minnie had ignored the poverty and pain of her village in Russia. She had ignored American immigration laws and Czarist rulings and had sent for one cousin after another, marrying Alex. After she had transplanted an entire village of Lanskys, Minnie began work on the American system of government. Her personal method of revolution was the chain letter; each Lansky, forced by guilt, spurred on by memory, would write three copies of Minnie's original letter of protest—one copy would be sent to a government official, the others to unsuspecting Lanskys in New Jersey and Queens.

Everyone agreed—Minnie had certainly never asked anyone's advice on her choice of a lover, and she never minded that she was the sole admirer of her husband's poetry. For years, Alex had sat behind an oak desk in the round turreted room on the third floor. All of the Lanskys were wise enough to keep quiet when we walked past Uncle Alex's room; we had better, for Minnie guarded Alex's room like a sentry.

In the evenings, Minnie's long hair was unwound to circle her waist as she walked down the hallways, presiding over her poet's needed solitude. In those summers we did whatever Minnie asked; she was nearly six feet tall, and we children especially feared her anger. She, and not Alex, had organized the boarding house, and Minnie continued to manage the house after Alex's death, a death which came to him as suddenly as a sigh. Uncle Alex had collapsed at his desk, still writing about Minnie—his lifelong subject—still comparing her to a warrior whose armor shone like polished gold, to a rose that grew by the sea—still searching for words that rhymed with her name as he took his last breath.

Minnie had always believed she had cornered the market on love; she could not have imagined any woman not falling in love with a short Russian poet who longed for silence and the odor of the sea. No one else's love affairs were quite as passionate; no one else really knew the meaning of the word.

"Not everyone is crazy about poets," I said.

Minnie looked up at me quickly. "Oh," she said. "I see."

"I didn't mean it to sound that way."

Minnie reached for a piece of embroidery she had been working on. "I understand," she said. "I understand perfectly."

"No you don't," I insisted. "I didn't mean anything personal."

"Nonsense. Everything is personal. How could it not be?" Minnie stuck a needle through her embroidery ferociously.

"Listen," I said, wanting to make peace, "I like poets. I really do."

"Hah," Minnie said.

"Emily Dickinson," I offered.

"That hermit?" Minnie said.

I turned to the window, watching the harbor, trying to think of a poet, other than Uncle Alex, whom Minnie would approve of. It was then I noticed the change in the sky. It was nearly five o'clock, the time when the sky should have turned a deep blue. Instead there now seemed to be a peculiar border of light around each cloud.

"There's something out there," I told Minnie. The horizon seemed lit from within.

"Is Beaumont looking through the garbage cans again?" Minnie asked. "I've told him a hundred times he's more than welcome to look through the garbage while it's still in the house."

"It's not Beaumont," I said, going over to the window to push back the lace curtains. "It's the sky."

As soon as I spoke, we heard the explosion; it was ten times louder than thunder, and the echo alone made the floor vibrate with shock.

"Minnie, look!" I said. The sky had lit up with flames; sparks leapt above the harbor like dancers. Minnie ran to stand with me at the window; as our breath fogged the glass we watched the fire. Now sea gulls fled the harbor and dove to the sidewalks for shelter. The floor beneath us still shook, a soft tremor that touched our feet; Minnie's teacup fell onto the floor, spilling golden seal in an oblong puddle.

"It's happened," Minnie said. "Look over there." She pointed east; thick purple smoke rolled over the harbor.

I was as nervous as Minnie was, but my training at work had taught me how to deal with disaster, along with heartache and injury. "Let's stay calm," I told Minnie. "There's no reason to panic."

"Calm?" Minnie said, turning on me. "It's the power plant."

"Minnie," I said, watching the purple clouds move toward town, but smiling all the same. "Don't be ridiculous; Angel Landing Three isn't operating yet."

But Minnie wouldn't listen. "I wrote to Congressman Bruner ten years ago, when the plant was just a proposal. I told him this would happen."

Outside, the sirens had begun to scream; dogs gathered on

street corners and howled, their heads tossed back to the sky. We couldn't see the horizon anymore; the sky had become a terrible soup.

Minnie walked back to her chair and sat heavily. "This is it," she sighed. "This is how it all ends."

"This is certainly not the end," I said. I bent to pick up the fallen teacup.

"I always wanted to know how the end would come," Minnie said. "Not that I wanted to be there, you understand."

I stared at Minnie uneasily, hoping that she would not decide to give up breathing, or slow her heart until it no longer beat; by the time I discovered the explosion was nothing more than thunder, the flames no more than the backfire of a supersonic jet, it would be too late—Minnie would be motionless, her tall body grown too heavy for me to lift from the easy chair.

"Just stop it," I told my aunt. I went to the telephone. "I'm going to call Carter. He'll know if something's happened at the plant."

Minnie opened her eyes. "You're going to call *him?* I don't believe it."

I dialed the number; I let it ring seven times. "I'm sure he's there," I whispered to Minnie, my hand over the receiver. But after eighteen rings I knew the Soft Skies office was empty. Carter was neither asleep on the mattress nor at his desk addressing fliers about solar energy.

"He's not there," I conceded.

"Of course he's not," Minnie said smugly. "I wouldn't be surprised if he's already evacuated. People with money are always the first to go. I wouldn't be surprised to hear he keeps a private plane ready in case of nuclear accidents. He may already be on his way to Venezuela."

"How can you say that?" I asked Minnie. True, Carter was heir to the Sugarland fortune, money made in flour and wheat; the cereal named after his family had found its way onto most American breakfast tables. But Carter was estranged from his family; even in college he stayed in the dormitory during Easter and Christmas, refusing to join the family in Bermuda or Vail. "Carter's dedicated; he would never run away. My guess is he's at the power plant getting the story firsthand. I'll tell you what we'll do—we'll listen to the radio."

"The radio," Minnie said with scorn.

I dialed in jazz and a Bach concerto, but our local station, WSFF, stopped broadcasting after five. I couldn't find any news. "That's funny," I said.

"Funny," Minnie said bitterly.

"You're repeating everything I say," I fumed. "Did you know that?"

"Repeating," Minnie growled and then fell silent. We sat across from each other—Minnie in the easy chair, I in the rocker.

"Why don't we sing something," I finally suggested. "That will keep us busy."

"I'm seventy-four," Minnie said. "I think my life may soon end because of an explosion at a nuclear power plant. Just what is it you'd like me to sing?"

I reached for a knitted afghan to throw over my shoulders; I rocked back and forth in my chair. Certainly Minnie was wrong about the power plant; nothing like that could ever happen in Fishers Cove; the tides might shift, a new café might open, the flowers that grew by the side of the road might bud and open, but surely nothing more than that.

Minnie suddenly jumped from her chair, as if she'd been startled, as if she'd been bitten, as if her heart were about to give out.

"What is it?" I cried.

"Beaumont," she said. "Where is he?"

The old boarder had been the night watchman at Angel Landing III since the plant's beginnings. For Beaumont it was a job made in heaven; he hated daylight and loved uniforms. It was time for him to leave the house and walk down to the power plant. Minnie ran to the basement door.

"Beaumont," she called.

When there was no answer from the basement, I suggested that Beaumont was probably somewhere in the neighborhood rummaging through garbage cans before reporting for work.

"He was killed," Minnie sighed. "The first casualty of Angel Landing."

"He's probably having coffee at Ruby's Café."

"Coffee?" Minnie said. "Beaumont wouldn't touch the stuff."

It was then we heard the rattling in the kitchen; the noise was faint, as if a mouse were moving between boxes of granola in the far cabinet. Minnie nodded in the direction of the kitchen. When she switched on the lights, we found Beaumont just as he was reaching for a jar of molasses; the old boarder blinked and lifted his hands up to protect his eyes from the sudden flash.

"I don't understand how you see in the dark," Minnie said.

"I didn't do anything," Beaumont said, hugging the jar of molasses to his chest.

"Of course you didn't," Minnie said soothingly.

"I'll replace it next week," Beaumont said of the molasses. "I ran out."

"Listen to me, Beaumont," Minnie said. "We caught you just in time, we thought you might have already left for work, and you're not supposed to report to the power plant tonight."

"Yes I am," Beaumont said, squinting at us. "At six."

"No you're not," Minnie insisted. "It's a holiday today. The plant is closed, I'm sure."

"A holiday?" I said. "What holiday?"

Minnie eyed me gravely and then came up with, "Saint Elmo's Day."

"Oh," Beaumont said. "Nobody told me."

"Didn't you hear the fireworks?" Minnie asked Beaumont. "You know Elmo is this town's patron saint."

I kept quiet. I didn't dare to disagree, not only because Minnie quickly shot me a look of warning, but also because I, too, thought Beaumont would be better off at home, kept away from the explosion.

"I have the night off," Beaumont said. He turned to Minnie. "What'll I do?"

"You'll have dinner and then you'll listen to the radio," Minnie advised.

"All right," Beaumont nodded. "I'll have soup."

"Why don't you have dinner with us?" I suggested.

Minnie and Beaumont both looked at me, surprised.

"Oh, I couldn't," Beaumont said.

"He likes to eat alone," Minnie told me.

"Just this once," I said.

"I couldn't," Beaumont said, taking the borrowed molasses and heading toward the parlor and the basement door.

"I thought he might want company," I explained to Minnie.

"He doesn't," Minnie snapped. "Beaumont's been eating alone for twenty years. He likes it that way. There's nothing wrong in eating alone. He's a man of solitude; what kind of dinner conversation did you think he would make?"

"Well, I see that you and I can't have a conversation either. We never could. There's no point in trying." I left the kitchen, went back to the parlor, and stood by the window. Outside, the sky was finally still; there was no wind, no stars.

Minnie came up behind me and stood to my left. "I'm on edge," she said to me.

"Sure," I shrugged.

"I'm an old woman," Minnie said. "Sometimes I'm on edge."

"Listen," I said, "I understand."

My aunt held the lace curtain in her hand. "I think something's happened," she whispered.

By seven o'clock there was still no word about the explosion on the radio, and I began to wonder if perhaps Minnie and I had imagined the sirens and the smoke. But the sky was still violet, and water rings marked the wooden floor where the teacup had fallen. I made a fire in the wood-burning stove, and Minnie and I crouched in front of it, drinking sherry and eating crackers and cheese like two refugees. When the doorbell rang neither of us wanted to answer it.

"What could it be?" Minnie whispered. "Only bad news."

I went to the door anyway; Carter Sugarland stood on the porch. He hadn't bothered with a coat, he wore old jeans and a woven white sweater; he stamped his feet like a tired horse and rubbed his frozen hands together.

"Do you believe this?" Carter said, kissing me so quickly he kissed the air instead of my lips. "Do you believe this shit?" Carter whispered as he came inside.

"What happened?" Minnie cried when she saw Carter. "Was it the power plant?"

Carter shook his long hair and sat in the rocking chair. "Do you have any Seagram's?" he asked me. "With a little water?"

I went into the kitchen for whiskey and water, and when I returned Minnie was standing in front of Carter with her hands on her hips.

"Big shot," Minnie said to Carter. "You don't know any more than I do."

Carter took off his rimless glasses and cleaned them on a doily. "I know more about what happened tonight than anyone else in this country."

Minnie smiled. "Carter, darling, you're a wonderful boy, but you don't know any more than Natalie or I."

Carter reached for the whiskey and took a long sip. "I was one of the first down there," he told me. "I got to the gates of the power plant before the fire department got there." He turned to my aunt. "So don't say I don't know anything, Minnie. It took me fifteen minutes to get to the power plant; it took the fire department twenty-seven minutes. I timed them."

"What caused the explosion?" I asked.

"I get to the gate and show one of the rent-a-cops a phony pass. But it's no go, he won't let me by. 'Listen to me,' I told him, 'I'm going in. You can't stop me. I'm a friend of the earth, and I've got a right to know what's happening inside these gates.' "

"And?" I asked.

"And they wouldn't let me through the line." Carter drank more whiskey and then rubbed his hands together. "I waited around with the construction workers and the reporters but no one was talking. No one was saying a thing."

"Well I knew it," Minnie sighed. "I knew it ten years ago when I wrote to Congressman Bruner. Nothing but trouble."

Carter got up to put more wood on the fire in the cast-iron stove. "Don't be depressed," he told Minnie.

"I'm much too old to be depressed," Minnie murmured.

"This explosion may be a blessing in disguise. If this doesn't show Fishers Cove how dangerous their power plant is, I don't know what will. If that had been a working plant, hell, we wouldn't be here drinking whiskey. We wouldn't be here at all."

"You're the only one drinking whiskey," I said.

Minnie shook her head. "You're very naïve," she told Carter.

"Hey, I'm not naïve," Carter said. "That's one thing I'm not."

"They'll say this accident was one in a million, they'll say it can never happen again," Minnie said. "That's politics."

"Minnie, you're out of touch," Carter said, catching my eye and winking. "Why don't you leave politics to me?"

Minnie had gone to the window and stood in front of the white lace which had been draped there for nearly thirty years, long enough to begin to hold the scent of the harbor, just as if salt had been threaded into the fabric.

"Minnie?" I said. "Minnie?" I called again when she did not answer.

Minnie looked at me, and then turned back to the window. "The first summer we came here the harbor was so clear you could see the bottom, you could see the horseshoe crabs swimming in circles."

Carter stoked the fire. "Is it freezing in here?" he asked me. "Maybe I'm sick. Maybe I have the chills."

Minnie still hadn't moved from the window. I went to her and touched her shoulder. "I'll make dinner," I said. "I know it's late, but we should still eat. Even I can make a salad."

"No," Minnie said. She turned to face me. "I can't eat. Not tonight. It would stick right here." She pointed not to her throat but to her heart instead. "I'm tired," Minnie said. "I'm much too tired."

I called good night when Minnie left the room, but there was no answer. I heard her footsteps on the stairs, I imagined her fragile grip on the wooden banister, I worried about the rate of her heartbeat and her pulse. I went to sit by the fire; I turned to Carter. "I'm glad you're here," I whispered.

"Shit," Carter said. "So am I. Talk about being in the right place at the right time. I could have gone to California, I could have set up the Soft Skies office in New Hampshire, but I came here. At the right time, the perfect time."

Although Carter had misunderstood, I went along. "Are we in danger?" I asked.

Carter looked at me fondly. "I've told you a hundred times— the whole planet is in danger." Carter cleaned his glasses again. "There's going to be a lot of work to do. A lot of organizing."

When Carter pulled his notebook out of his back pocket and

began making a list of antinuclear organizations to contact, I went into the kitchen and brought back the bottle of Seagram's. When I returned, Carter was already on the phone.

"No long distance," I warned him.

"Just send the bill to my office," Carter told me as he dialed New Jersey and Maine.

I sat in front of the fire, drinking Seagram's from Carter's glass. I didn't bother to add more wood, I didn't stoke the embers or add more kindling when the fire began to die. On the other side of the harbor, firemen watched Angel Landing III simmer and spark. And here, in Minnie's house, the only sound was Carter's voice and the hissing of bits of white birch turning to ash in the cast-iron stove.

Much later Carter hung up the phone receiver and came to sit next to me on the floor. "I'm feeling pretty good," Carter announced. "Pretty damn good."

"I'm not," I said. I took Carter's hand. "Stay here tonight," I asked.

"Tonight?" Carter said. "I've got fifty or sixty more phone calls to make. I'll be up half the night."

"That doesn't matter."

"No," Carter said, pouring himself the last of the whiskey and drinking it quickly. "I would never ask you to do that. You've got work tomorrow. So do I."

"I don't mind," I said. "I don't feel like sleeping. I'll stay up with you."

"I'll tell you something." Carter touched my face with his fingertips. "I think I'm on the brink of something, Natalie. I can feel it. Something is going to happen."

"Carter," I said, "just tonight. I don't want to be alone."

"You're not alone," Carter said. "Minnie's right upstairs."

"Just tonight," I said.

Carter shook his head. "You should understand better than anyone. I've got to go home."

I thought of trying to hold him there; I would refuse to open the front door, I would beg, throw myself down on my hands and knees, whisper every fear into the polished wooden floor, whisper into Carter's ear. But instead I quietly kissed Carter's cheek, and then walked him to the door.

"I'll call you," Carter promised. "Wish me luck," he said as he walked down the porch steps jauntily, not hindered by a coat or a scarf, not hindered by me.

But I did not wish him luck; I stood in the open doorway, wrapping my sweater tightly around myself. Carter got into his old MG and turned on the engine; as I watched him drive away I wished that he was the kind of man who would have stayed till morning. We could have made love all night long, we might have chased away the phantoms who whisper in tongues when the night is too quiet, and not even the sea gulls call. I waited a little longer, wondering if Carter just might be the sort of man who would make a quick U-turn in the middle of the street, a man who might suddenly know as much about my fear of darkness as he did about the politics of kindness. But Carter did not return, and I closed the front door and went up to my room.

I had always remembered Minnie's house in August, now I couldn't imagine summer in these rooms; perhaps that always happens when a house settles, when there aren't enough boarders. I turned down the hand-sewn quilt on my bed, then went to the window. The sky was still not right; a purple cast clung to the clouds, alien particles had been left behind.

I pulled down the window shade; I didn't want to look outside again until morning, when the horizon would once again be a calm blue. But once in bed I found it difficult to sleep; after the hours of noise and confusion, the harbor seemed unnaturally quiet, and the house seemed to breathe, wood and walls exhaled slowly. Waiting for sleep, I thought of Minnie, just down the hallway, and of Beaumont standing over a hotplate in the basement mixing up a snack of molasses and oatmeal.

When sleep finally came I dreamed of white horses locked in a paddock racing close by a wooden fence, in circles, over and over again. They left their footprints in the sand; their hooves were phosphorescent, trailing ribbons of light behind them. I awoke before dawn, hours before the alarm clock sounded, as if I had been awakened by the clamor of hooves and quick heartbeats. Then I dressed hurriedly, to escape the chill, to avoid my bed and those horses which seemed to have left their mark on my pillow, and their restlessness on my sheets.

TWO

RUMORS DRIFTED THROUGH town. Angel landing III had been closed for nearly a week, paid construction crews watched as a troop of laborers cleaned up the debris. The explosion was no longer referred to on the front page of the *Fishers Cove Herald*, but purple smoke still seemed to hang in the air. Everyone in town was interested, everyone had caught the same disease: an all-consuming interest in the power plant, a driving need to find out what had happened, a passion for gossip. There was talk that a lunatic was loose: a radical fringe walked the streets at midnight, a cult whose members wore black met secretly at the edge of the harbor.

Even at Outreach, where therapists prided themselves on cool rationality, there was an odd excitement. In the days that followed the explosion Outreach was busier then ever; people in town had gone wild. Life decisions were made in a flash, bad checks were written, cars were stolen, marriages dissolved overnight. But though new clients streamed through the waiting room, I refused to be caught up in the frenzy. I stuck with my old reliables: an anorectic girl, a sad teenager who had been truant from school for most of his life, and one or two others who wandered in and out.

All of my cases had been forced into therapy by the courts, none really cared to break into the evenness of our sessions with private stories of sorrow and betrayal. To my mind, this was just as well. In these months at Outreach I had come to distrust the methods and techniques I had been taught in graduate school; none of the theories seemed to apply. My original passion for social work had not done a bit of good. Each day I was more and more convinced that my clients would never be cured; I had little hope that any of them would speak more than two sentences once they had walked inside my office. And so, I refused to let the power plant explosion affect me, though even I could not help standing at my office window, watching the sky and the harbor.

On the day when one of the networks sent a news crew out from Manhattan to interview local residents, Lark Perry walked into my office without bothering to knock. Lark had been a therapist at Outreach for more than two years; she had her eye on the job held by our supervisor, Claude Wilder, in time perhaps an agency of her own. Lark sat on my desk and ran a hand through her curly brown hair.

"I've been watching you, Natalie," she said, "and I'm worried. You haven't had an in-take in ages. You have fewer clients than any other therapist."

"I thought I would leave the new in-takes for you," I told Lark. "I know you like a heavy caseload." I smiled then. "I know you're easily bored."

Lark raised one eyebrow. "I wonder where your anger is coming from."

"Anger?" I said.

Lark smiled knowingly. "And envy."

In truth I had met with absolutely no success, and Lark had already begun EMOTE, a therapy group based on original techniques; she had admirers throughout the state, Claude Wilder spent most of his time covering his tracks, making certain that Lark did not walk right into his supervisor's position.

"I really think we should talk," Lark went on. "With your anger and envy, how can you hope to be a decent therapist? Something has to be done."

"You think I'm envious?" I asked.

"Do you know what I want you to do?" Lark said. "I want you to come to EMOTE."

I shook my head. "I'm not interested in cults."

"Cults!" Lark said. "Well, because of a 'cult' not one of my junkies is on drugs anymore, not one of my car thieves would even look at a Mercedes now. I'm meeting with enormous success." Lark twisted the silver ring on her finger, she began to calm down. "But that's not the point," she went on. "Sooner or later you're going to have to deal with your own failure."

"It's true," I agreed. "My work hasn't been going well."

Lark jumped from the desk and came to give me a hug. "Don't you understand?" Lark said. "You're wonderful, you're the best. But you have to get rid of your self-doubt. See yourself from the EMOTE point of view."

"I don't know," I sighed.

"I do know," Lark insisted. "I can help you."

"Do I need your help?" I asked.

"Are you kidding?" Lark said. "Listen to me, there's room for both of us at EMOTE. I could use a good assistant, I can't possibly keep up with all the cases referred to me. I want you to try it. I want you to promise me you'll come to an EMOTE meeting."

"I'll think about it," I said.

That wasn't good enough; Lark shook her head. "Promise," she said.

"All right," I finally agreed. "One of these days I promise to come to a meeting."

"And you'll take on more clients here at Outreach?" Lark smiled.

I buzzed Emily, the secretary in the waiting room, and told her I would be glad to see the next client who walked through the door.

"Satisfied?" I asked Lark.

Lark shook her head as she walked to the door. "I won't be satisfied until I see you at EMOTE. Maybe then you'll learn something about social work. Maybe then you'll learn something about success," she said as she walked out the door.

Each time I compared my feelings about work with Carter's I grew depressed. He was dedicated to a job nobody paid him for, nobody wanted him to do, yet he was happier than if he had sat on the board of directors of his father's cereal company. But now when I thought about Carter I wondered if I might also have a chance for the same sort of fulfillment. If I became immersed in work, if I followed Lark's lead, I might start to sing in the shower, I could find joy in social work, reasons for dedication. If Carter had not been a man who thought of his work not as a job but as a passion, and if Lark had not needled me and forced a second wind of hope into my sagging professionalism, I might have spent that day like any other. I would have studied the naked blackberry canes in the frozen ground outside my window, I would have thought about writing my letter of resignation to Outreach's board of directors, I might even have imagined a move to California or the Southwest. But it was not like any other day, and so I got Michael Finn.

When Emily buzzed me and announced that a new client had just walked through the door, I thought it would be a small-time thief or a junkie, perhaps the court had sent over a fisherman arrested in a local bar or an abusive mother forced into therapy by the law. I never thought, as I opened the door and reached for the case file Emily handed me, that it would be anyone special. When I went back to my desk Michael Finn stood by the open door, hesitating. His long hair fell over the collar of his leather jacket. He leaned on the door and looked in at me.

"Why don't you sit down?" I said, pointing to the chair on the other side of the desk.

"No thanks," Finn said, but he did come into the office then; he closed the door behind him.

The only facts Emily had written into the file were his name, his address, and his age—twenty-nine. I looked over the top of the manila folder. "You haven't been referred by the court?" He would be my only client not forced into therapy, not ordered to produce his psyche at a given hour, legally bound to bare his soul twice a week.

"That doesn't mean I want to be here," Finn told me.

His eyes were the kind that could electrify with just one look.

"Why don't you have a seat?" I suggested. "We'll never be able to talk this way."

Finn shrugged and sat down. He stretched out his legs and crossed them, obviously waiting for me to make the first move.

"Cigarette?" I offered the pack on my desk. I, kept it there for new clients under stress, though sometimes I, too, needed to smoke.

"No."

"Why did you decide to come to Outreach? You must have had a reason."

"I didn't know where else to go," he said.

"I hope I can help you," I said reassuringly.

"I doubt that," Finn said as he took a pack of cigarettes from his pocket. He lit a match, inhaled. "I don't think anyone can help me."

"If you really thought that, you wouldn't be here," I smiled.

"I am here, aren't I?" Finn agreed.

"Let's start," I suggested, but neither of us spoke. A thin scar ran across Finn's cheek, from his left eye to his ear; his wrists were knotted with long, blue veins. "Why have you decided to come for therapy?"

"I have to talk," Finn said simply.

"All right," I nodded. "Good," I said. "About what?"

Finn looked at me carefully. "I'm the bomber," he said.

I had been scribbling notes in Finn's file—"anxious," I had written, "extremely ill at ease." Now I looked up and met his eyes. "What?" I said. "What was that?"

"The power plant," he said. "I'm the bomber."

I put down his file and reached for one of my cigarettes. Carter had always warned me against the danger of nicotine, and it now seemed my breath was terribly irregular.

"Actually," Finn continued, "it wasn't a bomb. It was a valve

I reworked, and when it blew the gas tanks caught fire. But in court they'll call it a bomb, so I might as well do the same."

"Court?" I said.

"Eventually they'll figure it out," Finn said. "I've already been taken to the police station for questioning."

"Just a minute," I said. "Wait one minute." Michael Finn looked nothing like the bomber I had imagined. That bomber was taller, he walked with a limp, he carried a briefcase full of dynamite, and he wore black gloves. "Exactly how did you gain access to this valve?"

"I work at the power plant," Finn explained. "I'm a welder."

I shook my head. "I'm sorry. I find your whole story difficult to believe."

Finn brightened, he very nearly smiled. "Really?"

Perhaps he was one of those desperate characters who felt the need to confess to crimes they never committed. He would then be a client with a string of interesting pathologies, a borderline psychotic, a case of intrigue and neurosis.

"So you're the bomber?" I said. "And you say you've already gone to the police?"

Finn smiled briefly. "The police came to me."

"I see," I said. "They knew right away to come to you."

"I think they plan to question every power plant worker, they just happened to bring me in with the first bunch of workers. But it's only a matter of time before they figure out it was me. Every welder stamps the work he does with his initials. As soon as they find the pipes I welded, they'll know."

He sounded quite rational; truth was a vague possibility. "Have you gone to your family? Have you told them what you did?"

"My family?" Finn said. "They don't want to know. They think the worst without being told anything at all."

"You can't be sure of that until you tell them," I said.

"I can't be?" Finn said mockingly. "Yes I can. I certainly can. The police came to pick me up for questioning at my parents' house. My folks were ready to guess I was wanted for murder, manslaughter at the very least."

"Murder?" I said warily. "What's this about murder?"

Finn ignored my question. "Listen," he said. "Every thing I say here is confidential, right?"

"That's right."

"You can't repeat anything I tell you?"

"Morally and legally, I'm bound to keep every word confidential," I said, but I was beginning to feel cornered, I wasn't so certain I wanted the information Michael Finn might offer. Of course, in the same situation, Lark would have jumped, she would have shivered at the prospect of an interesting case, she would have delighted in stories of passion and crime. "All right," I said, "why don't you tell me more about yourself."

"What should I say?" Finn asked.

"Whatever comes to mind."

Finn looked around the room cautiously. His hair was the color of lions; his eyes narrowed with suspicion. He leaned forward conspiratorially.

"I can't talk about myself," he whispered. "Not here. Your office could be bugged."

"Who would want to bug my office?" I laughed, though I had sometimes wondered if Claude Wilder's desire for total power at Outreach would lead him to electronic devices and wiretapping.

"The government?" Finn guessed.

"Do you sometimes feel that you're being followed?" I asked.

Finn scowled. "Of course not. I'm not paranoid."

I wanted to keep him talking, I wanted to get to his dreams and delusions; I wondered if there might actually be enough material in his case for a journal article, perhaps the first chapter of a book.

"So you insist that you're the bomber?" I asked.

"Did I say that?" Finn said.

"You certainly did," I nodded.

"If I did have anything to do with the explosion I wasn't in my right mind," Finn said. "I could have been temporarily insane. Of course that doesn't mean I'm saying I did it." Finn paused. "I'm not saying anything at all."

I wanted to gain his trust. "Look," I said finally, "I didn't ask you to come here, you decided that on your own. Now you say you don't want to talk."

"Not here," Finn agreed. "I can't talk here."

"No one is comfortable at the very beginning of therapy," I said. When Finn didn't answer I tried another tactic. "Maybe you don't really want to start therapy at all."

Finn studied me carefully. "Meet me tonight," he suddenly said.

"Are you kidding?" I said. He had caught me off guard; my hand shook as I reached for my appointment book. "I can see you, starting next week, every Tuesday and Thursday. Sometime in the afternoon?"

"Tonight," Finn said. "If you really want to talk, if you want to know what happened, you'll meet me tonight."

"If you're the bomber, if you're really serious, you'll tell me what happened right now. Right this minute," I challenged. But Finn smiled and shook his head no. "Why should I believe you?" I asked. "Why should I meet you?"

Michael Finn stood. "At the high school," he said as he reached over and crushed his cigarette out in the ashtray on my desk. "Behind the bleachers at eight o'clock," he told me as he walked to the door.

"It's out of the question," I said.

Finn shrugged and opened the door into the waiting room. "I'll be there," he said before he walked out of my office, "even if you're not."

"Wait a minute," I called, but he kept right on walking. I went to the door, Finn was on the far side of the waiting room, he had already opened the door. "What about Tuesday?" I cried.

He left the door open behind him; leaves and sand drifted over the floor. At her desk, Emily was deeply engrossed in a paperback novel; a client, a young girl, waited on the couch until the time for her appointment with Lark. My voice still echoed, calling Finn back, but neither Emily nor the girl bothered to look up at me. Neither had even looked up as Finn walked across the room; it was possible that I had imagined him, perhaps nothing had crossed the linoleum in those few minutes but a few faded birch leaves, sand the color of pearls.

I went back into my office and closed the door. Finn had disappeared as suddenly as he had come. In his file were white sheets of paper, clean, hungry for facts. If he was telling the truth, if he was a man with no loyalties, a stranger with smoke on his hands, he might very well soon be quite famous. If he were to be my client I might be interviewed during the course of his trial; the *New York Times* would contact me, *Newsweek* would telephone, the *Fishers Cove Herald* might ask for a daily psychology column.

In the chair where Finn had sat, the impression of his body remained; the odor of his brand of tobacco clung to my clothes. Even hours later, when other clients sat in the chair, Finn still seemed to be there, no one erased the lines he had left behind.

Later, between appointments with the anorectic, who refused to eat anything more than grapefruit, and an elderly shoplifter who could not ignore the urging of vague demonic voices whenever she set foot in a department store, I called Carter to cancel our Wednesday night together.

"It's not that I don't want to see you," I explained, "I just have too much work."

"I understand perfectly," Carter said. "I don't have time to breathe. A busload of demonstrators is coming out from Manhattan tomorrow. We're going to storm the power plant at midday. I wish you could be there with me."

"Too much work here at Outreach," I said. "Much too much."

Tonight, while Carter arranged a protest at the power plant, I might be meeting with the bomber himself. I would hear information so privileged no one else could be told; I would be as close to the truth as an accomplice. If Finn was indeed the bomber. If he was not merely trapped by delusions, a man who wanted to confess but did not yet have a crime. Perhaps he was only planning a crime: a murder behind deserted bleachers, a rape in the football field, an assault, a disappearance.

"Maybe we should meet tonight," I now said to Carter. "I

can come over to your place. We could make dinner together. We could make love."

"Do you want to know what I think?" Carter said, "I think the best thing you can possibly do right now is dig into your work."

"Really?" I said.

"Really. Then you might better understand why I'm so wrapped up with Soft Skies. You might even decide to be a part of the series of demonstrations I have planned for next summer."

"I didn't know you were already thinking about summer," I said, more hurt than interested.

"I have to make plans if we don't want any more plants like Angel Landing Three," he said.

"Oh Carter," I said, annoyed. "You can't stop an entire industry single-handed."

"I know that," Carter said. "Hey, I know."

"Where do you plan to be?" I now asked. "Next summer."

"I want you to go with me," Carter said.

"Where?" I asked.

"I'm not certain. I'll be here until Angel is closed down, and then who knows? California, Oregon, wherever I'm needed."

"I see."

"I want you to go with me," Carter said.

"And just quit my job?" I asked.

"I have enough money for both of us. Two can live as cheaply as one."

"I see, you want me to dig into my job and then quit it."

"I love you," Carter said suddenly. He sounded so far away, so sad.

"Really?"

"I'll miss you tonight," Carter said. "I always do."

"Is that true?" I asked, but he had already hung up. By the end of the day I had made up my mind. I would leave Outreach and stop at the Mercy Home; Minnie would be finished calling out Bingo numbers, she would have read her last story in faulty Russian to an old woman who longed for lumps of sugar in her tea and the language she had nearly forgotten. As Minnie and I walked home together, there would be no reason to wonder if what I planned to do was right or wrong, because I had decided before I left work that day, before I locked the office door behind me: I would do what Finn asked; I was ready to meet him.

THREE

HE MERCY HOME HAD once been a bordello. In the early nineteen hundreds, when Fishers Cove was a whaling town, sailors who planned to stay in port for a week often did not leave for months. Sometimes, after meeting a particularly beautiful woman, they did not leave at all; instead they opened taverns and grocery stores and shoe repair shops, and even though they listened to the sea, they no longer really heard it; they had begun to see the outline of Connecticut across the harbor much more clearly than they could see the waves.

Now, very little of the house's past was left, except for the blue Victorian turrets. It had been gutted; stained-glass windows were shuttered behind iron bars; where there had once been a redwood dining table, a reception booth staffed by nurses now stood. In the dayroom, which had once been a parlor filled with velvet and flesh, a television set blasted to a line of captive viewers, an audience strapped into wheelchairs, too exhausted to move out of the line of the newscasts and the game shows. Just behind the double glass doors which had replaced carved oak, Minnie was waiting for me.

"Over here," Minnie signaled with a wave of her hand. "Here."

The nursing home had once been painted in bright, cheery colors, but that paint had faded years ago, and beneath sharp fluorescent bulbs the whole place looked dismal.

"Are you deaf?" Minnie whispered from the doorway. "Over here."

"What are you doing?" I asked. When Minnie raised an annoyed finger to her lips, I dropped my voice to a whisper. "I thought we would walk home together," I said.

"There's something I want you to see," Minnie told me.

"Tonight's my night with Carter," I reminded my aunt, though it wasn't at all our night any longer, not since Finn.

"Don't worry about that," Minnie said. "This will take a minute."

I agreed to follow Minnie into the dayroom. Inside was a row of elderly residents, most of them women. Though they faced the TV, none of them actually watched the screen; instead their milky eyes were directed at the wall.

Minnie crossed her arms angrily. "So now you see," she said to me. "Is this the way to treat senior citizens?" She shook her head sadly. "Very nice." Minnie turned to make certain no nurses approached us, then she poked me with her elbow, she lowered her voice below a whisper. "Their stockings," she croaked.

"What?" I leaned my ear closer to my aunt.

"Stockings," Minnie whispered. "That's what I wanted you to see."

Nearly every one of the old women's stockings had fallen;

there were folds bunched around their knees, drooping nylon gathered around their blue ankles.

"Don't they wear garter belts?" I asked.

"Garter belts?" Minnie laughed. "These old ladies don't remember their names, how can they remember garter belts?"

"They must be freezing," I said. "Somebody should do something about it."

"Hah," Minnie said gloomily as she signaled me away from the dayroom.

"Why do you have your coat on?" a nurse behind the reception booth called to Minnie as we prepared to leave.

Minnie stroked her camel's hair coat. "I'm Mrs. Lansky," she said.

"How nice for you," the nurse said as she approached Minnie.

"She's a volunteer here," I explained. "My aunt."

"A woman her age?" the nurse said.

"That's right," Minnie said. "A woman her age."

"My shift starts at five-thirty," the nurse explained to me. "I can't be expected to know all the day volunteers. Especially not by name. Isn't that right, Mrs. Lansky?" the nurse said sweetly to Minnie.

But sweetness was no use on Minnie now; she refused to answer the nurse; she growled low down in her throat.

I took Minnie's arm and led her to the door. My aunt looked back at the nurse. "That woman knows nothing about suffering," Minnie said.

Outside, there was a stiff harbor wind which coated our lips with salt; we walked quickly, Minnie took giant steps, I trotted to keep up with her.

"The situation at Mercy isn't good," I called to my aunt. "But I certainly hope you don't expect me to get into it. Outreach has nothing to do with other agencies in town."

Minnie stopped at a street corner. "You?" she said. "Not you. Me. I intend to do something about it."

"Really?" I said. "Just what do you intend to do?"

But Minnie didn't answer; she had covered her mouth with her long woolen scarf; she walked faster toward home and I followed closely, up the porch steps and then into the kitchen. Minnie immediately began cutting up carrots and broccoli, without even bothering to remove her scarf or her coat.

"The director of the home thinks I'm there to play Bingo," Minnie said as she threw the bamboo steamer onto the stove and lit the burner. "To read off Bingo numbers." Minnie shook her head. "But I have a plan. And I wanted a witness to see how bad conditions are at Mercy. Just in case."

"In case of what?" I asked, suspicious of what a woman who had spent fifty years writing nasty letters to congressmen might now do if provoked.

"They may ask me to give up my job," Minnie continued. "I wouldn't think of quitting. But whether they like it or not, I'm going to make sure that every woman at Mercy is wearing knee socks by the end of the week."

"Do you think it's wise for you to work so hard at Mercy?"

"Wise?" Minnie handed me a washed carrot. "Who cares about that? I'm talking about something important, I'm talking about warm legs." She started cutting up the rest of the carrots. "Eat that," she instructed me.

Right then Minnie seemed stronger than I, younger somehow. "Are you planning other reforms at Mercy?"

Minnie's knife was now poised over a bunch of radishes. "I sure am. This is just the beginning."

"All right," I agreed. "I'll write up an unofficial memo at Outreach. I'll be your witness."

"Naturally," Minnie said. "How could you say no?"

Suddenly I was tired. I had been trying not to think about Michael Finn, but it was nearly seven o'clock and Finn might already be pulling on his boots and starting to walk toward the high school, he might already be waiting.

Minnie stirred the steamed vegetables into a large cast-iron pot, she added tomato sauce and tapped the wooden spoon on the rim. "You don't look so good," she said to me. "Did you take your brewer's yeast tablet today?"

"Someone came into Outreach today and told me that he had bombed the nuclear power plant."

Minnie scowled. "Stay away from him," she told me.

"He's probably a liar," I said. "He's deluded."

"It might be true," Minnie warned. "But bombers can bring you heartache. Believe me."

"Oh, Minnie," I said. "What do you know about bombers?"

"Plenty," Minnie said. She poured the vegetable stew into a blue-rimmed bowl. "I used to be in love with one."

"You?" I said.

"He was a union man, a presser; he made bombs for the union strikes. In the summers, when he wasn't on strike, he came out here to stay with his brother." Minnie tasted the stew and pursed her lips. "He fell in love with me."

"While you were married?" I asked, astounded, not thinking Minnie had ever looked at a man other than Uncle Alex.

"Not everything has to be sex," Minnie snapped. "I know

what you're thinking. Nowadays everything is sex; back then it was love."

"Did the police ever catch up with him?" I asked. "Did he go to trial?"

"The police?" Minnie laughed. "This was the thirties. There was so much union trouble, so many bombers, nobody even bothered to look for him. Later, he became an antique dealer. He had a shop in Manhattan, on Seventy-second Street. He stopped coming to Fishers Cove after I gave him the brushoff. He never visited his brother again. But what could I do? I was too busy to fool around with him. I was married."

"That was a long time ago." I smiled. "The old days."

"Old days, new days, a bomber is a bomber. You want to be smart?" Minnie said to me. "Don't see him again."

During dinner I found that I could barely eat, although the vegetable stew wasn't as bad as usual. It grew closer and closer to eight; by the time we were having tea I had begun to watch the minute hand on the clock above the stove. I had to go; rules of etiquette, rules of the heart all seemed out of place; Michael Finn was too special a case, and if he was already waiting, he might become more and more nervous, he might even be thinking about leaving the field before I got there. Much too soon the time came; I lied to Minnie, assuring her I would be back early from Carter's, then I walked out into the cold November night.

The high school had been built between the old and new sections of town; it was a good walk from Minnie's, and by the time I reached the field my nose was running, my fingers were numb. There was a slight moon that night and the bleachers cast long shadows in the hard autumn dirt. When I had walked halfway across the field I thought I heard breathing, but no one was there, the only things moving were the oak trees which bordered the field. I waited for Finn behind the bleachers, standing among fallen leaves and empty beer bottles, watching the moon's reflection in the narrow glass panels of the auditorium.

It was after eight and Finn had still not arrived. If I had headed back across the field, if I had run, I could have made it back to Minnie's in ten minutes. I remember, then, that Lark's EMOTE group was meeting that night; I remembered I was in the field for a reason. When I closed my eyes it was as if Lark had found me. Envy touched me, purpose made me hold ground; I tried to think of the book that might spring from my work with Michael Finn. I wondered how high the fees were on the social-work lecture circuit. While I was thinking about fortune, anticipating fame, I suddenly heard something move, something was out there. I noticed now that there were owls in the oak trees; their wings fluttered above my head. When the earth behind me was crushed beneath someone's step, I turned as quickly as I could.

"Michael Finn?" I called.

"It's me," he answered.

I looked closely at the man who now stood beside me. He could have been anyone, an impostor, a criminal.

"I'm glad you're here," Finn said. "I thought you might decide not to see me."

The owls suddenly took flight; they hooted and called across the clear sky.

"This is a ridiculous place to meet," I said.

Finn nodded solemnly and went to sit on the lowest rung of bleachers.

"Sugar?" he said. He had brought two cups of coffee with him in a paper bag and now offered me one. I sat across from him on the bleachers; the night was so frigid, even the coffee didn't seem hot.

Finn's head was bowed. "I wish I had someone to talk to," he said.

Although he didn't seem to be addressing me, I answered anyway. "You do. That's why I'm here, isn't it?"

Finn looked up at me. "You?" he said. "I don't know," he shook his head. "I'm going to jail. I'm going for a long time."

"Why don't you get some of your fears out," I suggested. "Talk about it."

Finn smiled. "Going to jail isn't just a fear. It's going to happen." He spoke quite softly, but his words were fragments of iron. His eyes now seemed dangerously wide. I was there, sitting across from a stranger, I was conversing with a criminal in a forgotten, deserted place. The longer we sat together the more certain I was that Finn was who he claimed to be. His honesty and guilt were evident in every word, in the tension of his body. The man I spoke with was the bomber, the lunatic of everyone's dreams, the man our town feared most.

"Relax," I said.

Finn's eyes focused. "I'm scared," he admitted. "This isn't the way I was supposed to feel."

Slowly, Finn's voice was taking me over, entering my bones.

"Well, here's your chance," Finn laughed. "Do some therapy. Tell me that fear is normal."

"It is," I nodded. "It's perfectly normal for you to be anxious about the possibility of prison."

"Possibility," Finn smiled bitterly. Finn looked like a nearly perfect statue which had been damaged. "When I first came to you at Outreach I had a plan," Finn now told me. "If I acted crazy enough I thought you would agree to be a witness at my trial. I'd plead insanity, you'd give the evidence. But I don't want to do it," Finn said. "I don't want to act crazy, because I'm not." His breath poured out like steam, like the hard breath of a runner. "I don't feel like I'm crazy," Finn whispered. "I'm not," he said.

"Of course you're not," I agreed. I had to agree; if I had thought he was crazy, even for a minute, I could never have stayed with him. I could never have asked him to tell me what happened.

"I want to know everything," I said. "Everything that happened that day, everything that happened afterward."

Finn nodded, resigned. Then he reached for a cigarette, one of the dozen he would go through that night; his fingers were long, the fingers of a painter or a pianist, skin and bones much too fine for dynamite. When he exhaled, the smoke moved upward, encircling us, then drifting higher, to the oak trees. There were still some crickets who had survived the first frosts, but their song was slow, not at all a sound of summer.

"All right," Finn agreed. "I'll tell you what happened. But you don't have to testify for me when I come to trial. You don't even have to believe me."

That's what he told me, and I nodded, but I knew, even before he began to speak, as I sat shivering, that I would believe every word he said.

F O U R

INN'S BOOT HEELS ECH-
oed as they hit the cement when he walked from his car to the
gates of the power plant. It was too early for Finn to talk: he
was a man who was used to solitude, and any kind of conversation jarred at such an early hour. So, he simply nodded when
he recognized another welder; he nodded again to the shop
steward when he picked up his brass and the stamp which
engraved each welder's initials into every piece of work he did.
It was the first Wednesday in November. Finn had recently
turned twenty-nine, and he had already begun to think about
being thirty.

Michael Finn was a loner, and sometimes it got to him. He
spent his lunch hour by himself in his car, and he refused in-
vitations to meet other welders at the Modern Times Bar after
work. But today Finn didn't feel lonely. His bootsteps were
steady; and, although he hadn't bothered to shave and had had
very little sleep the night before, he felt alive. He felt ready.
When he reached his locker, he slipped a brown paper bag
inside before reaching for his protective suede jacket. Anyone
watching might have thought the bag contained Finn's lunch.

But Finn never ate lunch; instead he sat in his car, smoking cigarettes and listening to cassette tapes of the Rolling Stones.

Finn slammed the metal locker shut. When he walked down the corridors to the room he had been assigned to, no one would have had any reason to be suspicious. Other workers thought him strange, but not as much so as ten years before, when they found his long hair a personal insult. If Finn was not accepted, he was never baited or bothered. Even if he was known for his unfriendliness, even if he could work for days without talking to anyone, his father, Danny Finn, who was the foreman of the second unit of the plant, could be found at the Modern Times Bar every day at lunchtime; and Finn's grandfather, John, had been one of the union's founding members.

Michael Finn had been a welder for nearly eleven years. He felt like an old man, he wondered if he was aging too quickly, or if, perhaps, each working day somehow had lasted months. He was missing something; he had become different, had grown apart from the friends he once had. These friends had gone off to state universities upstate, or they had gotten jobs in stores, or joined the police department, one had opened a health food store in East Hampton. But after graduating from high school, Finn had gone to work with his father, and from that day on his back was in pain, as if the spine had somehow curved with sadness. And although Finn had rented his apartment above the sporting goods store on the day of his eighteenth birthday, although he could have invited someone up to his place for marijuana or to listen to records, he never had company. He was, suddenly, much too old for anyone his age. Even the women he dated rarely agreed to go out with him a second time; Finn was too peculiar, too wrapped up in silence, and his eyes were too blue. Often, the women he dated grew afraid, and when they talked about Finn to their friends they laughed in the hopes that laughter would help them forget Finn's piercing eyes.

Sometimes, when he looked at his own hands, Finn was amazed; they seemed more like his father's hands than his own—they were callused, and the nails were split. But that day in early November, the feeling of age did not surround him; his eyes in the mirror were filled with passion. His knees did not ache as he climbed down from the scaffolding when the lunch whistle blew; his hand seemed smooth and strong as he turned off his welding machine. By the time he walked down the corridor and opened his locker door, Finn felt truly young; he was dizzy with possibilities. It was then he knelt and picked up the brown paper bag.

If he had been caught, if someone had wrestled him to the floor and ripped the paper bag from his hands, nothing could have been proven against him. There was no dynamite, no TNT, not one Molotov cocktail. Finn knew nothing about dangerous explosives; it would have taken him months of study to learn how to make a bomb, and Finn hadn't had the idea for months. What he intended to do was not even a plan; it was more like a storm of thoughts that encircled him, so that every step he took was soft and far off the ground, as if his ideas had sprung from the sky.

When he first began taking a check valve apart in the basement, beneath the sporting goods store, Finn did not know exactly why he had brought home the two-inch black iron valve. The reason came to him slowly: he would create a fault. He reversed the tappet, and reamed the valve until it was half of its original thickness. The steam that poured through the piping system during testing would build up pressure and blow out the valve Finn had tampered with. An oxyacetylene torch unit was stored nearby. There would be an explosion. Suddenly, simply, all of the work that had been done on the second unit would be blown away.

Finn tucked the paper bag into the front pocket of his suede jacket. He walked in circles in the parking lot through the half-hour lunch break. He couldn't stand still, he couldn't sit down, he dared not talk to anyone. When the whistle blew once more, and other men returned from the Modern Times or the deli on Route 18, Finn climbed back up the scaffold carefully, as if he carried a sack of diamonds, or a bag of gold.

It was one-thirty by the time he had welded the valve into place. He admired his work; the welding was beautiful, as neat as a dime—so neat that the inspectors wouldn't think to X-ray the welds for porosity. Finn's work never showed the little air holes that could appear between the welding beads. No one had any reason to be suspicious. His initials would be in place. And what fool would stamp his own treason? Only a man like Finn, after eleven years with the taste of iron in his mouth and the smell of metal caught in his nose. It was not so much a calculated act as it was a last-chance effort; if his life kept on the way it was going, Finn couldn't have survived. He would not have wanted to.

That afternoon, at the end of the working day, Finn said hello to men he usually ignored. He thought, briefly, of joining some other welders at the Modern Times; but he knew he would have ordered only one beer, and he would have left it untouched. So, Finn left the power plant right on time—at four—and he walked across the parking lot to his car. That day Finn was certain that there was nothing left of him that anyone could take away. He sat in his Camaro, but he did not start the engine. And, as the other men began to drive away, Michael Finn waited.

It happened quickly. Only one apprentice, who lost half his thumb, was hurt—everyone else had already left for the day when the testing crew turned on the steam. Finn was not alone when the roof blew; other welders were gathered around the coffee truck, and Finn got out of his car and raced toward the truck. And he watched just as innocently as the others, as if some other man had caused the spark.

The first thing to go was the roof; Finn had not known a roof could blow so high. And when the fire on the second floor began, Finn had not imagined that the fire had a sound, its own hissing voice.

"Holy shit," the men gathered around the coffee truck said. "Fucking incredible."

Finn stood still as the sirens began to scream. "Was anyone hurt?" he asked.

"Who the hell knows," another welder shrugged. "Fucking incredible," he whispered.

The fire trucks pulled up, and their hoses began to splash water on the burning plant. Finn watched with real amazement as the sky filled with fire.

"This will put the schedule back a while," someone said, "and give us another year's worth of work." He grinned.

"Well, then," the coffee vendor said to the shivering group. "It must be an act of God."

Finn stood without speaking. But whenever he thought someone might have spoken to him, he turned quickly, as if he held his heart in his hand. When the other men tired of watching the explosion, when the firemen had drenched the plant leaving only sticky ash behind, Finn felt he had to turn away. He did not want to seem suspicious, but he could have watched for hours, forever. When he drove out of the parking lot, Finn realized for the first time that he had not thought beyond this one act of treason. To the other welders the explosion meant that their work would last longer—months longer, perhaps even a year. But to Finn the explosion meant only that he would not be able to sleep that night.

Finn did not go back to his apartment; and although he drove past his parents' house in Harbor Heights, it was just to make certain that his father's Buick was in the driveway. Finally, he wound up at a Burger King on Route 18, where he ordered a hamburger; but he found he could not eat, he couldn't even chew. He wished that he had somewhere to drive to, or that something special would happen, so that the feeling he had when the purple smoke filled the sky wouldn't go away. But he had nowhere to go, so he drove his Camaro to the service road alongside the Long Island Expressway. Because he had no one to race, he drove alone at seventy miles an hour, at eighty; the tires screamed when he made a fast U-turn and dust covered his windshield. And even though the heater in the car was broken, Finn slept in the Camaro that night. He pulled off the road, parked in the dirt, and covered himself with the blanket he kept in the truck to put under the tires whenever the car got stuck in snow or mud.

He rested in the back seat, a gypsy, a thief. Although the traffic on the expressway was like a moving lullaby, Finn hardly closed his eyes. In the morning, he drove to Harbor Heights.

He drove there every Thursday, giving his father a lift to work, so that his mother could have the car one day each week. It was the same as any Thursday morning. The only difference, when Finn pulled up to his parents' house that morning, was a patrol car in the driveway parked next to his father's Buick.

Finn didn't think twice, he didn't even imagine an escape. He parked on the street and got out of the Camaro. He walked up the gravel driveway, past the patrol car, past the Buick. Pieces of old engines Danny Finn had taken apart but never put back together again were scattered over the brown lawn like vines. The walk to the front door had never seemed so long, Finn's steps never sounded so quiet. And, if he had thought faster, Finn could have run then. He could have slipped behind the wheel of the Camaro and taken off to New Jersey; he might have gotten as far as Canada. He could have let his beard grow, and changed his name. But Finn did not think that way; his thoughts were too hazy and too slow.

Danny Finn was waiting for him when Michael Finn walked up the porch steps and opened the glass door. When Finn looked past his father, he could see his mother and two uniformed officers drinking mugs of coffee at the Formica table. Still he did not panic. He felt nothing at all, except for the tightness he often had inside his chest, as if something pulled at his heart.

"Now you're going to get it," Danny Finn said, and he kept a cigarette between his lips, so that when he spoke his breath was hot. "I don't know what you've done, but if you've done anything at all, if you've fucked up, I'm going to let you have it."

Finn didn't answer; he couldn't. He wondered if he was slowly disappearing.

"I'm going to make you sorry that you ever lived," Danny Finn said. "That's what I'm going to do."

But Finn saw his father's arm move. He knew Danny Finn's punch, and he had picked up his timing from the beatings he had had as a boy. And so, Michael Finn was able to sidestep out of his father's aim, and Danny Finn put his fist right through the door. The crash surprised both men; they stood watching as bits of glass fell on their shoes. Danny Finn's cut hand spilled blood onto the pile carpeting and both men watched the blood as if it were an intruder. Neither of them moved; not even when one of the officers ran over and tied his handkerchief around Danny Finn's hand.

"We just want to ask your son a few questions," the officer said as he kicked away pieces of glass. "That's all. Nothing to get excited about. We'll be questioning every welder sooner or later."

Neither man answered; neither moved. The sky was gray and pink, and down by the harbor, where the gates of the power plant stood, two construction workers were absent. And as if they had made a pact, these men did not look at each other, not even as Michael Finn was taken away.

FIVE

"THE POLICE QUESTIONED me for half an hour, then they let me go. But they know it was me," Finn whispered. "It's only a matter of time."

"Be positive," I suggested. "A lot may depend on your attitude. If you would try and think of yourself as innocent, other people might also believe it."

Finn shook his head. "They'll go over the power plant inch by inch. All the welders have been laid off for two weeks, but the company could have the plant cleaned up in two days. If they wanted to, if they didn't need more time. They know it's someone from the inside. They know it's me."

"It could have been an accident," I insisted. "How can they know?"

"They'll find the exact spot in the pipe that triggered the explosion. They'll find my initials. Then they'll know."

We sipped coffee; like passengers aboard a ship, we discussed the weather: storms and bombings and seas. Finn seemed without hope, totally lost in the aftershocks of his own explosion.

"What you should do right away," I said, "is get yourself an attorney."

"An attorney?" Finn smiled. "And how am I supposed to pay him?"

"Or her," I said. "It could be a woman."

"Well I couldn't pay her either," Finn said. "After they arrest me I'll get a court-appointed lawyer."

"But you need someone special," I said. "Someone who can handle your case; someone who can win."

"I could never afford someone who could win," Finn sighed.

Now I thought of Carter: he could still command a fortune with one telephone call, he could hire an office full of New York attorneys by selling off one small bit of Sugarland stock.

"Soft Skies can afford an attorney," I told Finn.

"No dice," Finn said. "Uh uh. I'm not getting mixed up with a group like Soft Skies. I don't want people to think what I did was political. It wasn't; it had nothing to do with Soft Skies."

"What does that matter?" I asked. "Do you want a good attorney or don't you?" Finn shrugged. "Do you want to go to jail?" I then asked.

"All right," Finn said. "But how am I supposed to get in touch with Soft Skies? What makes you think they'll be interested in me?"

"It's not a they. It's a he. Carter Sugarland. And he'll be very interested; he'll probably be willing to pay for the entire defense."

Finn eyed me suspiciously. "How do you know?"

"Carter's a friend," I admitted.

"Oh," Finn nodded. "A good friend?"

"Yes." I shrugged.

"I see," Finn said. "What do you get out of all this?" Finn now asked me.

"I really don't know what you mean," I said.

"You don't even know me. I could be a liar, I could be insane. Why are you willing to help me?"

"Your case is one in a million," I said.

"Thanks," Finn nodded.

"Of course you're more than just a 'case.' I'm interested in you, as a person."

"As a person, huh?" Finn smiled.

"All right," I said. "Having you as a client would be great for my professional reputation."

"Reputation," Finn repeated.

"I might get a promotion at Outreach," I said. "There could be some journal articles, maybe a book—of course, only if you agreed."

"I'll think about it," Michael Finn said. He stood and stretched his legs.

Now I was worried that I might never see him again. "If you come to my office on Tuesday I can arrange for you to meet Carter."

Finn ran his hand through his hair. "I don't know," he said. He spoke so softly I had to strain to hear. I concentrated on Finn alone; Fishers Cove might have been miles away, the field we were in could have been moving slowly in space. "I never even thought of being afraid when I installed the valve," Finn whispered. "Never."

When he spoke that softly, I grew confused, I nearly forgot why I had come to meet him. I nearly forgot the articles and books; I couldn't quite remember the importance of succeeding at Outreach. It now seemed to me that I was there in the field because I wanted to be there; I needed to be comforted. I needed to talk just as much as if I'd been wanted for a crime, just as much as Finn.

Finn had gathered the coffee cups together. Now he shook his head, and as he did he seemed to shake off his sadness as well. He turned to me and said, "It's late."

"It is," I agreed. I wanted time to move backward so that the night could be just beginning, so that there was nowhere else I would have to be. I had gotten lost in Finn's sorrow, in every word he had said; I wondered how it could be possible for me to ever find my way back.

"Do you want me to walk you home?" Finn asked.

"Better not," I said. "A therapist and a client are supposed to meet only in the office."

Finn nodded. "All right."

"Don't forget Tuesday," I said as Finn walked away so quickly that he seemed to disappear before his shadows had passed over the beer bottles and the fallen leaves. "Good night," I called, not knowing whether he could hear.

I walked through town, past the shuttered library, past Ruby's Café. When I reached Minnie's the porch light was still on. Even though the wind was strong, I stayed out on the porch for a while. Finn might have gone home to his apartment, or he might have decided to park his Camaro on some deserted beach, he might be looking at the same stars that I looked at. From where I stood on the porch, I could see through the lace curtains into the parlor; it was nearly midnight, but Minnie was still awake.

She sat in the easy chair, her feet stretched out in front of the fire in the wood stove. She was waiting up for me the way she had done ten years before. That was the last summer I spent at Minnie's, I was eighteen, far too old for the curfew Minnie imposed on all her nieces and nephews.

"You're home," she would say when I sneaked in the door at one or two in the morning. "Finally," Minnie would say with a sniff.

I turned the key in the lock and walked inside, expecting an argument. Minnie would ask me where I'd been; I would inform my aunt that I simply refused to be treated as I had been ten years earlier. I paid eighty dollars a month for my room; not a fortune, still, I expected some privacy. But when I stood in the hallway and hung up my coat, Minnie didn't rush from her chair to accuse me for my late hours. There wasn't a sound from the parlor; Minnie must not have heard me come in.

I went to the parlor doorway and looked in. The fire in the stove had burned down low; Minnie's shoulders were hunched over, tears ran down her face. Immediately, I retreated to the entrance hallway; I had walked in on too private a time, I had seen too much—much more than Minnie would have ever allowed. I went to the door, opened it, then slammed it shut. I wanted to give my aunt time to collect herself; I would come in again, I would avoid her tears.

"Minnie," I said after I had slammed the door shut. I thought I could hear her moving. "I'm home," I said loud.

"That's nice," Minnie called from the parlor. "That's fine."

"Is there anything I can get for you?" I asked as I threw my coat around, creating as much noise as I possibly could, arranging it so that my aunt and I would not have to meet face to face. "How about some tea?" I called. I had never before seen Minnie cry; I had not imagined that she could. Even when Uncle Alex died, she had stood stoically at the gravesite.

"I don't want anything," Minnie said from the parlor. "I'm reading a novel. Historical. About the Greeks."

My aunt was lying; there had been no book on her lap, only a white linen handkerchief. And Minnie never read novels, historical or not. "All right," I called to my aunt. "I'm going upstairs."

I put my hand on the banister and then stopped; I could see Minnie's profile, she looked like any one of the old women I had seen earlier, at the Mercy Home.

"Good night," I said. I didn't want to leave her alone, but I didn't want to force Minnie to explain her tears any more than I would want to explain the confusion which had been growing from the moment Michael Finn appeared behind the bleachers. "Good night," I called again.

"Yes, yes," Minnie answered, her voice urging me to hurry, to get up the stairs before any questions arose, before we had to confront each other. "Very good. I'll see you in the morning." Minnie sounded as if she could not wait to be alone once more, then she would hold the linen handkerchief to her cheek, she would return to whatever thoughts kept her awake at such a late hour.

I went right to bed, but I couldn't sleep. Between the sheets, beneath the quilt Minnie had stuffed with goose feathers, I tossed and turned; I could hear the waves in the harbor as clearly as if water were rising right outside my door. Somewhere Michael Finn slept uneasily; and here, in our tall house at the end of Main Street, something was happening, to Minnie and to me. That may have been the time I should have rushed back downstairs; I could have returned to the parlor, thrown my arms around Minnie and wept with her, I might have borrowed her handkerchief and asked for some comfort. If I had gone back, Minnie might have confessed some bad dream, and when her new tears washed over me I could have dried them.

There was nothing I wanted more than sleep; I would not have even minded dreams. But I couldn't seem to erase Minnie's tears, or the sadness that had lined Michael Finn's face. If I could have drifted off beneath the heavy feathered quilt Minnie had sewn years before I had ever come to Fishers Cove, I might not have been overtaken by a terrible feeling of being alone. There was no point counting sheep, and not even warm milk and honey would have helped; what was to happen had already begun.

ON ICE

ONE

*T*HE NEXT WEEK THE HAR-
bor froze solid. Sailboats and sloops were caught until the spring
thaw, the ferry to Connecticut would not sail again until April.
Winter settled, the tulips and orange day lilies seemed buried
forever beneath the soil. Slowly the temperature began to drop;
and on the day I told Carter I knew who had bombed Angel
Landing III, there was the threat of the first snow.

Carter was recuperating from the demonstration he had organized; protesters had been forced back by barbed wire and
mace, and Carter had been one of a dozen members of Soft
Skies who had been arrested. The protesters had been released
after forty-eight hours, on bail posted by one of Carter's attorneys. When the other Soft Skies workers had gone home, to
New Hampshire and Manhattan, Carter stayed on, planning the
next attack on the power plant and nursing the wounds barbed
wire had left on his skin. That morning I arrived at the Soft
Skies office at eight-thirty; I unlocked the door with my key
and found Carter still asleep on the mattress on the floor. He
had slept in his clothes, and because the radiator in the office
was faulty he had wrapped himself in two army blankets. When

I sat down next to Carter on the mattress I noticed that he had forgotten to remove his glasses.

"Carter," I whispered, "wake up."

Carter opened one eye; his glasses were smudged, he smiled slightly. "Waffles," he guessed. "You brought me waffles."

"When did you eat last?" I asked. The office had no refrigerator or stove, and Carter usually ate potato chips and cottage cheese. Occasionally he heated a can of soup or beans over the flame of a cigarette lighter.

"I'm glad you're here," Carter said, pulling me toward him.

"It's eight-thirty," I said. "I have to be at work in fifteen minutes."

"That's enough time," Carter nodded. "Come into bed."

"Listen to me," I whispered. "I know who the bomber is."

"Did you bring your diaphragm with you?" Carter asked.

"I'm serious," I said. "I've set up a meeting for you with the man who bombed the power plant."

Carter sat up and adjusted his glasses. "You know who the bomber is?" he asked.

"I do," I confessed, embarrassed that I had known for a week without telling Carter. But something had kept me from sharing Finn with anyone, including other workers at Outreach, and Minnie, and most of all, Carter.

"The bomber just happened to come to you?" Carter asked. "He just walked into Outreach and said, 'I have to talk to someone'?"

"That's right," I nodded.

"Holy shit," Carter said. "I'd better hurry." He jumped up and started looking for his shoes.

'You can't meet him until four-thirty," I said.

"But that's not for hours," Carter said.

"I can't help it," I explained. "That's the time Finn and I agreed on last week."

Carter stared at me. "Last week?" he said. "Last week?"

I cleared my throat, I shifted my position on the mattress. "That's when I first met him," I admitted.

"You've known all this time?" Carter said.

"Listen to me," I said, "we're talking about an extreme paranoiac. I worked hard to convince him to meet with you."

"All right, all right," Carter said. He sat down on the mattress and put his arm around me. "I know you wouldn't intentionally keep anything from me."

I looked the other way; the truth was I didn't want to share Finn with Carter.

"Where can we meet?" Carter asked.

"Outreach," I suggested.

"You've got to be kidding," Carter said. "We've got to find a place where nobody knows us. Down by the harbor?"

"Not there," I said. Our words would get lost beneath the gulls' cries and the waves; there was too much open space there, Michael Finn could run away.

"The Cove Theater," Carter smiled. "That's it. Perfect."

"A theater?" I asked.

Carter got up and leafed through an issue of the *Fishers Cove Herald*. "The early show," he said. "It begins at four-thirty-five." He came back to me and held both my hands. "I can't believe this," he said. "You're wonderful. I don't know how you set this all up."

"I just want to warn you," I said, "before you get too excited. He's not political."

Carter smiled sweetly. "Of course he's political. How can he not be? Bombing a power plant is a political act."

"All right," I said, "but let's just say it wasn't political, let's say it was a personal act, would you still help him?"

"I consider him my brother," Carter said. "Whatever his reasons were."

"Then I'd better tell you what he wants," I said. "He wants an attorney. A good one."

"I'll set it up," Carter said.

I got up from the mattress and straightened my clothes. "I'll see you at the theater," I smiled.

"Now, I know what he wants," Carter said to me, "a good lawyer. But does he know what I want, Nat?"

I stopped at the door. "What could you possibly want from him?" I asked.

"I want to use him," Carter said simply.

"For what?" I asked.

"The cause," Carter answered.

"I told you he's not political," I said.

"I don't care." Carter shrugged.

"Charming," I said.

"I'm just being honest," Carter said. "This bomber of yours can be instrumental in closing down Angel Landing Three, and he has to realize that if he takes help from Soft Skies he's automatically one of us. He just is."

"I'll tell him" I said as I walked to the door. "But he may not agree."

When I kissed Carter goodbye I felt as though I'd just betrayed him. I left him wrapped in delight, overjoyed at the prospect of meeting the Fishers Cove bomber, unaware that I had somehow been unfaithful, that my loyalties had shifted.

Now I felt as removed from Carter as I did from Minnie. Since the night I had met Finn, that night when I had found Minnie crying in the parlor, my aunt and I had avoided each other. We still had breakfast and dinner together, but we were polite, our conversation was no more than small talk. It had been six days since that meeting in the field and nothing that had happened since seemed real, time moved differently now, as if the second hand on every clock was stuck in honey. I was conscious of waiting, aware of every hour that passed.

On that Tuesday we were to meet again I watched the street from my office window. I wondered if Finn would really return, or if he would appear to me only once. My morning appointments each seemed to last hours, days; and at lunchtime, when I went across the street to Ruby's Café, I found I couldn't eat the sandwich I ordered, even coffee seemed much too heavy. My three-o'clock appointment was with Jack, the young truant, and I dreaded our meeting; often Jack failed to speak one word during our fifty-minute session. This week, however, was quite different; this week he had decided to talk about his aspirations.

"What I'd really like," Jack confessed, "is a motorcycle."

I didn't bother to turn from the window to answer. "Oh, Jack," I said, annoyed that he was no more realistic than he had been on the day he was first dragged into my office by the high-school truant officer. "It's eighteen degrees out there. No one drives a motorcycle in this sort of weather."

"Not for now," Jack said dreamily. "I'd ride it this summer."

"Really?" I said. "Your family can't afford anything like that.

With no education and no job, how are you ever going to get yourself a motorcycle?"

Jack blinked. "I know I'm not really going to get one."

I looked over at the boy, wondering if I had been too rough.

"It's all up to you," I said. "I'm sure if you really want something badly enough, you'll manage to get it."

"No," Jack said softly. He ran a hand through his fine long hair. "I'll never have a motorcycle. I was just dreaming about it."

Jack stared at the carpet, but his eyes blinked rapidly, holding back tears.

"I'm sure you'll have a motorcycle someday," I said.

Jack shook his head. "No, I never will."

There was a knock at the door, and I was grateful to have reason to look away from poor Jack.

"Yes?" I called.

Emily opened the door a crack and peered inside. "I'm sorry," she said. "I didn't want to interrupt, but there's someone here who claims to have an appointment."

I bit my lip; it had to be him: early for his appointment, Michael Finn.

"Jack," I said, "would you mind if the session ended now?"

"Okay," Jack shrugged.

"That won't be necessary," I heard my aunt Minnie say. "This will only take a minute."

"You'll just have to wait," Emily said, blocking the door with her body.

Minnie slammed a shopping bag against Emily's shins. "You're blocking the door," she grumbled.

"You're damn right," Emily cried, unglued and rubbing at her shins.

"It's all right," I said. "This is my aunt."

"Really?" Emily said, raising her eyebrows as she backed out of the office.

Minnie closed the door tightly. "Don't worry," she told Jack as she put down her shopping bag and dragged a hard-backed chair next to him. "This won't interfere with you. You stay right where you are," she nodded as she unbuttoned her camel's hair coat.

"You can't do this," I told my aunt.

"I wouldn't unless I absolutely had to. This is an emergency. I don't think he minds," she pointed at Jack. "Do you mind?" she asked the boy.

"Me?" Jack said.

Minnie nodded. "Because as far as I'm concerned, you're the boss. If you say stay, I'll stay. If you say go, I'm on my way," she told the boy confidentially.

"Please stay," Jack said.

"What do you want?" I said. "Briefly."

"This is the place to go when you're depressed, so here I am," Minnie said.

"This is the place," Jack agreed.

"But you haven't mentioned this to me at home," I said, thinking of our polite dinners and formal teas. "You've been avoiding me."

"So?" Minnie shrugged. "You've been avoiding me, too. And this is business. This isn't chitchat over dinner. I need professional help."

"I'll make an appointment for you," I said. "But I really think you should see a therapist who isn't related to you."

Minnie waved her hand in the air. "If you can't trust your family, who can you trust?" She turned to Jack. "I never thought I'd see the day when I needed therapy."

Jack nodded solemnly. "I know what you mean."

"Jack," I said, "is this really all right with you?"

"Fine," Jack smiled.

"I'm very depressed," Minnie told us. "Very." She stared at the ceiling with watery eyes. "Some nights I start crying and I just can't stop."

"Oh, no," Jack said.

Jack had stopped blinking; he watched Minnie carefully, and with real concern.

"Go on," I said to my aunt.

"Frankly, it's the nursing home. I've always been involved in this and in that," she explained to Jack. "Writing letters. Mobilizing my family. But this is different. Every day when I go there, there's another empty bed."

"Someone's died?" Jack asked.

"You've got it. Sometimes the bed is made—all tucked in very nicely, as if no one had ever slept there. Sometimes the sheets are rumpled. Once I saw a pillowcase stained with blood. Every time I see one of these empty beds I imagine myself lying there, not able to speak; I can't even call out or scream. I'm trapped in an old body. In a bed."

"You're identifying too closely," I warned.

"Of course I am," Minnie snapped. "I'm old."

"You're not that old," Jack said to Minnie, but he was too shy to look at her as he spoke.

Minnie smiled, but when she saw Jack light a cigarette she poked his arm. "At your age, you smoke? I bet you drink Coke, too. What are you doing to yourself?"

"Me?" Jack said.

"Take my advice," she said. "Fast for three days. Then cut out all cigarettes, meat, and chemicals."

"We were talking about your problem," I said. "Jack has the right to make his own decisions about his life."

"I could get into fasting," Jack said.

"Just water," Minnie told him. "And a little fruit juice in the morning. It will pick you right up."

"Doesn't it make you feel better to know that you're helping some old people?" I said, wanting to move on, away from the topic of Jack's diet.

"Old people," Minnie sighed.

"What about the socks you were going to bring for the ladies?"

"Those ladies don't know if they're coming or going. Those ladies are tied into their wheelchairs."

"The socks," I said.

"The socks are still in the drawer at the reception booth. The nurses don't want to be bothered."

"That's terrible," Jack said.

"Of course it is," Minnie nodded.

"You have to be realistic," I said. "You can do some things to help, but you can't fight the entire bureaucracy."

"Oh, no?" Minnie smiled. "I got myself some very interesting information. When the nurses were between shifts, I went to the supervisor's office and discovered that even though Mercy is funded by the county, it's privately administered. This morning I went to the library and looked up the board chairman in the Fishers Cove social register. The fellow's name is Allen Crest, and the most interesting thing is that he's married to Congressman Bruner's sister, Yvette Bruner Crest."

"For someone who's so depressed, you certainly have been doing a lot of research," I said.

"Oh sure," Minnie shrugged. "I intend to find this Allen Crest and see to it that he makes some improvements."

"There you go," I nodded. "You're helping other people, you should feel great about yourself."

"But who'll do something for me? Who'll take care of me? The Lanskys? I never even get a phone call from any of them. Not even from Ephraim Lansky, and that old man used to write to me once a week until his son bought a condominium in Atlantic City. Who's going to watch out for me when I get taken to Mercy?"

"You're perfectly healthy," I told my aunt. "You're not about to go into a nursing home."

"Not today. Not right this minute. But what about tomorrow? I could fall down the stairs and break both of my hips. That's how brittle bones get when they're old," Minnie confided to Jack.

"You can't worry so much about the future that you're paralyzed in the present," I said.

"Oh yes I can," Minnie said softly.

I looked at my aunt carefully: her hands, which were once powerful enough to direct a whole house full of Lanskys with one wave, were now an old woman's hands; the lines on her face ran together to form a creviced graph; her long legs were never warm, not even when she wore three pairs of woolen knee socks. There might soon be a day when Beaumont moved out of her house; I certainly didn't plan to stay forever; and then Minnie would be alone. The house would be empty; one day Minnie would be so frail that she would no longer be able to lift wood into the parlor stove. Death would come to her slowly; when she was found, weeks, perhaps months later, Minnie would be lying on the hardwood floor like a lonely artifact, her skin would be blue, and when she was carried from her parlor, the ice which had formed on her skin would melt in huge drops, and all that would be left to be taken down the porch steps would be an old woman who had frozen to death in her own house.

"Oh, Minnie," I said.

"I've never felt sorry for myself. Not in my entire life," Minnie said. "Not until now."

"I'll take care of you," Jack volunteered.

Minnie sat up straight. "At the moment I'm quite capable of taking care of myself, thank you."

"When you can't."

"He's cute," Minnie said to me.

"I mean it," Jack insisted, his eyes glowing with dedication.

"No," Minnie shook her head. "You have better things to do."

"I don't have anything better to do," the boy confided.

Jack spent his days avoiding school, drinking gallons of soda in coffee shops and diners; at three-fifteen he returned home to a family who would not have noticed if he never returned.

Minnie glared at the boy. "Do you think you'll live forever? Do you think you can just waste time?"

I cleared my throat. "Well," I said, "I think our session is over."

"This is it?" Minnie said. "This is therapy?"

"Did you expect to come to terms with death and old age in five minutes?"

"Yes," Minnie nodded, "I had hoped to."

"You can't expect miracles," I said.

"Well, if this is it, I'm very dissatisfied," Minnie said. "Very."

"Me, too," Jack sighed.

"You?" Minnie said to Jack. "You're too young to be dissatisfied. What you need is the proper diet. The right vegetables would fix you right up."

"Jack has other problems," I said. "School. His family."

Minnie ignored me. "Do you know what happens to people who don't get enough vitamin E?" Minnie asked Jack. "They disappear. Their skin becomes as thin as tissue paper."

"Minnie," I warned.

"My dear, it's a fact," my aunt said.

When Minnie reached over to my desk for paper and pen so that she could write out a personalized diet for Jack, I walked to the window.

I cleaned off the window with my palm and looked down at Main Street. Suddenly, he appeared; his face was hidden in shadows and I almost overlooked the man with the turned-up collar who shivered in the doorway of Ruby's Café, the man who looked into my window. It was Finn. "You've got to go," I said to Minnie and Jack.

"Just a minute," Minnie snapped, but she did stand up to button her coat. "I'm going to take an extra spoonful of brewer's yeast with dinner," she whispered to Jack. "It's marvelous for depression."

By the time Minnie had put on her hat and gloves, and picked up her shopping bag, Emily knocked on the door. I rushed past Minnie and Jack, and slid the door open.

"Do you have group therapy today?" Emily asked. "Because there's someone else who says he has an appointment with you."

"Send him in," Minnie called.

When I opened the door wider, there was Finn, peering inside the office cautiously, like a thief ready to run.

I went over to Finn and took his arm. "I'm so glad you're here," I said as I led him inside. Then I closed the door quickly to block any quick escapes.

Minnie handed Jack his diet, and then looked up. "Oh," she said. "Is this the bomber?"

Finn looked betrayed. "What is this?" he said, his voice breaking like a teenager's.

"This is my aunt, who was just leaving. And this is Jack— he has a problem with school—who was also just leaving. This is Michael Finn, who is here because of marital problems," I lied, hoping that Finn would not panic and flee.

"Ah," Minnie said. "He's married. Too bad."

Finn stood as still as a wild animal; he watched Minnie with wide eyes.

I opened the door and nodded to Minnie. "Your time is up," I told her.

"I'm going," Minnie said. "I've got some vitamin C in here that I'm taking over to the nursing home." She rattled her shopping bag. "But I think you could use a bottle yourself," she told Jack as they left the office together. After Jack and Minnie had gone, and the door was shut behind them, I could still hear my aunt's voice in the waiting room, prescribing five hundred milligrams of vitamin C each morning, and advising Jack never again to drink a carbonated beverage.

"I trusted you," Finn whispered.

"I wasn't certain if you really did," I said, feeling both pleased and surprised.

"You told her," Finn said. "You told that old woman about me."

"She's not an old woman, she's my aunt," I said. "I did once mention that someone came to me claiming to be the bomber, but I never told her who. I never even mentioned your name."

Finn paced across the room. "What if she tells someone about me? What if she goes to the police?"

"Minnie?" I said. "She would never go to the police."

Finn looked at me carefully. "Who else have you told?"

"Now wait a minute," I said, "I could get in trouble, too. I could lose my job for not reporting your activities to my supervisor. Outreach has rules about this sort of thing. I'm taking a chance, too, you know."

Michael Finn sat down and ran his fingers through his hair. "I'm so goddamned nervous," he said. "I'm falling apart."

Instead of walking behind my desk to my usual chair, I sat where Minnie had sat. "Please don't worry so much," I said. "Carter's going to meet us in forty-five minutes at the Cove Theater. He'll have gotten you an attorney by then."

"A movie theater?" Finn said, surprised.

"He has a tremendous fear of being followed," I explained, and Finn nodded knowingly.

"I'd like to turn myself in," Finn said. "I'd like to get the whole thing over with."

We sat side by side, not looking at each other. Still, from the corner of my eye, I could see that he was shaking, as if the office were filled to the ceiling with danger. I reached out without thinking; when I touched his wrist I felt his skin jump beneath my fingers.

I moved my hand away, and Finn looked down at his wrist. "I don't want to go to jail," he said.

"Carter will find you a really good lawyer," I said. "Of course, you may have to do a little something for Soft Skies in return."

"Like what?" Finn asked. "I'm not going to any demonstration."

"Just some publicity," I guessed. "A few personal appearances after the trial."

"After the trial," Finn smiled.

"After today your lawyer will take care of everything. You just have to relax and trust him."

"Oh yeah?" Finn said. He reached into his pocket for a cigarette. "Trust a lawyer?" He quickly lit a match and inhaled. "Listen," he told me, "there's a lot you don't know about me."

Immediately I found myself wondering if Finn was married; he had never said he wasn't. There might be a woman waiting for him in the Camaro right now; perhaps children, a son with the same blue eyes. "What don't I know?" I asked.

"I've been in trouble before," Finn said. "I've been arrested."

For all I knew, Finn might have been guilty of a dozen horrible crimes, perhaps even murder. In his crazy youth he might have set fire to one of the old sailors who slept on the beach or in the doorway of the rundown Fishers Cove Hotel. There might have been a crime of passion—the stabbing of a woman who had refused his advances. Perhaps a fatal knife fight inside one of the roadhouses on Route 18.

"What were you arrested for?" I asked.

"Does it matter?" Finn said. "I'm just telling you that I've had enough experience with lawyers and courts to know I don't have a chance."

"It matters to me," I said. "What happened?"

Finn smiled and shook his head. "Everything that shouldn't have. Or maybe I was lucky," he said. "Maybe I found out right away, early in my life, that there was nothing out there for me."

As Finn began to speak I wanted to reach out and chart his pulse, to feel his skin with careful fingers. Instead I sat back in my chair and waited to discover what had been lying in wait out there, so long ago, when Finn first lost himself to the terrible sadness which had, by now, become even stronger than his own flesh and blood.

TWO

$\mathcal{T}$HE SCREEN DOOR SLAMMED.
Finn was running away for the twenty-second time, and all he
had with him were the clothes on his back, and the anger which
cut through his chest each time he breathed. That morning, the
last time he tried to escape from his parents' house, Finn was
sixteen. Already he was certain, even as he was walking out the
door, that there was nothing for him to run to.

Still, running away had become a pattern, a habit he couldn't
break. He had been running since the summer of his eighth
year. Finn's mother, Ada, was a cook in the hospital cafeteria,
and his father drove straight to the Modern Times Bar as soon
as the whistle blew to end the workday, and so Finn was alone
a great deal of the time. He enjoyed coming home from school
to the empty house; soon he learned to cook dinner for himself,
although each meal was an experiment, and often a failure. The
day the kitchen wall was set on fire, Finn was cooking spaghetti
for the first time when the flames from the gas stove had leapt
up; Finn ran to the bathroom for a towel, and he beat the towel
against the wall until the flames were out. But, the wallpaper
above the stove was ruined; a huge black hole wrecked the

pattern of yellow daffodils. Water and spaghetti had boiled over and trailed down the stove in stringy wet puddles. It was an accident, but that would not matter to Finn's parents. Finn knew already, in the summer when he was eight, that he was not allowed any accidents. Not even one.

As soon as Michael Finn heard his father's key turn in the door, he hid. He covered his ears when he heard Danny Finn's yells in the kitchen; he knelt down in the bathroom, between the toilet and the tiled bathroom wall. And that was where Danny Finn found his son, in the bathroom, crouched down low, like a rabbit. Danny Finn was as drunk as he was angry; Michael Finn weighed only sixty-two pounds, and it took just one swing of his father's arm to send Finn through the shower door. There, surrounded by glass and blood, Finn stared up at his father; he did not move or blink an eye, he did not even feel the cuts in his skin. Danny Finn had had seven beers at the Modern Times, but he was sober enough to know blood when he saw it.

"Oh, shit," Danny Finn said.

Michael Finn lay on his back in the bathtub; across his face was an enormous gash, and blood spurted from beneath his shirt where he had been cut across the back.

"Holy shit," Danny Finn said. He knelt down, picked Finn up, and wrapped his son in a large blue bath towel. By the time they reached the emergency room at Saint Elmo's Hospital, that towel was soaked in blood, and Danny Finn wondered if he would be charged with murder if his son should die. He prayed that his son would not accuse him in the emergency ward, when they were surrounded by doctors and nurses and Danny Finn would have no way to escape the charges of a terrible crime.

But Danny Finn had nothing to worry about; in the emergency ward, wrapped up in the bloody towel, Michael Finn didn't make a sound. The nurses did not accuse Danny Finn, they did not point their fingers at him and scream; they simply wrote on Michael Finn's records what his father dictated: the boy had slipped while taking a shower. No one asked why Michael Finn had been dressed while showering, no one noticed that the child's hair was not wet, no one mentioned that his shirt was slashed as if by knives. They cleaned the blood away, stitched up his back and his face, and sent Finn home with his father.

Danny Finn had scared himself; he had not expected to throw his son through the glass shower door; he was shocked by the huge gash across the boy's face. "Listen," Danny Finn said as they pulled into the driveway later that night, "it was an accident."

Michael Finn didn't answer; he knew it was nothing of the sort.

"I'm glad you understand." Danny Finn turned off the motor. "We wouldn't want to upset your mother."

Michael Finn turned his head slightly; he looked at his father and not one emotion slipped through.

"I'm glad you understand," Danny Finn said again.

Two days later, Finn ran away for the first time. It was not something he had thought about, or something he planned. He was walking home from school when he saw his father's car parked outside the Modern Times, and somehow, he had just kept walking. Right past the house, and through Harbor Heights. He walked for miles; through the old section of Fishers Cove and west on Route 18. Finn didn't stop until he had reached the edge of town, where this branch of the Long Island

Railroad ended at a small, wooden station beside a field of wild daisies. Finn sat down on a green bench outside the station; as he watched trains come and go and kicked his shoes against the bench, he began to feel his chest fill with something that swelled. After midnight, Finn was still there, sitting alone, with nowhere to go.

Danny Finn pulled into the station parking lot early in the morning. The station door was locked tight and no train tickets had yet been sold. Michael Finn had fallen asleep; he was curled up on the green bench, his face resting against the cool wooden slats. Danny Finn shook his son's shoulder roughly.

"Let's go," Danny Finn said.

Finn opened his eyes; his father was watching him, and his mother sat in the front seat of the car. There was no choice, and because he was eight years old and the stitches in his face and back hurt, Finn followed his father. That morning, Danny Finn didn't hit his son; Michael's stitches were still so new they looked like fresh tracks of blood across the boy's face. Now Danny Finn was afraid of blood, and hospitals, and his own anger, though years later, he wondered if he hadn't been too soft, if his palm hadn't left a strong enough imprint on the boy. For although Michael Finn was beaten each time he fled again and was returned home, nothing stopped him from trying, not even the scar across his face, which marked him for life, or the welts his father's belt left on his back and legs.

Finn never had a plan, he had no destination, and he never really had any hope of success. Each time he ran away he knew he would be caught, he would be returned home, and after he was beaten, he would promise never to do it again. One day, when he least expected it, Michael Finn's feet would take charge; before he knew it, before he had time to think, he was walking away from his parents' house. And then, quite suddenly, he would be running.

To Ada, Finn's running away had become a joke—a quirk in her son's personality, a sign of a wanderlust, a lark. But to Danny Finn it was no joke, Danny had lived his life without running away, and there had been plenty of times he would have liked to pack up and head west, leaving everything behind, including his memories. But he had stayed on, even when he felt next to nothing for his wife, and less for his son; he had done his duty, he had stuck it out, he considered himself a moral person, a man. He planned to make certain that his son would not grow up to be the running-away sort. And so, each time Finn ran, his father grew angrier. That anger forged together and settled in Danny Finn's heart and in his fists; and finally, it exploded the last time Finn ran away.

Michael was sixteen; it was Indian summer when he picked up the keys to his father's new Oldsmobile. In his fingers, the keys stirred; they fluttered and moved. Later, Danny Finn would report the car stolen, but Michael Finn was not thinking of stealing as he slid behind the wheel and started the engine. He was not thinking of anything more than moving fast along the highway. He pulled the car out of the driveway and drove through Harbor Heights. Finn had known how to drive since he was fourteen; there had been nights when friends of Danny's would call from the Modern Times to report that Danny could not find the ignition of his car, no less the road. On those nights Michael Finn did not want to wake his mother. Ada now slept alone in the third bedroom which had always been used for storage before. She and Danny Finn no longer slept in the same room, and they no longer spoke to each other at the breakfast table or in the living room where together they silently watched color TV on Sunday nights. So Michael Finn would walk the half mile to the Modern Times; he would watch as his father was loaded into the back seat, and then he would slowly drive home. Finn was a good driver, he was sure of himself behind the wheel; so on that hot September day Finn took the curves in the road easily; and without any premeditation, he drove off and left Fishers Cove behind.

Finn drove east. No police cars pulled the Oldsmobile off the road; Finn looked older than his age, and he kept well within the speed limit. The gas tank was full, the radio blasted out tunes he knew by heart, and Finn felt as if his chest had opened up; and what escaped propelled him east; he was flying. Because Finn had not planned his escape, the land gave out when the gas tank was still half full. He was only two hours from Fishers Cove, but it was the farthest Finn had ever run and he glided into the rest area above Montauk Point as if on wings. He parked the car, opened the door, and breathed so deeply that he nearly lifted himself off the ground. At sunset, Finn hiked down to the ocean; he walked far out on the black rocks. Sea gulls hung above him, a new moon appeared in the western sky; and after he had climbed back up to the parking area Michael Finn slept soundly, dreaming about the Atlantic, curled up in the back seat of the Oldsmobile with a new feeling of safety.

He had enough money to buy coffee and potato chips the first few days at the refreshment stand near the lighthouse. But after that, he liked the feeling hunger brought on; it seemed to Finn that he was seeing more clearly—the sky looked brighter, he could actually spot the red glow of a sea gull's eye as it flew above him. He did not care if he ever ate again. He was free; perched on the hood of the Oldsmobile, he watched the ocean at daybreak and at dusk. He crouched in the woods near the rest area like a deer, and he slept better than he ever had in his parents' house. He wondered if he might live the life of a hermit forever—sleeping in the woods, eating the bark off pine trees in winter, wandering over the dunes long after the Oldsmobile had turned to rust in the rest area and all signs of Michael Finn had disappeared.

But Finn did not have a chance to live his hermit's life. In less than a week he was found. In the days above the Point, the anger in his chest had all but disappeared. Now Finn had nothing but peace. When he was awakened late one night, when the glare of a flashlight in his face brought him back from his dreams, and the peace was shattered, Finn did not cry out. And when a man's hand shook his shoulder, Finn did not strike out or struggle, he did not bolt from the car. He sat up quietly, nightblinded, unable to see anything but the beam of the flashlight.

"The party's over," a young policeman said to Finn.

"Let's go," a second officer said.

Finn got out of the Oldsmobile and followed the two officers into the patrol car; as soon as the door was closed behind him, it locked shut. Still, Finn was not afraid; he really had done nothing wrong. He had thought of flying, he had driven without a license, he had watched the moon rise, and gone without food. While the older officer radioed for a tow truck, the young one turned to Finn and offered him a cigarette.

"The next time you steal a car," the officer said, "drive west.

You head east on Long Island and you're a sitting duck. Nothing waiting for you but the ocean."

"I don't steal cars," Finn said, accepting the cigarette and noticing how peculiar his voice sounded; he had not spoken for days and his words were thick and slow.

The young policeman, who introduced himself as Morrison, shook his head. "This car's reported stolen. I have the report right here."

He showed Finn some papers, which the boy could not read in the patrol car. Finn's chest had begun to tighten.

The older policeman turned to him. "Do you have a license?"

Finn shook his head; he had only a permit.

"That's not a federal offense," Morrison shrugged, remembering his own youth. "The real problem is the stolen-car rap. Your father called in and gave the report. Once that report is filed and on record, there's nothing anybody can do about it. You're a car thief."

Finn was read his rights and driven to the Montauk station house; he waited while Danny Finn was called and asked to take the train out and identify his Oldsmobile and his son.

Morrison brought Finn a cup of coffee. "You'll have to wait a couple of years to get your license after pulling this stunt. Poor planning is what I'd call your activities."

"I'll never have my own car, so it doesn't make a difference," Finn said. "I don't need a license."

What made a difference was Danny Finn. He arrived at the station house in a little over an hour. He looked hard at his son.

"That's him," Danny Finn said. "He stole the Oldsmobile."

Finn stood up; he was taller than his father, in a fair fight the boy might have won. "I didn't steal anything."

Danny Finn might have asked that the charges be dropped against his son; he might have begged that the record be wiped clean. Instead he spit on the floor. "That's him," Danny Finn repeated. "That's the fucking thief."

Finn inhaled; his breath caught in his throat and refused to go through his lungs. "I didn't steal anything," Finn said. "I went for a ride. That's all."

"Don't look at me," Danny Finn said to his son. He turned to the lieutenant at the station desk. "I don't want him to look at me," he said.

"You're crazy," Finn said, as his father signed the papers identifying the car and the thief; charges against Finn for grand auto theft would be pressed automatically by the state.

"What are you doing?" Michael Finn said.

"You'd better learn your lesson," Danny Finn said without looking at his son.

"Let's go," Morrison said to Finn.

"Wait a minute." Finn shook off the officer's hand. "Don't I get a lawyer?"

"Come on," Morrison said easily.

Finn felt the old gathering of anger in his chest; there it was in his lungs and under his skin, circling his heart.

"I have rights," Finn said. "I'm entitled to something."

"I'll give you something." Danny Finn advanced toward his son, waving his fists.

"I want a lawyer," Finn said to Morrison.

"You'll get one," Morrison answered.

"Court-appointed," the lieutenant called from the desk. "All minors are entitled to court-appointed attorneys."

"I'm not moving," Finn said. "You can't make me."

Morrison touched Finn's arm lightly. "Don't cause trouble," he said to Finn. "Believe me. It's just not worth it."

There was a circle around Finn: Morrison was to his right, the older officer was behind him, his father stood in front of him, and the desk lieutenant had begun walking toward the circle.

"All right," Finn said. "I'll go." As he followed Morrison, Finn's face was quiet, but inside no part of him was calm.

Finn stayed in the County Juvenile Holding Center for two weeks, but not until the morning of his court appearance did he meet his lawyer. Finn walked into the meeting room, and the thing inside his chest weighted him down like lead. The court-appointed attorney was studying Finn's folder; he didn't look up when the boy sat across from him.

"Car theft," the lawyer said. Finn sat still and waited; finally the lawyer looked up and slowly removed his glasses. "Car theft," he repeated.

"That's right," Finn shrugged. "That's what they say."

"You'll get one to three at a school upstate."

"Do you want to hear what happened?" Finn asked.

"I know what happened," Finn's attorney said. "Car theft."

Finn turned away. He had nothing else to say to his lawyer, and there was no point in talking, or in trying to explain, not even once they were inside the courtroom. The judge was fidgety, anxious for his lunch hour, and the hearing was soon over. After the arresting officers made their statements, Danny Finn was called to the bench. He was dressed in a blue pin-striped suit he had not worn since the funeral of an uncle in Brooklyn; while he gave his testimony, he eyed his son as if Michael were a wild animal who might spring at any moment. Danny Finn spoke slowly; he hoped only that his son would be taken someplace where the boy could learn his lesson, and learn it fast. Finn, himself, paid no attention to what his father said, he didn't listen to a word. Instead, the boy looked out the window and watched a row of bluejays sitting on a telephone wire.

By this time, Finn had no hope. He no longer dreamed at night, and he couldn't remember the time when his dreams were filled with the sound of the ocean. When the judge announced Finn's sentence, the boy did not have to listen to know he had been sold out—by his father and his court-appointed attorney, by the judge and by laws which he knew were not made to protect him. It did not matter to him that he had been given a short sentence—only one year upstate—with good behavior he would be back in his parents' home, back at his old high school, in less than eight months. Finn did not hear the name of the institution he would be sent to; he did not care how far outside of Albany the place was or what facilities they had for boys like him. He was too busy to listen to the judge; he was watching the sky, through the courtroom window, concentrating only on the low clouds which moved like a white sea right outside the courtroom.

THREE

FINN'S PAIN HAD TRANS-
formed the room; his memory had leapt across the white walls,
the frost on the window was the same shade of blue as his eyes.
I watched him without daring to breathe: he was still the child
bleeding in the emergency room, still that boy listening to the
slam of the screen door behind him. Outside, it had begun to
snow, but here, in my office, it was as hot as that Indian summer
day when Finn ran away for the last time.

"I'm sorry," I said to that boy who stood above Montauk
Point, waiting for night to fall. He was there, in the parking
lot edged with freedom, surrounded by a secrecy sweeter than
oranges and honey.

"Don't be sorry," Finn said. "I didn't tell you that for pity.
That's just the way it was. The way it still is," he said. "When
you're dangerous they can sense it. When you're angry they
know. And they'll know about Angel Landing, they don't need
any proof."

"You can fight them," I said. "Carter will help."

"How do I fight?" Finn asked. "How do I plead? I'm
guilty." He shook his head sadly. "I am."

It was true and there was no way to change it, even if he was only guilty of anger in the first degree, guilty of a rage purer than heat.

"I wish I could just make your anger disappear," I said. "And maybe, in time, it will."

"I think I've had it," Finn said. "I want to stop talking now."

I looked at my watch; it was time to meet Carter. "We have to go," I said.

"I don't know," Finn whispered. Beads of light fell across his face, but the scar on his left cheek was hidden; he looked like a man who had been trapped between the darkness and the light.

I put my files away, reached for my coat, and then went to the door. "We really have to go," I said. We left Outreach together. On Main Street the snow was heavy; we walked blindly to the lot where Finn's car was parked, we were close to each other, fighting the wind, inhaling flakes of snow each time we breathed. When we reached the Camaro I waited inside while Finn cleaned off the windshield with his hands. We could have been anyone: friends, a couple, two people who had known each other for years ready to drive to the market, to dinner, to another state.

Alone in the car, I grew curious. I examined the leftovers from Finn's life which littered the Camaro. Empty soda cans and crushed cigarette packages, a toolbox on the floor of the rear seat, a woolen blanket. Only the barest signs of life. Quickly, still watching as Finn went around to clean the rear windshield, I opened the glove compartment. There were no clues: a Rolling Stones tape, a map of New York; matches and maps instead of souvenirs and mementos. I clicked the lock shut just as Finn opened the door. When he sat behind the wheel and rubbed his frozen hands together his breath filled the car, it steamed up the mirror, the windows grew foggy and the world outside grew oddly dim. On the way to the Cove Theater the streets were slippery, drifts had already begun to form on the sidewalk. We didn't say a word until Finn parked in the movie theater lot.

"Don't worry," I said to Finn. "Carter is easy to talk to."

Finn held tight to the steering wheel, paralyzed, rooted. I touched his shoulder. I left my hand there, lingering. "I'll be with you," I said.

We walked hand in hand to the ticket booth, but we didn't dare look at each other; we pretended that our hands were crazy rebels, our fingers had minds of their own, they alone had decided to touch. The film playing was a French drama, subtitled; the price of admission was only a dollar fifty, but I refused to let Finn pay for me. And when I had convinced him that I didn't mind paying for myself I realized I didn't have a cent in my pocket; I hadn't had time to think of anything as practical as money.

"Just this once," I whispered as Finn paid for our tickets. As if there would be other times, as if we would continue to go to movies together, monthly, weekly, every night.

The theater was nearly empty: a few old women in heavy winter coats, a teenaged couple sat in the last row, already whispering and sighing. Carter sat on the left side, his boots propped up on the seat in front of him.

"That's him," I nodded as I led Finn down the aisle. I sat in the middle, between Carter and Finn; introducing them just as the lights went down.

"I was starting to get worried," Carter said, stroking my leg. "I thought you two had decided to run out on me." He reached across and shook Finn's hand. "I've been looking forward to this. Natalie has told me all about you."

"Oh?" Finn said, staring at me.

"Not all," I whispered. "Just some basic information."

"Aren't you going to ask me if I've found a lawyer?" Carter said.

"Have you?" I asked.

"I haven't found a lawyer," Carter grinned. "I've found *the* lawyer. Reno LeKnight."

"That's amazing," I said. Reno LeKnight had defended some of the most famous criminals on the East Coast; one year he had flown to Utah to defend a man known as the Saline Killer. LeKnight had worked for activists of the left and the right, and although his politics were questionable, his winning streak wasn't—he played for keeps, his record was a hundred percent.

"You're going to have Reno LeKnight defending you!" I beamed at Finn.

"Who is he?" Finn asked.

"He defended the Saline Killer," I said. Michael Finn shook his head. "The antiwar activists in New Haven?" Finn shrugged. "Well, he's famous," I said. "And he wins."

"How much does he charge?" Finn asked.

"Don't worry about that," Carter told Finn. "Reno will have to contact you. I'll need your phone number." Finn wrote his number on a scrap of paper Carter had handed him. "I've got to tell you," Carter said, "I think what you did was terrific. A really courageous act."

"Oh yeah?" Finn said cautiously.

Carter slipped the paper with Finn's number into his work-boot. "For safekeeping," he explained. "You know, I can arrange to get you on the Soft Skies speakers' roster after your trial," he told Finn. "We might be able to work something out. I've been looking for a good assistant. Someone with your sort of background."

"I'm not interested," Finn said quickly.

"When I think of the political implications of your trial my head spins." Carter sighed.

"I'm not interested in politics," Finn said.

"Oh?" Carter said, annoyed. "What about the fate of mankind? Interested in that?"

"Carter," I warned, "this hasn't been easy for him."

"It hasn't been easy for any of us," Carter said. "Do you know anything about radiation?" he asked Finn.

I could almost see Finn retreating, swallowed up in distrust. It was too much for him to think about the fate of mankind, he could barely stand or examine his own dreams.

"I don't want to talk about this," Finn said, too softly for Carter to hear. "I can't talk about it."

"I can give you statistics that will make your hair curl," Carter went on. "The stillborn children and animals, the deformed lizards and birds; radiation levels that will last forever."

"Forever," Finn said, slowly, as if tasting the word.

Carter grew more and more excited. As I often did, I now envied Carter his ability to care; somehow he was convinced that he would change the world. "You can really help," Carter was saying to Finn. "You can get on the witness stand and let people in this town know how easily accidents can happen in a power plant."

"Please," Finn said. "Please."

"Your trial is going to blow this town right open," Carter grinned.

"Listen," I said to Carter, "I think we should go home." As Carter's voice rose, moviegoers began to notice us. An usher patrolled the aisles, glaring at Carter's boots resting on the faded velvet seat in front of him.

"Home?" Carter said. "I've got to go to Manhattan to see Reno LeKnight."

"Right now?" Finn said. "Tonight?"

"Can't you do it tomorrow?" I asked Carter.

Carter shook his head, then he leaned over and kissed me. "Thank you," he whispered into my ear. "Thank you for giving him to Soft Skies. You don't know what this means to me." Carter threaded a scarf around his neck. "LeKnight will want to meet with you this week," he told Finn. "Either at his office in Manhattan or his beach house. But don't worry—I'll arrange the meeting, I'll take care of everything."

Finn and I both stood to let Carter pass. "You're terrific," Carter whispered to me. "I'll call you tomorrow," he nodded to Finn as the two men shook hands once more.

When Carter had gone, Finn and I stayed on. We sat side by side, aware of the absence of Carter's body, the absence of his hope.

"Do you want some popcorn?" Finn asked.

"I don't think so," I answered. Carter was out in the parking lot, starting his old MG. Although the roads were treacherous, and the drive would take nearly two hours, Carter would sing all the way into Manhattan, he would step on the gas, a man with a mission.

"I don't feel so good," Finn whispered. "I can't breathe."

The air inside the theater did seem too heavy, as if it was years old, breathed in one too many times.

"Let's get out of here," Finn said.

We stood and found our way back up the aisle. Once outside, breathing was much easier; the snow came down harder than before.

"Don't forget our appointment on Thursday," I reminded Finn. "At two."

"I'll drive you home," Finn said to me.

I shook my head. "Someone could see us together. I have to remain objective if you want me to be a witness at your trial."

"But it's snowing," Finn said.

"I can walk."

Finn nodded and turned up his collar. I watched as he went to the parking lot; I could see him beside the Camaro, his long hair as wet as if he'd just stepped from a shower. Without bothering to make certain no one was watching, I walked to the car and got in. Finn didn't look up as I walked across the parking lot, he didn't smile when he saw me get inside. And when he got in and sat behind the wheel he didn't flinch or say a word; he started the engine and we left together.

"Toward the harbor," I said. "The last house on Main Street belongs to my aunt. That's where I live."

"And Sugarland?" Finn asked as he strained to see the road through the falling snow.

"Carter lives in his office. That's where he's happiest."

I borrowed a cigarette from Finn and lit it. "What do you do every day now that the plant is closed?" I asked, still curious about the details of his life.

Finn glared at me. "I do a lot of things," he said.

"Of course," I said, frightened by his sudden anger.

"I've got every minute of the day planned," Finn continued. "First, in the morning, I'm nervous. That takes up a lot of time. In the afternoon I'll start to get anxious and that'll be good for a couple of hours. And then, by the time night comes, I'm just plain scared."

Finn had pulled up in front of Minnie's house; smoke rose from the chimney. Finn stared straight ahead, on edge, on fire, ready to step on the gas the minute I was out of the car, ready to drive away, racing toward the center of his own dark fears. The car was in neutral and I could have gotten out without looking back. I could have said goodbye, good luck, I'll see you at the office, I'll see you in court. I could have asked Finn to stick with the facts and keep his sorrow to himself. Instead, just before opening the car door, I turned to him. "Come in and have a drink," I said.

"What?" Finn said, turning to look at me.

I repeated my offer and then waited for Finn on the sidewalk; the Connecticut wind was still rising, blowing drifts across the front lawn. Inside the Camaro, Finn looked out at me. Then he turned off the engine and took his hands off the wheel. I was facing the other way, but I heard his door slam shut, I heard him follow me across the lawn and up the porch steps. As I opened the front door I saw that Minnie was watching us from the parlor window, but when I took Finn into that room to wait while I went to look for something to drink, the parlor was empty.

"I'll be right back," I told Finn. "I hope Scotch is all right. There's only that and some sherry."

"Scotch?" Finn said, as if the word was terribly foreign, too difficult for his tongue.

"Wait right here," I said.

I found Minnie in the kitchen, washing dishes.

"What are you doing with a married man?" Minnie asked casually, without bothering to look up.

"I'm going to borrow some of your Scotch," I said, reaching for glasses.

"I don't like it," Minnie said. "Not one bit."

"The truth is, he's not married."

Minnie scowled. "First you tell me he's married, now you tell me he's not. What should I believe?"

"What's the difference," I said, heading for the door. "Married or not, he's only here for a quick drink."

Minnie pointed a finger at me. "He's the bomber," she nodded. "I was right. I knew it the minute I saw him."

"All right, all right. He's the accused bomber, although nobody's actually accused him yet. But he has decided to turn himself in; Carter's arranging it all."

"Carter?" Minnie said. "Couldn't you find someone a little more reliable?"

"I want you to keep quiet about all this," I warned my aunt.

"Who would I tell?" Minnie said as she poured boiling water into the teapot. "As far as I'm concerned, good luck to him. It's too bad he didn't have a bigger bomb, because before you know it they'll have Angel Landing going again."

"It wasn't a bomb, it was a valve. And the whole thing was really an accident."

"An accident?" Minnie shrugged. "Sure. If you want to believe that, sure. But what I want to know is, why are you suddenly going around with a bomber? After everything I told you."

"I'm not going around with anyone," I said as I walked into the hallway. "Except for Carter," I added.

Minnie followed me into the hallway, drying her hands with a towel. "Did you invite this bomber into my house or didn't you?"

"I'm entitled to have guests, whoever I want. If I want to invite a murderer over for tea, I'm entitled," I told my aunt. I was afraid that if Minnie approached Finn the way she had in my office she would frighten him away. "You can't really complain," I said to Minnie. "I rarely have guests."

"Have some guests." Minnie shrugged.

"Why shouldn't I?" I said. "I have no strong connections, no real responsibilities. I should be having more guests than I do, and I should be able to entertain them alone."

Minnie turned away from me. There, in the entrance hallway of the empty boarding house, as the cold draft sneaked in beneath the door, Minnie seemed to be shrinking, she was losing inches with every second.

"Oh come on," I said, backing down. "Have your tea with us." Minnie glared at me. "I want you to."

"Do you really expect me to believe that?" Minnie said.

"Yes," I said. "Yes. Join us."

Minnie shook her head. "I never had children," she said, "because I never wanted them. I was busy, I had my husband, what did I need them for?"

"How often do you get a chance to spend time with a bomber, Minnie," I said, afraid of what secret sorrow had just been triggered.

"Of course," Minnie went on, "even if you have children, there's no guarantee. I see it all the time. Do children visit their parents at the Mercy Home? Do they even know they're alive? No," Minnie shook her head, "there's never any guarantee."

I balanced the Scotch and glasses in one hand, and with my free hand I reached for Minnie. I touched her to reassure myself; she wasn't fading, she was still blood and bones, still Minnie. "What's gotten into you?" I said. "Come on."

When we reached the parlor, Finn was still standing in the spot where I had left him; still wearing his leather jacket, hands in his pockets, ill at ease.

"Here we are," I said. "You've already met my aunt."

"I'm having my tea with you," Minnie said to Finn as I poured out drinks, "but don't expect me to talk. You're my niece's guest, not mine." Minnie sat in the easy chair, she leaned her elbows on the frayed lace doilies.

"Why don't you take your coat off?" I asked Finn as I handed him his drink.

"I don't think so," Finn said. "I'm nervous all the time," he explained to me. "I like to be ready to get up and leave."

"Nervous," Minnie laughed. "You should have thought of that before you bombed the power plant."

I cringed and tried to smile. "She guessed," I told Finn.

"Revolutionaries, criminals, and saints all need a certain sort of character," Minnie said. "They can't afford to be nervous."

"It wasn't a bomb," Finn said. "It was only a valve."

"You want to take my advice?" Minnie said. "I'm old, so I know a thing or two. Forget about being nervous, you don't have any control over what will eventually happen to you. So save your energy, because if you want to know what it is that's going to happen, I'll tell you." Minnie smiled sweetly, as if she had a marvelous secret. "You just get old. That's what will happen. No way around it."

"Thank you," I said, regretting having invited Minnie into the parlor, "for that wonderful advice."

"On the other hand," Minnie went on, "people have to use their energies before they kick the bucket."

"You just said exactly the opposite," Finn told Minnie.

Minnie looked at him, surprised. "So?"

Finn shook his head. "For an old woman you seem very confused."

Minnie glared. "For a young man you seem very mixed up. First you bomb a power plant, then you regret it. Make up your mind."

Finn gulped down his Scotch.

"Another?" I asked him.

"But let's not argue," Minnie said to Finn. "I like you," she nodded. "And I approve." She smiled, first at Finn, and then, even more broadly, at me.

"What are you talking about?" I asked.

"I approve," Minnie said. "The two of you." Finn and I both stared at her dumbly. "Your affair."

"Don't be ridiculous!" I said to my aunt. "There is no affair."

"Hah," Minnie said, knowingly.

"Can I have another drink?" Finn asked.

I poured him some; we didn't look at each other. I tried to think of a way, short of murder, to get Minnie out of the room. "Can you get some crackers and cheese?" I asked her. "I don't want to make a mess in your kitchen."

"Certainly," Minnie said, "but I'll be right back."

When she had left, I turned to Finn. "My aunt," I explained, "is eccentric."

Finn sipped his Scotch. "She's different," he agreed.

"She's not crazy or anything like that."

"Oh, no," Finn said quickly. "Nothing like that."

Perhaps Minnie had guessed that I'd fallen for Finn's blue eyes; she assumed I wanted to be closer to him than I dared, but she had no proof, none at all; and if my heart beat quickly, just a little too fast, it may have been something as simple as a slight fever.

"One thing I don't understand," Finn said. "Why doesn't Carter live here?"

"He's dedicated to his work," I said. "He's more complicated than anyone would guess," I added.

Finn shrugged; finally he decided to sit in the easy chair, he leaned back and finished his drink. As soon as Finn had relaxed, Beaumont began to rattle his pots and pans, like a convict wrapped in chains.

Finn's body tightened; he sat up straight. "What is that?" he whispered.

"Nothing." I smiled. "Just Beaumont."

"Is he hiding down there?" Finn pointed to the basement below.

"He's lived in the basement since nineteen fifty-six; he's one of my aunt's boarders."

"Oh yeah?" Finn said. "How do you know that? How can you be sure?"

"You don't believe me?" I smiled. I went to the basement stairs and opened the door.

"Don't do that," Finn said, following me to the door. "You don't know who's down there. I may have been followed."

"I know who's down there," I said. "Beaumont," I called. We heard pots clatter; the odor of cabbage drifted upward.

Beaumont peered up from the basement.

"It's me," I told him, "Natalie. Come on up."

"I didn't do anything," Beaumont called back.

He walked up the stairs, and when he reached the parlor the old boarder blinked like a mole. He was dressed in the gray shirt and trousers that were his watchman's uniform. Beneath his shirt his back was hunched from years of ducking under the pipes in the basement.

"What's he wearing?" Finn asked suspiciously.

"This?" Beaumont squinted down at his shirt. "It's my uniform."

"What kind?" Finn whispered. "What does he do?"

"He's a guard," I said. Beaumont nodded as Finn looked more and more uncomfortable. "At Angel Landing," I confessed.

"Oh, shit," Finn said. "Great."

"I've been there for seven years," Beaumont told Finn. The old man walked to the wood-burning stove and held out his hands. "Sure would be nice to have a stove like this downstairs."

"Why didn't you tell me?" Finn asked.

"He's only the night watchman," I said. "He probably doesn't even know there was an explosion. Take a look at him; he's only a guard."

Finn watched Beaumont carefully. "Still working?" he asked Beaumont.

"Oh, sure," Beaumont said. "I'm there every night."

"But the plant's been closed down," Finn said.

Beaumont blinked. "I don't know anything about it. I'm still there every night."

Minnie returned to the parlor; when she saw Beaumont crouched by the stove she glared at me. "Did you force him to come upstairs?" she asked me. "He likes his own room; he doesn't need a social worker." She turned to Beaumont. "Has my niece been harassing you?"

"Oh, no," the old boarder answered.

"No social work with my boarders," Minnie said, waving a finger at me.

"Boarder," I corrected. "You have only one aside from me."

"Everything's fine," Beaumont said as he edged toward the basement door.

"I think I better go," Finn said. He placed his glass on the silver tea tray near the stove.

"That's right." Beaumont nodded to Finn as the old man made his escape to his lair. "It's late. I have to get down to the power plant."

I followed Finn to the front door. "I'm sorry about all this," I said. "My aunt gets carried away."

"I think I shouldn't have come here," Finn said. "You asked me to have a quick drink because you felt sorry for me, because you're polite."

"I'm not polite," I insisted.

Finn opened the front door; snow swept over the polished floor, icicles hung from the roof like daggers, just above Finn's head. "Good night," he told me, softly, quietly, as if his words were some long farewell meant to last years.

"Don't forget our appointment Thursday," I called.

"I'll think about it," Finn said as he walked out on the porch. "I can't promise anything more. I can't promise you I'll be there."

I watched as Finn got into the Camaro and drove away, then I went back to the parlor. Minnie had taken out her sewing box and was repairing the torn doilies which covered the arms of the easy chair. I stood at the window, behind the glass and the lace; I imagined the apartment where Finn would sleep that night: I was certain the room was not well heated. Finn would sleep in his clothes, and would shiver beneath a thin cotton blanket; in the early morning, when the sky was still black, he would call out in his sleep, his own cry would wake him.

I went to the stove to warm my hands; when I looked up, Minnie was watching me. She tore a piece of thread with her teeth and then tied a knot. "So?" she said.

"You were rude to him," I said.

"Old people can get away with that." Minnie smiled. She crisscrossed stitches across the doily. "What do you think?" she asked me. "Do you think this Finn is for you?"

"He's my client," I said.

"So?" Minnie said.

"You're being ridiculous," I said. "He may be a very important case in my career. If he continues therapy."

"Is that why you invited him here for a drink?" Minnie asked.

"You don't know what you're talking about," I said.

"The first time I saw your uncle Alex," Minnie now recalled, "I knew he was for me. Right away. I knew."

"It's not like that," I said.

I barely knew him; he was only another case, and probably

dangerous. And there was Carter, and there were rules: he was my client, and it didn't matter if his eyes were blue or gray, or that my pulse grew weak when Minnie even suggested there was something more than there ever could be.

"That's exactly what I told everyone after I met Alex," Minnie told me. "I said, 'What the hell would I do with a poet? That man is certainly not for me.' But, I just didn't want to tell the truth. Was it their business? But I knew, from the minute I first saw him."

Although I shook my head and laughed and didn't believe a word Minnie told me, when I said good night later and walked upstairs, I worried about Michael Finn. He might disappear; he would forget his Thursday appointment and run off to Canada or Mexico. I watched the harbor from my window; the later the night grew the more convinced I was that Finn, too, was looking at the same harbor, watching the same falling snow.

I was certain that Minnie was wrong; she was an old woman, with an old woman's desire for nonexistent romance. And he was a stranger, nothing more. But all the same, by the time the snow stopped falling, I was still thinking of Finn, still drowning in a stranger's eyes.

FOUR

$\mathcal{C}$ARTER AND I HAD BEGUN
to miss our Wednesday nights together; he was busy organizing
a second protest at Angel Landing and I was busy with Michael
Finn. Instead of disappearing, Finn now came to my office twice
a week; he was never late for his appointments, but there was
no way to call what went on between us therapy. Finn was as
uncomfortable with his past as he was with the future, and so
we avoided everything like sorrow and pain. Instead, we talked
about the everyday, at times we let a sweet, comfortable laziness
take over; we would sit, with cigarettes and coffee, occasionally
mentioning the weather or the world outside. It was easy to
forget that he was a client. But each time we met we could not
help but remember that sooner or later there would be a trial.

Finn would take that long walk to the district attorney's
office; there would be no quiet Tuesday afternoons together, no
private Thursdays, we would no longer be able to pretend there
had never been an explosion. When Carter finally called me, to
come to the Soft Skies office on a Wednesday night, I had nearly
forgotten that Wednesdays had ever been important to me; I
charted the weeks by Tuesdays now, I had given myself over

to Thursdays. Still, I agreed to meet Carter; refusing to admit that something between us had disappeared, I even took my diaphragm with me.

When I arrived at Soft Skies, Carter was waiting for me in the hallway outside the office door, pacing.

"You're here," Carter said, taking my hand.

"I don't know what's happened to us," I said. "Wednesdays have disappeared."

"That's all right." Carter kissed me lightly.

"But tonight is different. We'll be together," I said, though I knew I couldn't stop thinking of Finn, even when I was in Carter's arms.

"Forget about tonight," Carter said sadly.

"But you invited me."

"I don't have time," Carter explained. "I have to get organized for next week's demonstration at the plant."

"You called me," I said.

"That's right." Carter nodded. "Because there's someone who wants to meet you," he said as he opened the office door and led me inside. "Reno LeKnight."

The attorney sat in the only chair in the office; he was dressed in a long suede coat, his shoes were Spanish leather, his cologne was a strong mixture of roses and lime.

"Natalie Lansky," Reno LeKnight said, in a controlled courtroom tone.

"Why does he want to meet me?" I asked Carter.

"Why don't you sit down," Carter said to me.

There was only the chair LeKnight sat in, that and the unmade mattress on the floor.

"I don't think so," I said.

"I'm glad we could get together to talk," Reno LeKnight said to me.

"I don't see why," I told him. "I don't know anything. I can't help you at all."

Now that we were in the same room, I could imagine the chalky odor of the courthouse; alibis danced on the lawyer's skin.

"I think you can help me," LeKnight said. "Eventually you'll be a witness for Mr. Finn, and I want to know exactly where you stand."

"What do you mean?" I said to him. "Is he implying that I'm not one hundred percent behind Finn?" I asked Carter.

Carter sat on the bare wooden floor; his hand stuffed fliers into addressed envelopes the way other fingers turned to needlepoint or worry beads. "Natalie," he said easily. "Just relax."

"What's your relationship with Michael Finn?" Reno LeKnight asked.

"I'm his therapist," I told LeKnight. "I don't see why this is necessary." I turned to Carter.

"But it is necessary," Carter said. "I've had to appear in court seventeen times, and believe me, you can never be too prepared."

"Why did Mr. Finn first come to see you?" LeKnight now asked.

"Who can tell why a client first decides to go into therapy?" I shrugged. Any fact about Finn seemed too personal to share, the tiniest bit of information was much too powerful.

"You're going to be asked this in court."

"He wanted to work on his feelings of anger and guilt," I said.

"Anger and guilt," LeKnight nodded. "Good. And you knew about the explosion?"

"Do I have to answer that question?" I asked Carter.

"You do," Carter said.

"I knew there had been an accident. But I didn't know all the details."

LeKnight dropped his voice, the courtroom polish fell away. "Is that really true, Natalie?"

"I didn't know," I said. "Not right away."

"Now this is important," LeKnight said to me. "Would you say Finn was emotionally damaged when he first came to Outreach?"

"Oh, who's to say?" I whispered.

"Natalie," LeKnight said. "It's important."

The scar down Finn's cheek, the icy calm of his eyes, the anger that moved deep inside and finally rose up like a serpent, devouring itself. "Yes," I said. "He was emotionally damaged."

"So much so that he may have been distracted while at his job, he may have accidentally made a crucial error?"

"I suppose so," I said.

"Yes or no," LeKnight said. "It's as simple as that."

Simple as pain, easy as a one-word answer. "Yes," I said. "He was that emotionally damaged."

LeKnight sat back in his chair and smiled. "She'll do," he told Carter.

Carter got up and hugged me, but I thought of the witness stand and shivered.

"I told you she'd be terrific," Carter said proudly.

"What will happen to him?" I asked LeKnight.

"We'll go to the district attorney and plead innocent to the charge of criminal tampering in the second degree, and we'll simply enter a guilty plea to reckless damage of property," Reno nodded at Carter. "Soft Skies has generously offered to put up bail so Finn won't have to await trial in jail."

"Can you afford to do that?" I asked Carter.

"Bail can't be more expensive than Reno's fee."

After I had said good night, Carter walked outside the office with me. "Are you sure you don't want me to stay?" I asked. Under the fluorescent hallway fixtures Carter looked tired and drawn.

"I don't have time to sleep," Carter explained. "As soon as Reno leaves I have to get back to work."

"When was the last time you slept?" I asked.

"I stayed up all last night," Carter admitted.

"Should you be working so hard?" I asked.

"I have to," Carter told me as we kissed goodbye that night. "I can't help it."

Reno LeKnight was ready for the courtroom battle, Carter had begun to raise bail; I knew my afternoons with Finn were just about through. I looked forward to seeing Finn all that day, but when he walked into the office at three o'clock he refused to sit down, he paced around the room. The time had come; I was about to lose him, I could feel it in my blood.

"What's wrong?" I asked.

"Reno LeKnight called me this morning," Finn said. "It's going to happen."

"When?" I asked.

Finn lit a cigarette and inhaled, but he refused to sit. "To-day," he finally said.

My skin grew tight.

"I'm going to jail today," Finn said softly.

I shook my head. "Carter's going to raise bail."

"Until he does," Finn said, "I'll be in jail. And afterward. If I lose I'll be in jail for a long time."

"You're not going to lose," I said. "You have a terrific lawyer. The best around."

"Ten or fifteen years for one act of stupidity," Finn said. "I never even thought of what would happen after. I never thought at all." He crushed his half-smoked cigarette in the ashtray on my desk. "If I have to go to jail, I might as well give up. I'll die."

"You will not," I insisted.

Already Finn seemed farther and farther away. "I won't string myself up. I won't slit my wrists. I'll just die." He snapped his fingers. "That'll be the end for me."

"You have more strength than that."

"More strength than what?" Finn said. "You don't know anything about it. You've never been in jail."

"Neither have you," I said.

"Oh?" Finn said. "Oh, really?"

"The Stockley School?" I said. "Don't tell me that's jail. I was there on a field trip with a graduate-school class. I saw the school: it has basketball courts and color television sets."

"A field trip?" Finn said. He laughed once, but it was too short a laugh, too dry. "You didn't see anything," he told me. "Did they show you how once you're in you begin to feel less and less, until nothing is left inside? Once that happens, there's nothing left to keep you from collapsing when you get pushed."

"We were just there for part of one day," I said softly. "Really only for an hour."

"An hour," Finn smiled. He went to the window and pulled back the shade; he watched the street like a fugitive. "You think terrible things can't happen because they've never happened to you," he told me. "But they're out there, all the time, every day. They happen to someone."

There was the possibility that he might be convicted; he could be put away for years. Finn would grow old and fade; and one day, as he passed by a mirror, there would be no reflection, nothing at all but a spot of light where a man once had been.

"Not you," I said. "Nothing like that will happen to you."

Finn ignored me; he shook his head. "It's bad enough outside, but in jail you can never let your guard down. You pretend to feel nothing, you have to. You pretend it day and night, and then suddenly, it's true. There's nothing left inside."

His memories moved so close to the surface I began to fear that Finn might now try to escape all that he had felt and forgotten: he might leap through the window to the street below, he might slowly become invisible, turning more transparent with each second, until I could look right through him.

"Please sit down," I said. My voice sounded sharp, as if it might break or dissolve.

"I can't," Finn said. He closed his eyes for a second, but even that was too long a time for an outlaw who did not dare relax long enough to rest his blood. He opened his eyes wider and blinked, as if any minute, if he wasn't terribly careful, he might fall under a spell. I went to the window, I touched his shoulder and tried to get him to turn to me.

"You were once in jail and there's still something left inside you," I said. "You didn't lose everything."

"It will be worse this time," Finn said.

"What happened to you?" I asked. "What did you lose?"

Finn shook his head. "You'll never be able to see the things I tell you; you'll never understand. It could never be the way it was. It will only be a memory. That's all it will seem like, but it's not," Finn whispered. "It's still with me."

Finn finally agreed to tell me; but when he turned from the window and began to speak, I stayed where I was, just to make certain that no one would come for him and take his fugitive heart away from me too soon.

FIVE

E HAD BEEN DRIVEN UP TO the Stockley school by a county probation officer. Because Finn would not answer any questions, because he simply would not speak at all, the probation officer had slipped a Beatles tape into his cassette player, and they had listened to that one tape over and over again, all the way up to Albany. When they finally reached the school, Finn moved as slowly as a sleepwalker. He tried to listen, but when the probation officer and the head-master talked to him, they spoke in tongues, and Finn did not understand a word they said. Still, Michael Finn nodded when he was addressed; when he was told where to go, he moved his feet, he walked; there was no point in arguing, there was not even a reason to think; if he could have, Finn would have quietly stopped breathing, he would have collapsed to the floor in a pile of ashes.

Finn had emptied himself, so that he would not be frightened; and he felt nothing at all as he was given a medical examination, issued clothes, and led to the dormitory. Finn was not certain whether or not he was dreaming that night when his new roommates advanced toward him ready to fight. And although Finn's lip was split, and blood filled his mouth when he tried to eat breakfast the next morning, he had not really been hurt; he had only been told that he was new, and the last in line. That fight was the first of many; Finn never won, he just didn't care enough to fight hard, sometimes he didn't bother to protect himself at all. He kept to himself, he was a loner, and soon the other boys grew to ignore him. He was assigned to a job in the machine shop, which he went to each day after classes with no resentment and no joy. And each night, alone in his bed, Michael practiced not feeling until everything inside seemed flat and dry. After a month at the Stockley School, Finn had perfected his method of walking through his daily routine without thinking; of course, he was disguised—he looked real as anyone else as he strode across the campus of the Stockley School; although no one knew it, Finn was invisible, he was never really there.

It was not until he was attacked in the toilet of the machine shop that Finn felt anything, and then suddenly there was a sharp shiver of emotion when they held him up against the cement wall. Two boys held him and a third, named Caesar, unzipped Finn's jeans and pulled them down below Finn's knees.

"Are you a queer?" one boy asked, much too close to Finn's ear, so that each word was like an explosion.

"What are you talking about?" Finn said, wondering if his supervisor in the shop would miss him, wondering if anyone would miss him if he disappeared.

"You know what he's talking about." Caesar, who had been at the Stockley School for three years, smiled. "You like to do it with other guys."

Finn's exposed penis grew smaller and smaller, as if he could withdraw into himself protectively.

"Are you crazy?" Finn said, unable to pretend he was invisible, unable to stop his stabs of panic.

"He wants to know if I'm crazy," Caesar smiled.

"We're going to let you do what you like to do so much," said one of the boys holding Finn up against the wall.

And as Finn watched, terrified, still as stone, Caesar unzipped his own jeans. "That's right," he said. "And be careful not to bite," he warned. "Or we can remove every tooth in your mouth."

Finn had eleven more months to serve at Stockley; and that day, in the toilet, eleven months might as well have been the rest of his life. He might have shouted out or screamed, but Finn was certain that no one would hear him, no one would answer. He rested his head against the cement wall and concentrated on his breathing; he closed his eyes and tried to make his heart die. But his heart was still moving when one of the boys forced Finn to go down on his knees; and Finn was resigned to anything that might happen to him, when the toilet door opened. Finn's attackers looked up, uncertain, ready for a fight.

Herman, a tall black boy who had been sent to Stockley on charges of armed robbery, closed the door behind him. "Now what the hell are you doing?" Herman asked softly, but his eyes were as mean as thunder, and there weren't many at Stockley who dared to talk back to Herman, especially when his hands, which were stronger than those of men twice his age, were clenched into fists.

Caesar smiled vaguely. "Nothing," he said.

"What do you mean 'nothing'?" Herman said. "This," he pointed to Finn on his knees, "looks like something."

"He likes to do it with guys, so we're going to let him do it," the boy who held Finn around his throat said, but he loosened his grip and eyed Herman nervously.

"How do you know that's what he likes?" Herman asked. "Did he tell you that?" When no one answered, Herman snorted and shook his head. "Get your pants up," he told Caesar. Caesar quickly pulled up his jeans and zipped them. "That's right," Herman nodded. "Now get out of here." Finn's attackers stood their ground, but they shifted their weight from foot to foot. "You heard me," Herman said. "Go on." He smiled as the boys edged toward the door. "Scat."

Finn and Herman looked at each other. Finn's heart fluttered and jumped, and if Herman took one step toward him he was ready to close his eyes. He would simply float away and leave his body far behind; he would soar until no one could touch him.

"You sure look like a fool," Herman said finally. "You're bound to trip on those pants when you walk if you don't pull them up."

Finn eyed Herman cautiously.

"Go on," Herman nodded. "Get up. I'm not going to do anything to you."

Finn stood, pulled his jeans up, and went to the sink; he poured green liquid soap all over his palms. Finn listened carefully; he was ready to give up if Herman should come after him in a flash. But when he turned from the sink, Herman leaned against the wall and shook his head.

"Don't you ever fight back?" Herman asked.

"They were queers," Finn said, softly, testing the word out.

"Oh yeah?" Herman said. "And is that bad?"

Finn shrugged his shoulders; he had not thought of good or bad, he had only thought of panic.

"Because that's what I am," Herman said.

"Oh?" Finn said, surprised that one stranger would admit something like that to another.

"That's right," Herman said. "Everybody's entitled to something. Even in this place it's nice to get love. But I get mine from David, because me and David are together. I don't scare little boys in toilets."

If Finn had not been so detached from everyone at the Stockley School he would have known what everyone knew: that a sixteen-year-old boy named David was not to be fooled with, he was protected by Herman's reputation, by Herman's love.

"Well thanks," Finn said uncomfortably, "for walking in and everything."

"You should thank me, and you should be embarrassed that you have to thank me." Herman reached into his pocket for a pack of cigarettes, and offered one to Finn.

"Where did you get this?" Finn said, amazed and hungry for the taste of a cigarette.

"You are very naïve," Herman said. "Your family can send you cigarettes any time they want to. Just write and ask. Don't you know anything? You've got to understand, even if you don't know something, you better act like you do. If you're not a fighter, you better let people think you are."

Finn thought over Herman's advice while they finished their cigarettes.

"What are you in for?" Herman asked.

"Nothing," Finn said. "I was charged for something I didn't do."

"You've got a lot to learn," Herman sighed. He tossed his cigarette butt into a urinal and looked hard at Finn. "I said, what are you in for?"

"Car theft," Finn answered this time.

"That's more like it," Herman nodded as he walked toward the door. "You better learn to say what it looks like, not what it is. Don't bother with the truth."

Finn took Herman's advice. He got through the next few months easily: when he couldn't keep away from everyone else, when he was forced to, he confronted other boys, he no longer pretended to be invisible. He pretended to be tough, at times he could look menacing. But more and more, Finn was afraid; he believed that something would surface in him. He wondered if feelings might someday overcome him, so that suddenly, without any warning, he might break down in tears.

It was not only the pretense of toughness that protected Finn against ridicule or violence, it was his association with Herman. They were not really friends, they had nothing in common, they rarely even spoke; still, Herman made it clear that Finn was not to be bothered, and Finn repaid his debt with the cigarettes his mother now sent him, or with the racing magazines and comic books he was able to buy on rare trips into Albany to the dentist's office. Herman and Finn did not work side by side in the machine shop; there they ignored one another, they were acquaintances who nodded a greeting and sometimes sneaked out for a shared cigarette. It was after work, in the evenings, that Finn would find his way to Herman's dormitory room. There Finn would sit, with Herman, and sometimes with David as well, as if Finn could gain a strength that could only be found in Herman's room.

One evening, as Finn and Herman leafed through magazines, Herman watched Finn carefully.

"You're not close to anyone, are you?" Herman said.

Finn looked up from his magazine, surprised. "I'm doing all right," he shrugged. But in truth he was feeling worse and worse every day.

"How can you take it?" Herman shook his head. "It's one thing to act tough, and it's another thing to be so tough inside," Herman said as David walked into the room and began to complain about his job in the kitchen.

Finn could not stand his aloneness, and in spite of himself he had grown close to someone, and that someone was Herman. Finn passed algebra and eleventh-grade English, in the machine shop he learned how to use a drill and a hammer, but the only time he felt real was in Herman's room. There, he was himself. And Finn himself did not even know how important Herman was to him until Herman started avoiding him.

It began with Herman's decision to ask for a transfer from the machine shop to the kitchen. Soon after, Herman chose a different table to sit at in the dining room. Then after several evenings of feeble excuses why Finn could not visit his room, Herman finally took to walking out on Finn; he would leave his own room without saying a word. Now Finn could no longer pretend to be invisible, he could not levitate above the Stockley School; he found himself thinking about Herman, not occasionally, but all the time, as if Finn had become possessed. The evenings were long, and Finn spent his time wondering what he might have done to turn Herman away from him. On a Friday night, in the recreation room, Herman walked away from a card game when Finn sat down. This time Finn followed Herman out into the hallway; this time he stood his ground.

"Tell me what I did," Finn said.

"Did?" Herman said. "You didn't do anything."

"You're mad at me," Finn insisted. "Why are you mad?"

"Nobody's mad," Herman said. "The problem is David is jealous," he said simply. "That may sound foolish, that may be foolish, but David wants me not to talk to you. And if that's what he wants, that's what I'm going to do."

The nights were so long now, and no one at all knew Finn, no one but Herman. "I can come to your room tonight," Finn said suddenly. "It can be that way with us," he said without looking at Herman.

"I couldn't do that," Herman shook his head. "I could lose David by doing that. David's jealous, understand?"

Finn's loneliness came at him in a rush; it was all through his blood. "I've got to see you," he said to Herman, and his voice didn't sound like his own, his words broke, his words were sobs.

Herman took Finn's arm and led him to a corner of the hallway, where no one could see when he held Finn close. "Maybe you do have feelings," Herman smiled. "Maybe you fooled me with those blue eyes."

Finn did not move; Herman's touch went right through his shirt, his skin was electrified, currents flowed straight to his heart. "I don't want to lose you," Finn admitted.

Herman held him tighter, but after a while, he dropped his arms and backed away. "You've got to understand," Herman said. "David and me are both here for another year. You'll be getting out soon. You'd be leaving me. And I just can't risk that. It would just be too lonely to be alone."

Finn nodded, he said he understood and he watched Herman walk away; and later, when he was in bed, alone, Finn told himself that he was glad Herman had turned him down. He pretended that he had never meant the offer, that it had all been a joke. But Michael Finn didn't make jokes; alone, he faced the terrible truth: that he wanted to make love to Herman, and worse, he wanted to be held, to be rocked, just like a child. From then on, David had nothing to worry about: Finn kept away from Herman. He did not want to see Herman's face or hear his voice, and he did not want to know what stirred him.

Now when Finn walked down the halls of the Stockley School, he watched the other boys carefully; he wondered if everyone knew about him. He might easily be discovered; Herman might have talked about Finn's proposal, or Finn's feelings might show in his eyes. But no one paid any attention to Finn, and once again he tried to keep all of his feelings in check; after months of practice, weeks of being alone, Finn was again in control of his feelings: nothing escaped.

And Herman had been right; before he knew it, Finn's time at Stockley was up; he was released two days before his seventeenth birthday. There was no one for Finn to say goodbye to on the day of his release; he packed his bags and walked across the lawn to the administration building, where his parents waited. Less than a year after he left Stockley, Finn tried to contact Herman, on a whim, without thinking first. He had gone to a phone booth in Ruby's Café on Main Street and called long distance; it took quite some time before the clerk at Stockley found Herman's record, and by the time Finn was told that Herman had been picked up on burglary charges two months after his release from Stockley and then sent to Attica, all of Finn's change had run out. But Finn never imagined Herman in an upstate prison; he always remembered him as he had last seen him on the evening when Finn walked toward the administration building, and Danny Finn's waiting Oldsmobile.

That evening the sun was setting and crickets had begun to call; Herman was walking back from the dining room to the dorm. His arm was thrown over David's shoulders as they walked; and then Herman stopped for a moment to look up. He reached to point out something far above, a hawk or a cloud. And as he watched, secretly, from a distance, Finn could not imagine that any face could be as sweet as the one that looked upward in the middle of a huge lawn, in a school outside of Albany from which no one ever really escaped.

Finn waited until Herman was out of sight, until he could no longer see his friend, and then he walked on across the lawn, carrying his bags, not daring to look back. In the headmaster's office, Ada and Danny Finn sat awkwardly in leather chairs.

"Here he is," the headmaster shouted when Finn came through the door. "Here's our boy."

Ada Finn rushed over and kissed Michael's cheek; Danny Finn stood and shook his son's hand; but even though Finn greeted his parents, he was thinking about Herman, he was wondering why everything hidden inside himself had escaped once Herman had touched him.

"I hope things have changed," Danny Finn said. "I hope you've made a man out of him."

"Oh yes," the headmaster nodded. "I'm sure we have."

Again, Finn took Herman's advice; he pretended that there were no tears inside; he had learned to act the way he was supposed to be, not the way he was. And so, instead of running back across the lawn and searching for Herman in every room, instead of dropping to his knees on the thick wall-to-wall carpeting of the headmaster's office and howling until all of the pain inside evaporated, Michael Finn reached out and shook his father's hand, and he left the Stockley School, supposedly a free man.

SIX

"So DON'T TELL ME I don't know about prison," Finn whispered after the story had been told. "I was in prison when I walked through the doors of the Stockley School, and I was still in prison when I left."

"But it's over with now," I said.

"It's never over with," Finn told me. "Sometimes when I wake up in the morning I don't know where I am; I expect to find myself in the metal bed I had at Stockley. How can you say it's over when my heart never worked right again?"

Finn had been so alone that last day when he stood on the lawn on the Stockley School. If Herman had turned and run to him, what would Finn have done? What would he do now if I touched his face, if I held my arms around him and let him know he was not the only one to ever be lonely?

"You're starting to have feelings," I said.

"Hah," Finn said. "Fear."

"That's a start," I insisted.

"So what?" Finn said. "What does it matter? I'm going to jail." Finn lit another cigarette and inhaled.

"No," I said.

"Yes," Finn said tiredly. "Today. I'm going today."

"I don't want you to go," I said.

"You?" Finn laughed. "How do you think I feel?"

"I'll have to tell my supervisor about your case," I said.

"Yes," Finn agreed.

"I'll have to say I found out about your criminal activities today," I explained. "Otherwise I could be fired for withholding evidence."

"Of course. I never wanted to get you in trouble."

"Of course you didn't," I agreed.

"I thought of not coming here today, but I didn't want you to think I had just disappeared."

We sat so far apart we seemed to be separated from each other by miles, the room filled with blue shades of regret. Finn cleared his throat. "I have to be leaving," he told me.

"Are you certain it's today?" I asked.

Finn nodded. "I'd better go," he said, though he didn't make a move.

I finally stood and offered him my hand. "Good luck."

Finn took my hand and held it just long enough to make me shudder when he turned to go. I closed my eyes so that I would not have to watch him walk out the door, and when I opened them again he was already gone.

I canceled my appointments for the rest of the day; a burning in my stomach grew stronger and stronger, it moved along my bloodstream making me dizzy and unable to work. At four that afternoon, when Finn had already turned himself in to the district attorney and I was still alone in my office, Lark opened the door and peered inside.

"Natalie?" she said.

"I'm here," I told her.

"Why is it so dark in here?" Lark asked. "You're depressed."

"No." I shrugged. "Headache."

"You know," she said, coming to sit in the chair where Finn had been, "I've been expecting you at EMOTE. I've been promising the group for weeks that you'd be there."

"I've been too busy," I said.

"Really?" Lark said nothing about my empty desk, the telephone which did not ring, my head in my hands. "I hope you're not too busy to come to the staff meeting. It's already started."

I followed Lark through the waiting room where Emily measured coffee into the pot and listened to her portable radio. Soon newscasters would call out Finn's name on every wavelength, bits and pieces of his story would be told at six and eleven. I walked into the supervisor's office behind Lark, and then sat in the rear of the room, in the shadows cast by the other social workers. Claude Wilder was at his desk; he concentrated on a navel orange which he peeled carefully. Through the open door I could hear the hum of the radio, the pitch growing higher and higher.

"Claude," I called from the rear of the room, "I have something I'd like to discuss."

Lark got up and went out to the waiting room to complain about the volume of the radio; I strained to hear each word that was broadcast.

Claude Wilder chewed his orange calmly; he had no idea who Michael Finn was, he couldn't possibly tell I was a traitor, a coconspirator after the fact, the sweet burning act. "You'll just have to wait until the monthly business is over with," Claude said.

"This is serious," I said, my voice rising along with the volume of the radio which Lark seemed to have turned even higher. "I've discovered one of my clients may have committed a criminal act."

Claude tossed the last of his orange peel into the wastebasket and wiped his hands. "What client at Outreach hasn't been responsible for a criminal act?"

"This is different," I said.

Lark now returned to stand in the doorway. "They've caught him," she crowed. "They may send him here to Outreach for psychological testing. I may get to run a battery of tests."

"This will have to wait until after the monthly business," Claude said as he leafed through a pile of financial statements.

"Didn't you hear me?" Lark cried. "They've got the bomber."

The other workers turned to Lark, but I avoided her eyes. "I know they have," I said to her.

"How could you know?" Lark said.

"He was my client," I whispered, too low for anyone to hear.

"Do you want to hear something amazing?" Lark went on from her post at the door. "He's from Fishers Cove. He lived right here in town. We probably all know him by sight."

I hoped for courage. "He was my client," I announced.

Lark turned to me. "What?" she said.

"Michael Finn," I said. "Tuesdays and Thursdays."

"What are you talking about?" Claude Wilder asked.

"Tuesdays and Thursdays," I repeated.

"You didn't tell us who he was?" Lark said. "You kept him to yourself?"

"You're supposed to report every unrecorded criminal act to

me," Claude cried. "It's in our guidelines, it's in our rules. We have to work with the police department, we depend on county funding."

"You see, Finn mentioned a criminal act, but he wasn't comfortable discussing it," I said.

"Comfortable," Claude said.

"I didn't want to push him," I said.

"Natalie!"

"He made vague references to the explosion, but he didn't tell me all of it until today."

"He was here today?" Claude cried.

Lark sat down in a hard-backed chair. "She knew," Lark said, "and she didn't tell."

I shook my head; he had been here, he was here still, in the corners of every room, rising up like incense flavored with cinnamon and the oil of despair.

"All right," Claude Wilder nodded, crossing his arms in front of his chest, "you've got a lot of explaining to do."

Once Emily had been called in to jot down everything I said in shorthand and the other workers had all turned to listen, I didn't know where to begin. I was forced to leave out too much: how Finn's eyes could grow sharp with fear, how his hopelessness had taken over suddenly, mysteriously, after years of quiet rage. There was no way to explain why his rare smiles were so important to me. Without all of these details, the man I spoke of was not even Finn. How could I tell them that although he had committed a crime, he was innocent; that innocence was as secret as my own heart, and just as impossible to lay down on the bare floor.

After the meeting, Claude insisted that I agree to a conference with Outreach's board of directors the following week. I got my coat from my office and then walked through the waiting room, where the other social workers had gathered in a corner to discuss my betrayal.

"Thanks," Lark said to me as I walked out the door.

"Did you want me to betray a professional confidence?" I asked her.

"You just wanted to keep him all to yourself," Lark said. "That's all."

I ran all the way home to Minnie's, hoping the fresh air would sober me and I would no longer feel such a tremendous loss. There would be bulletins on the radio, headlines in every local paper, and Finn would be alone, behind metal, behind bars, behind the blackest sun of doubt. At least there would be quiet at Minnie's—no radio, no TV, just hours of sleep.

The door shut behind me; I felt as though I were still running. When I found Minnie waiting for me in the kitchen, my hopes for quiet, for forgetfulness, grew dim.

"I just can't talk about it," I told my aunt. "It's true he's turned himself in, but I don't know any of the details, and I'm sick to death of it all."

"Take a look," Minnie said, handing me a copy of the *Fishers Cove Herald*.

"No," I said. "I can't bear to."

"Do you live in this world or don't you?" Minnie said. "Take a look."

Finn's name stretched across the headline; there was a splotchy photo of Reno LeKnight standing on the steps of the police station on East Main. "It's begun now," I sighed, handing the paper back to Minnie. "That's all anyone will be talking about. The bomber," I whispered. "Michael Finn."

"Wake up," Minnie said, refusing the paper. "Look farther down the page."

"Can't you understand?" I said to my aunt. "Every time I think of Finn in jail I feel sick."

"Look," Minnie said. "Just look."

I opened the paper. Beneath the photo of LeKnight there was another photograph, a smaller one; in the haze Beaumont cast a faint smile at the camera. I looked up at Minnie.

"That's right," Minnie nodded.

"This is ridiculous," I said. "Where is he?" I turned my ear to the floor below, listening for the familiar clatter of pots and pans.

"He's not here," Minnie said. "He's also turned himself in as the bomber."

I sat at the kitchen table and closed my eyes; there was no place that didn't seem shaky, no one who hadn't been touched by the purple smoke of the explosion. Beaumont and Finn were both in jail for crimes never committed anywhere but in their own hearts, and I could not think of one thing I could do to help. So when Minnie set a cup of peppermint tea with honey in front of me I didn't wave her away, I didn't bother to remind her peppermint was a flavor I had never cared for. Instead, I let the sweet-smelling steam rise up in my face, and then I drank it all down like medicine, even though I knew, as I tasted the honey on my tongue, that there was no remedy, no home-grown cure for what I had caught, and no hope of recovery.

HALF-LIFE

ONE

ON SUNDAY, WITH BEAU-
mont and Finn still in jail, Minnie decided to take matters into
her own hands. It was late afternoon when my aunt informed
me that we were both about to visit Fishers Cove's congressman,
Pete Bruner. I had not yet bothered to dress; I was on the floor,
surrounded by Sunday newspapers, cutting out articles about
Michael Finn, wishing that the *Herald* or the *Times* had printed
at least one photograph.

"Come on," Minnie said to me. "I'm going to get Beaumont
out of jail and I need a witness."

"Do you really think you'll get to see the congressman on a
Sunday?" I asked. "I have my ways," Minnie said with a smile.
There was only the slightest chance that the congressman would
agree to see us, let alone listen to what we had to say, but there
was the chance. I dressed and met Minnie out in the driveway,
where her faded violet Mustang was parked. We got in and
Minnie revved the motor. When we pulled out of the driveway,
we headed toward the harbor and then turned west on Route
18. A few miles outside town, Minnie turned off onto Shore

Drive; here the old estates still stood, perfect frozen lawns rolled down toward the water.

"I've never been here before," I said.

"Why should you ever have come here?" Minnie asked. She took her hand off the wheel to point toward a huge brick house. "Think of how many people could live in that house; you could fit a whole family into one of the closets."

When we saw the congressman's name engraved into a high wrought-iron fence, Minnie turned the Mustang down a secluded dirt driveway. We drove beneath a grove of mimosa and pines, and finally reached a stone house whose turrets reached to the trees. A greenhouse filled with orchids and palms was to the left of the house, and to the right a built-in pool had been circled with paths of slate.

"A public servant," Minnie said.

We followed the circular driveway and parked beside tall stone vases planted with ivy. At the front door, Minnie pulled a long metal chain which sounded a bell. "Let me do all the talking," my aunt told me as a young woman in a black uniform opened the door.

"Can I help you?" she asked.

"I'm here to see the congressman," Minnie said far too loudly, as if the housekeeper might be deaf. "Right away," my aunt said.

The housekeeper gazed from the battered Mustang in the driveway to Minnie's unruly white hair. "Do you ladies have an appointment?" she asked.

"Ladies," Minnie said to me. She leaned forward confidentially. "How well does he pay you?"

"What?" the young woman said as she drew back.

"I'm curious," Minnie explained. "When I first came to Fishers Cove I thought of trying to get a job in one of these houses. I'm a terrific cook," she told the housekeeper. "But they paid their help shit then, and I suppose it's still the same. What domestic workers need is a union."

"We do have an appointment with the congressman," I said in what I hoped sounded like a rational voice. "Perhaps he's forgotten. He definitely said at three on Sunday, and it's just about three."

"Just a minute," Bruner's housekeeper said as she closed the front door.

Minnie turned on me. "Why did you lie to her? We don't have to humiliate ourselves. Bruner works for us. We're the people."

"I thought you wanted to get inside?" I said. "What difference does it make now?"

"It makes a difference," Minnie cried. "We don't have to bow and scrape."

"No one bowed," I said. "Nobody scraped. I simply lied."

The housekeeper was back in only a few minutes to show us inside. "The congressman will see you," she said to me, but she kept her distance from Minnie.

We were led into Bruner's den. The ceiling was two floors high, bay windows lined the wall facing the harbor, there were white velvet couches grouped around a thick red rug. Congressman Bruner stood behind his desk; he bit off the top of a cigar.

"I don't think you two ladies really have an appointment." Bruner smiled. "But I love it when my constituents feel they can just drop in on me. That means we're close, and closeness is what counts in government."

"This isn't a social call," Minnie said, refusing to shake the congressman's hand and going instead to sit on a velvet couch.

"How do you do?" I said.

"He does very well, can't you see that?" Minnie said, waving her hand at the furniture and rugs.

"What brings you ladies here today?" the congressman asked.

"You don't have to be polite with me," Minnie smiled. "I know you from way back."

"And do I know you?" Bruner asked.

"Minnie Lansky," my aunt said proudly.

"Lansky," the congressman said. "The letters. I remember you." He nodded glumly. "Your whole family, too."

"I never had anything to do with those letters," I explained.

"I've had my eye on you for a long time," Minnie told Bruner. "And now I've got you."

Bruner sat behind his desk. "All right," he said. "Let's not spend time fooling around. What do you want?"

Now that the congressman had begun to look more uncomfortable, Minnie relaxed. She took off her gloves and unbuttoned her coat. "This is my niece." She pointed to me.

"Very nice to meet you," Bruner said cautiously.

"The truth is," Minnie said, "I'm here because I want D. F. Beaumont released from jail." She paused and smiled. "Today."

"Oh you do, do you?" Bruner said. He turned to me. "Who is Beaumont?"

"This takes the cake," Minnie cried. "What kind of politician doesn't know what's going on in his own town? Don't you read the news?"

"Now just a minute," Bruner snapped. "I'm very busy. I can't be expected to know everyone in the county by name."

"That's what they all say," Minnie nodded.

"Beaumont has been a boarder at my aunt's house since nineteen fifty-six," I explained. "Now it seems he's been arrested."

"And he's sixty-three years old," Minnie said. "Sixty-three."

"All right," Bruner said, reaching for a notepad. "What was he picked up for?"

"Nothing really," Minnie said. "He says he's the bomber."

"The bomber?" Bruner frowned. "That weasel? Does he think he can stop progress?"

"Progress?" Minnie sniffed. "Hah."

"We'd like him released in our custody," I said.

"You'd like the bomber released?" Bruner said. "You've got to be kidding."

"Beaumont wouldn't know how to make a bomb if you paid him. He was in my house at the time of the explosion, I can vouch for that. The truth is he's just an old eccentric," Minnie explained.

"He's innocent," I said. "There's no doubt about it."

"That may be," Bruner said. "But there's nothing I can do, even if I wanted to. And I don't really think I want to," he said pointedly.

"All right," Minnie said. "Fine." She began to button her coat, she reached for her gloves. "If you can't help, maybe your brother-in-law can."

"What brother-in-law?" Bruner said.

Minnie smiled and patted the mohair scarf around her throat. "Let's go," she said to me.

"What does Allen have to do with anything?" the congressman asked warily.

"Your brother-in-law's a big shot, isn't he?" she said to the congressman. "Although to tell you the truth he does a lousy job running the Mercy Home, I can't see how he ever got the contract from the county in the first place." Minnie wrinkled her brow. "Does he have a degree in business administration?"

Bruner sat up straight in his chair. "The Mercy Home?" he said.

"I work there," Minnie said. "A volunteer."

"How do you know who runs the home?" I asked.

"What do you think?" Minnie said. "I looked through the records."

Bruner relit his cigar. "It's illegal to look through private records."

"So?" Minnie shrugged. "Send me to jail."

The wind rapped against the bay windows, sea gulls circled the wide, sloping lawn.

"Do you intend to make your knowledge public?" the congressman asked.

"Not necessarily," Minnie said.

"All right," Bruner sighed. "I'll see what I can do."

While Bruner reached for his phone and dialed the Fishers Cove station house, I watched Minnie; she was just like the woman I remembered, the one walking through all of my summers with giant steps. And no one who saw her, sitting on the white velvet couch, patting stray strands of hair back into place, would have guessed how strong she was.

Bruner hung up the phone and turned to Minnie. "Beaumont isn't the bomber."

"We know that," Minnie said.

"The police plan to send him back to the Veterans' Hospital, but if you're willing to take him on, fine. Naturally he no longer has his job at the power plant; he's too unstable to be a night watchman."

"Good," Minnie nodded. "That was no job for him anyway."

"Well, then, ladies," Bruner spread out his hands and smiled, "I believe our business is finished."

"No," Minnie said, settling back on the couch, "it isn't."

"Please, Mrs. Lansky," Bruner said, "my daughter and her family are driving out from Manhattan for dinner."

"Lobster?" Minnie said. "Because if it's lobster from our harbor, it's been crawling around in polluted waters."

"Steak," Bruner said grimly.

"Filled with DES hormones," Minnie said. "Do you really want your grandchildren to eat that?"

"Mrs. Lansky," Bruner sighed.

"A little favor," Minnie said. "In return for not spilling the beans."

"Spilling the beans?" Bruner said.

"That an unqualified person like your brother-in-law was made board chairman of the Mercy Home."

"Let's not talk about my brother-in-law," Bruner said. "All right?"

"If there were improvements at Mercy, I would never mention him again," Minnie said. "Better food and clothing and a recreation staff. I think it can be done by the end of the week."

"Mrs. Lansky," Bruner said, "these things take time."

"He's right," I said. "And the congressman might not even have the power to do what you're asking."

"My niece," Minnie said to the congressman. "Don't listen to her. What does she know? I know. You have more power than anyone else in the country."

The congressman looked at my aunt, pleased. "I wouldn't say that," he said.

"I would," Minnie insisted.

"All right," Congressman Bruner nodded. "I'll see what I can do. I'm not promising anything."

"Fine," Minnie said. "I have faith in you," she told Bruner. "I'm sure you can manage something."

"I should have been in politics," Minnie said when we followed the congressman's housekeeper to the door. "I'm hot stuff," she whispered.

Once we were out of the house I said, "You just blackmailed a congressman."

Minnie shook her head and opened the door of the Mustang. "Plea bargaining," she said. "Lawyers do it all the time."

"You're not a lawyer, Minnie," I said, but she had already closed her door and turned on the engine. When we drove back down the driveway, past the wrought-iron fence, I was envious because Minnie had managed to spring Beaumont from jail while I couldn't even manage a visit to Michael Finn. I wanted to bake Finn a rich chocolate cake with concealed hope and a file, but I was helpless, able only to ride shotgun with an old woman who seemed strong enough to bend metal bars.

Minnie was so thrilled with her own success that she insisted on treating us both to dinner before she continued on to the station house where Beaumont was being held. We stopped at a small Szechuan restaurant on Route 18, just outside town.

"Chinese food," Minnie told me, "because they wouldn't be

caught dead using chemicals. Order something with bamboo shoots—they're great for anxiety."

We ordered black mushrooms and rice, and a dish called Three Vegetable Delight; though none of the ingredients looked familiar to me, Minnie insisted bamboo shoots were included. During dinner my mood grew worse; over and over again I thought of how Finn had walked out of my door.

"Tea," Minnie prescribed when she noticed I was sad.

But I drank only a sip; I played with the fortune cookies the waiter had set down before us, afraid to read any of the slips of paper inside.

"You should be happy," Minnie said. "We've had a victory."

"You've had a victory," I told my aunt. "You'll have Beaumont out of jail tonight, and I can't even go down to the station house."

"Why can't you?" Minnie asked.

"I'm supposed to be an objective witness for Finn," I said. "I can't go and visit him as if I were anything more."

"Of course you can," Minnie said. "You're the man's social worker, you're entitled to see him."

"He may not want me," I said. "There's nothing between us, you know," I informed my aunt.

"Oh, please," Minnie said. "Not that again."

"Ask him if you don't believe me," I said. "Ask him."

"Listen to me," Minnie said, reaching across the table to hold my hand, "there's nothing wrong in making certain he's all right."

"I've never been inside one of these places," I told Minnie as we walked up the stairs of the station house.

"The first time I was here was in nineteen-fifty-one to report a missing person," my aunt said. "Alex went for a walk one day and he didn't come back. I knew he didn't have a girlfriend, he wasn't the type; so where could he be? I came here and reported him. They found him all right, asleep in the library; he had gotten locked in. What a night for a poet like Alex! Sleeping surrounded by all those books." Minnie pinched my cheek as we walked inside. "There's nothing to it," she whispered. "Just walk right in and act like you belong."

While Minnie signed for Beaumont's release, I went up to the desk lieutenant and asked to see Finn.

"Who are you?" the lieutenant asked. "A reporter?"

When I said I was Finn's social worker, the lieutenant grudgingly agreed to let me into the detention cells for a few minutes. I followed a young officer to the row of cells where prisoners were held before going on to the county jail, or to an upstate prison, or in a few cases, back to the street, released by a miracle or bail. The iron door slammed shut behind us; inside, the walls of the corridors had been painted green, an imitation of spring. When we walked by the first cell I saw that Beaumont was there; he sat on the metal rim of his cot and stared mournfully at the ceiling.

"Do you mind stopping?" I asked the officer who led me to Finn. "Beaumont," I called through the bars. "Get ready to go. Minnie's signing for your release."

Beaumont was startled to see me; he straightened his rumpled shirt. "I can't go," he said shyly. "I did it. The explosion was my fault."

"He's been saying that all day," the young officer shrugged.

"Beaumont, you're not responsible," I said.

"Sure I am," Beaumont said. "And I'm sorry. I really am."

"You placed a bomb in the second unit of the power plant?" I asked.

"No," the old boarder said.

"A lunatic," the officer behind me whispered. "We get them all the time."

"Did you tamper with any of the machinery?" I now asked. "Have you ever been inside one of the buildings?"

"No."

"Then why do you keep confessing?" I asked.

"He's crazy, that's why," the officer explained.

"I was the night guard," Beaumont told me. "If I had done my job, the explosion never would have happened."

"The explosion happened before five in the afternoon," I said. "Whoever is the day watchman is responsible. Not you."

"Not me?" Beaumont tilted his head like an old dog.

"It was the day man's responsibility," I said. "You're the night man. You're innocent."

"I'm innocent." Beaumont smiled. "I'm the night man, and I didn't do it."

"That's what we've been telling you all day," the officer sighed.

"Minnie will be here soon," I told Beaumont as I followed the officer farther down the corridor. The metal bars of empty cells shimmered, the odor of stale cigarettes stung. When we were nearly to the end of the row I finally saw Finn; he stood with his back to the wall. Pretending to be quiet, he almost looked calm, but he pounded his fist against his thigh, as if he hoped eventually to break through to the bones and the blood. The officer rapped on the metal bars.

"Someone's here to see you," he told Finn.

When Finn looked up and saw me, his expression didn't alter; he looked right through me.

"Can you unlock the door?" I asked the officer.

"Sorry, no," the officer told me. "This one's the real bomber." But he did walk back down the corridor to smoke a cigarette and give us some privacy.

"It's perfectly normal for me to visit you," I said to Finn.

"Yeah?" Finn said.

"It is," I said. "It's perfectly normal."

"Why?" Finn asked.

"I had to make certain you were all right," I said.

"Well, here I am. I'm not going anywhere."

"Carter's probably raising bail right now," I said.

Finn's lips moved but I couldn't hear him; the iron bars caught every word. "Come closer," I said.

"I can't," Finn said. "I can't move."

He stood against the wall, rigid as wire. If he moved an inch he might not be able to stop, he might climb right over the bars; if he opened his mouth too wide he risked a shriek or a sigh.

"I want to help you," I said.

"You can't."

"Please," I said. I had moved so close to the bars that I could feel the metal and rust in the back of my throat. "Just talk to me."

The officer who had led me to Finn now tossed his cigarette on the floor and crushed it beneath his heel. "Time's up," he called to me. "He really shouldn't have any visitors at all."

Minnie had followed the desk lieutenant into the holding center to retrieve Beaumont.

I turned to that last cell. "Michael," I said, "just come closer." But Finn refused to answer me; he leaned his head against the wall and closed his eyes.

When the officer wouldn't wait any longer, I followed him back down the corridor. Beaumont was stepping out from his cell. "Thank you," the old man said when I reached him.

"It was nothing," I said. "Just a mistake."

"You saved me," Beaumont said, looking from Minnie to me. "You rescued me."

"From now on you'll have to be more careful," Minnie said sharply. "We can't go running after you, we can't keep rescuing you."

Beaumont hung his head. "It was a mistake," he said.

"That's right," Minnie said, linking her arm through his. "That's all it was."

The desk lieutenant opened the door back into the station house and Minnie and Beaumont stepped through. But before I left the rows of detention cells, I looked back. Through the bars I could see that Finn had finally moved. His face was hidden, he was too far away for me to look into his eyes, but before I stepped through the doorway, I saw that he had wound his fingers around the bars, and he held on tight, as if there were enough power in his hands to lift him right up through the roof, straight into the starless night.

TWO

On the morning when I was to meet with Outreach's board of directors, Beaumont presented Minnie and me with a gift; breakfast was ready and waiting on the table. Minnie frowned at the oatmeal, she scowled at the glasses of prune juice and tapped the steaming mugs of peppermint tea suspiciously.

"Who asked Beaumont to do this?" Minnie said. "Who needs him messing around in my kitchen?" My aunt picked up a glass and studied the juice. "And what does he mean by this? Why is he feeding us prunes?"

"I think it was lovely," I said. I tasted the oatmeal, then pushed the bowl away, and got up to make coffee. "It was a very nice gesture," I insisted, though the oatmeal was horrid, and my stomach was too jumpy for juice.

Minnie tasted a spoonful of cereal. "Not too bad," she shrugged.

"A gift of love," I said as I measured out coffee.

"Now that he doesn't have a job, all Beaumont can give is love," Minnie said. "Unless he has a new job. Unless someone hires him."

"Who would hire him?" I laughed.

"Me," Minnie answered. "That's who. I've got to spruce this place up, and I could use some help."

"This place looks fine," I said, settling for goat's milk to pour into my coffee.

"Not fine enough if I want to fill the house with boarders."

"Oh, really?" I said. "And just who do you expect to get?"

"Old people," Minnie said.

"Minnie," I shook my head. "You don't have the facilities for old people here."

"What am I?" Minnie cried. "Am I old? Do I live here without any facilities? There are plenty of people at Mercy who would love to live here. Good food, natural food, privacy and company both; and their Social Security would cover all the expenses and give me something on the side."

I sipped my coffee. "It will never work."

"I'll give you odds," Minnie said.

We cleared the table. Minnie undoubtedly thought about filling every room in the house with new boarders as she slammed plates into the sink, while I imagined the board of directors waiting for me dressed in black suits, filling Claude Wilder's office with judgment. When we had finished cleaning up, Beaumont appeared in the doorway, dressed in his uniform.

"You didn't like the breakfast I made," he said, when he saw Minnie pouring her juice down the drain.

"It was wonderful," I said, though I had scraped my oatmeal into the bucket of biodegradable trash.

"Not too bad," Minnie commented. "But as far as I'm concerned, none of us should ever need prune juice if our diet is right. I hope you're eating enough fresh fruits and vegetables, Beaumont."

"You know," Beaumont told us shyly, "I'm not the bomber."

"Of course you're not," Minnie said, nodding. "You never were. But now that you've been fired from the power plant, you'll need another job."

"My raft," Beaumont said. "I plan to retire to Florida as soon as my raft is ready to go." The old man had been tinkering, working for years on a raft I was certain existed only in his imagination.

"Your raft," Minnie's voice rose impatiently. "You'll still have plenty of time for that. But I'd like to hire you. Free rent if you agree to work for me. Floors, windows, a lot of hard work."

"Minnie," I said as I reached for my coat, "don't you think you're rushing things?"

Minnie ignored me. "Bring the floor waxer up from the basement," she told Beaumont. "If it's not too heavy for you."

"Too heavy?" the boarder smiled. "For me?"

"Is he your indentured servant now?" I asked.

"This is none of your business," my aunt told me. "Beaumont is only too happy to have something useful to do."

Beaumont nodded. "But I'll have to work at night."

"Night, day, what's the difference?" Minnie said. "As long as we get this house into tiptop shape."

When I left for work, Minnie was leading Beaumont down the stairs in search of the floor waxer, which had long ago been stored behind the washing machine and the old Hoover freezer. As I walked to Outreach, I worried about Minnie. She had been young when she had called all the Lanskys together to flock to her house in summer like crazy Russian birds. Her heart had been strong then; she could have carried the floor waxer up to the third floor without any help. Now she was old; a woman her age should not be planning a boarding-house renaissance, a woman her age should not depend on a thing as fragile as hope. As the last Lansky left with her, I would have to deal with Minnie's despair if her plans fell through and no boarders checked in. I might even find Minnie's feet dangling over the edge of her bed if, in some hazy depression, she decided to slip a bit of natural poison into a glass of raw apple juice. And then, what of Beaumont? Without Minnie he would wind up back at the V.A. Hospital, returned to the wide porch lined with rocking chairs, with no hope of ever seeing either his raft or the Florida waters he yearned for. My concern for Minnie and her old boarder overwhelmed me, and when I got to Outreach I sat on the couch in the waiting room like a tired client.

"They're all in there," Emily whispered to me from her desk. "They're waiting."

I rose with a sigh, and walked into Claude's office with my coat still buttoned. Inside, Claude was circled by the three Outreach directors: a physician named Johnson, who had first sponsored Outreach for county funding; Gerkin, our fund raiser, who attended dinners and lectures all through the state; and Sally Wallace, who had donated fifty thousand dollars of her own in the memory of her late son, Gideon, a boy Mrs. Wallace thought might have survived his heroin addiction had Outreach existed before his death.

"Here she is," Claude said when I entered the room. "Right on time."

"You've really done a very stupid thing," Sally Wallace said to me.

"There's been some bizarre behavior here at Outreach," Johnson said. "Some irresponsible behavior."

"Naïve," Mrs. Wallace said. "Naïve would be a better word."

"I haven't been irresponsible," I said. "If you're referring to the bombing at the plant, we have nothing to talk about. I have no information. It's true, Mr. Finn is my client . . ."

"Was," Claude Wilder corrected. "He'll see a court-referred psychiatrist from now on."

"He came to see me because he was having a problem dealing with his anger."

"I'll bet," the fund raiser, Gerkin, said.

"And when he came to see me, the bombing had already occurred, it was already water under the bridge," I said.

"The point is," Johnson said, "you have got yourself into a very controversial situation."

"Oh, no," I said quickly. "I don't think so."

"You're still a new worker," Claude Wilder told me. "You're still on probation. If you know what I mean."

"No. I don't know what you mean," I said to Claude, but my palms had begun to sweat.

Claude leaned far back in his chair. "I mean you can be fired for the slightest infraction of Outreach's rules."

"I don't understand," I insisted. "I didn't break any rules. I knew very little about the bombing until the day Mr. Finn turned himself in to the authorities." As if for spite, my left eye began to twitch as I lied. "To my knowledge, the bombing was an accident. It seems that Mr. Finn realized he had made an error in his work when it was already too late."

"It doesn't matter if it was an accident or if he was working with the Russian army. We just want you to be careful," Johnson said coldly. "Watch your step," he advised.

"You may be in the public eye," Sally Wallace told me. "You may even be called to testify at the trial."

"Do you really think so?" I asked.

"Quite possibly," Mrs. Wallace said.

"Some members of the board feel that you won't be able to handle the pressure," Claude said. "But I'm sure you'll do just fine. I'm certain that none of Outreach's state or county funding will be jeopardized by any stupid mistakes."

"Don't forget," Gerkin said, "this is a great opportunity for you if you deal with the situation correctly."

"One hand washes the other," Johnson nodded.

"We want you to come through the trial without any controversy, and with as little publicity as possible. We don't want Outreach linked with the bomber," Sally Wallace said.

"I'll try my best," I said.

"Just remember," Claude said, as the meeting came to a close, "we all have faith in you."

All the plans I had made for Finn's trial seemed petty; it barely mattered that the board of directors now warned me against publicity, all those articles I had planned to write would have been touched by emotion anyway. The lies I had told regarding how much I knew about the explosion and the agreement I had made to appear as Finn's witness would now bring me nothing, only a terrible loneliness I had never known before.

For all practical purposes, Finn and I were through with each other; he would be referred to a court psychiatrist, I would move on to other clients. Still, all that day I thought of him, imagined him walking on slippery ice. Finn may have been sending out a distress signal in the holding center of the police station, his fingers on the bars might have been a sign of passion, and trust. I had difficulty listening to the soft complaints of my clients that morning, and when Susan Wolf, the young anorectic, appeared for her afternoon appointment, I found myself drawn to the window, hoping that Finn might somehow appear, that he might stand in the middle of the street and look upward, into my window.

"Why is everything so difficult?" I said.

"I don't know a thing about it," Susan said.

Outside, on the window ledge, pigeons flapped their wings and cooed. He couldn't be out there, not waiting in a doorway or alone in his Camaro. I went to my chair and sat heavily. "I'm so confused," I said.

Susan looked alarmed, she sat far back in her chair. "It's not my fault," she said. "Don't tell me about it."

But it was too late, and Susan was too small and not strong enough to keep me from crying.

"Don't do this," Susan said.

Tears dripped down my cheeks, nothing was held back, not until every sob was out. I reached for a tissue.

"I'm sorry," I apologized, but Susan looked down at the floor and refused to speak. "Please," I said. "Sometimes these things happen."

"Not to me," Susan said.

"You never cry?" I asked.

"I don't want to talk about it," the girl told me.

"You've never felt like crying?" I asked.

"No!" Susan told me. When she shook her head her hair flowed out in long, bitter strands.

"All right, all right," I said.

"I don't have to listen to you, you know," Susan said. "I don't have to."

"No," I agreed. "You don't."

"And I don't have to stay here," Susan said.

"Unfortunately, you do," I said. Susan had been referred to Outreach by the juvenile court after an arrest at the new shopping mall on Route 18; she had been discovered in the dressing room of the children's department, filling her pocketbook with sweaters and shirts many sizes too small.

"I can see another worker," Susan said. "My parole officer told me I could." She reached for her coat and stood. "I don't have to stay here," she told me.

"Fine," I said. "That's just fine with me," I called as Susan slammed out of the office. When she had gone I reached for her file; already the girl would have run across Main Street, her footprints would lead down to the harbor where she would stare mournfully at her own reflection in the thick slabs of harbor ice. I had chased Susan away with my own flood of feelings; if she surfaced in a hospital ward where old women and young girls were forced to eat against their will, I would be to blame. Even after I wrote a memo referring the girl to Lark, I felt that I had betrayed Susan, as I had all of my clients; every bit of reason I ever possessed was gone. I no longer felt able to try and arrange the lives of my clients when I was so caught up with Finn.

It was then I called Carter; if I could spend the night with someone, someone whose skin and kisses I knew as well as

Carter's, my feelings for Michael Finn might disappear. I might wake up in the morning with Carter's arm around me and find there was no one else I wanted to touch, no one else whose touch I wanted desperately. I let the phone ring five times, and just when I was about to hang up, Carter answered.

"I'm so glad you're there," I said. "I don't know what I would have done if you hadn't answered."

"He's out," Carter told me, and as soon as he did my skin grew cold, and all the words I thought I would say disappeared. "I cashed in my mother's securities yesterday, and Reno put up bail today."

"Where is he?" I asked.

"Somewhere in town," Carter said. "Otherwise I'm a poor man, otherwise he's jumped bail."

"He wouldn't do that," I said. "He would never do that."

"I hope not," Carter said. "Listen, I can't really talk."

"Sure," I agreed. Finn had walked out the door of the police station only hours before. Reno LeKnight had walked arm in arm with his client, speaking of defense tactics and courtroom secrets with every step.

"I have to drive to New Hampshire tonight," Carter told me. "The Soft Skies office in Manchester asked me to come up and brief them."

"Of course," I said, already forgetting about Carter's kisses, not quite remembering the color of the sheets on his mattress.

"I'll try to be back by the end of the week," Carter said. "It's not that I like all this running around. It's not that I don't miss you."

A woman in love would have been much more disappointed, a woman in love would have cried and begged him to stay.

"Drive carefully," I said before I hung up.

Because Carter was unavailable, I decided to go to the nursing home at the end of the day. I hoped to walk the rest of the way home with Minnie; I needed a companion other than Finn's spirit. But when I asked for Minnie at the admitting desk, no one knew where she was. My aunt had finished calling off Bingo numbers at four; and although one of the nurses thought Minnie might still be in the dayroom, when I went there she was nowhere in sight. There was only the same row of captives, trapped in their wheelchairs, as if they hadn't moved since last time I visited Mercy. At the far end of the room, across from the color TV, a neat elderly woman sat watching the screen. Because her posture was straight and her eyes focused, I went over to her.

"Have you seen the news?" I asked, thinking Finn's release might have been televised.

"Oh, yes," the old woman smiled. "Many times."

"Today?" I asked.

"Sure," the old woman nodded. "Absolutely."

"Did they mention anything about the bombing?" I asked.

"Bombing?" the old woman laughed. "That was in nineteen forty-one. You're a little confused, aren't you?"

I excused myself, left the dayroom, and began to search for Minnie. I walked up and down the first-floor corridors; here, the very old and ill rested on hard mattresses, their eyes closed, their breathing soft and slow. Up on the second floor the old folks were healthier; they played checkers or chess, some listened to transistor radios or sipped tea. There, at the end of the hallway, I found Minnie.

My aunt sat on a hard-backed wooden chair; she spoke with

two identical old sisters and a bearded old man who mopped his brow with a linen handkerchief.

"It's so damn hot in this place," the old man said. "Are they trying to broil us alive?"

"It's that old myth," I heard Minnie say cheerfully. "The older you are, the hotter you should be. Although people are dying like flies in Florida, and they're living to a hundred and twenty in the Georgian mountains."

"Exactly," the old man nodded.

"Of course in Florida you have your oranges, you have your lemons," one of the twins said.

"And your grapefruits," her sister added.

"Filled with chemicals and coated with wax," Minnie said gravely.

When I knocked on the open door, all four turned toward me like thieves caught in the act.

"Relax," Minnie told the others when she saw me. "It's just my niece. We thought you were one of the nurses," she explained to me. "Although God forbid they ever get up the stairs to the second floor. It would be easy enough to die up here and not be missed for weeks."

Minnie then introduced me to the Fuller twins—Evie and Yolanda, whom I could tell apart only because Evie wore a lime-green pants suit and Yolanda a beige woolen dress. Arthur, the old gentleman, stood and shook my hand.

"You may ask what we're doing up here," Minnie said. "The truth is that we're conspiring."

"No better way to phrase it," Arthur nodded.

"These three are going to be my new boarders," Minnie said proudly.

"That's a nice idea," I said vaguely.

"It's more than an idea," Yolanda said.

"It's a lifeboat in the sea of old age," Arthur added.

Minnie wrinkled her nose. "Maybe not a lifeboat. But you've got to admit," she turned to me, "there's no reason for these three to be in a nursing home."

"Well, no," I said. The three old folks sat up straight and puffed themselves out like chickens showing off beautiful feathers.

"They look quite healthy," I agreed.

"You're damn right," Evie said, as she tossed her head and her long gold earrings chimed.

"And I'm even healthier than she is," Yolanda pointed to her sister. "I have all my own teeth."

"We're here because of poverty," Arthur explained. "None of us can afford our own home on Social Security."

"Now that you're here," Minnie said to me, "I can tell you the news. I saw your bomber on TV."

"Minnie," I said, "he's not 'my' bomber." Arthur looked away discreetly, but Evie and Yolanda now craned their necks forward to listen.

"You can trust them"—Minnie gestured at the twins— "they're old."

The sisters' heads bobbed in agreement, and because I longed to find out more about Finn, I asked my aunt, "What do you know?"

"He's out on bail. He was filmed walking from the station house to his lawyer's car. A Lincoln."

"How did he look?" I asked.

"How could he look?" Minnie said. "He looked tired." Minnie turned to her friends. "This bomber is a very young man," Minnie said, and the twins nodded as if everything was now explained.

"All I can do is sit and wait for the trial to begin," I said. "Outreach doesn't want any publicity."

"Your bomber is out on bail and you're not going to see him?" Minnie shook her head sadly. "Love," she said to her friends, "is not what it used to be."

"It used to really be something," Evie said wistfully.

"It used to be the sparkles in a naked woman's eyes," Arthur sighed.

"Nowadays," Minnie added, "everything is practical."

"Why do you keep insisting I'm in love with this man?" I said angrily.

Minnie looked straight at me. "It's obvious."

"Well, you're wrong," I said, afraid that the more Minnie insisted, the less I would be able to protest. "It's ridiculous to think I'd become involved with a client."

"Oh." Yolanda nodded. "A client. That's a different story."

"Nonsense," Evie said. "Love is love."

"What kind of client?" Yolanda asked.

"Are you coming home?" I asked Minnie.

"I can't," Minnie shook her head. "Beaumont's picking me up here. We're going to buy an elevator seat for the staircase. I don't want Arthur to strain himself walking up and down once he moves in."

"It's no strain," Arthur said self-consciously.

"Don't be silly," Minnie said. "Every house full of old people should have one of those contraptions."

After I walked home I would have dinner alone, but once I

had cooked the scrambled eggs, I would be unable to eat. My untouched dinner would congeal, the floorboards would creak, the clock on the kitchen wall would tick like a heartbeat.

"Don't wait up for me," Minnie now advised me. "I've got a million things to do. Beaumont's something like a werewolf," she explained to her friends. "He won't set foot on the street till after sundown."

I wondered if Minnie was right; perhaps Finn was mine whether I wanted him or not, maybe because I was the first one to hear his story or just because I cared. He would be with me no matter what I did; even if I tried to avoid him, his spirit would be waiting for me in the parlor, in every room, ready to turn to flesh and blood.

"He's got a thing about the dark," Minnie was saying. "Look, everybody's a little crazy." She shrugged.

I stood and interrupted my aunt. I was not nearly as afraid of that empty house as I had been just minutes before, the walk home didn't seem half as long.

"I've got to go," I said. "It was nice to have met you," I told Minnie's friends.

The conspirators called out their goodbyes as I went toward the stairs. I walked home slowly. When I got there I didn't hesitate at the door, I went inside alone, no longer resisting my thoughts of the hour when I would meet Finn again.

THREE

$\mathcal{A}$S SOON AS I COULD, I
went to see him. What had begun that first night we met in
the field had now come together; tendrils led to a pure, red rose.
Finn was more than just another client to me; I could no longer
pretend otherwise.

As I walked up to Finn's second-story apartment I was un-
sure of what his reaction might be when he found me at his
door. I was nervous, I listened for footsteps behind me, my
palms were wet. After I knocked, the door opened slowly; I
couldn't see who had answered, it might have been anyone.
Michael Finn might have jumped bail and left town.

"Who is it?" Finn's voice asked from inside.

"Hurry," I said. "Someone could see me here."

He opened the door just wide enough for me to slip inside.
Then we stood next to each other in the unlit entrance hall,
until Finn finally reached over and switched on the light. I could
see then he hadn't shaved for days; the scar across his face was
like neon, it marked him like a brand.

"What are you doing here?" Finn asked.

"For a minute I thought you might have left town," I said.

"You shouldn't have come here," Finn told me. "There could be trouble if anyone knew."

"Don't worry," I said. "I wouldn't do anything to hurt your case."

"My case?" Finn said. "I meant trouble for you. Your job."

"Don't worry about that," I said.

"Well, you've seen me," Finn said. "I'm out on bail, thanks to your friend Carter. I'm alive and well, and now that you've seen that for yourself, you can go."

"You could offer me a cup of coffee, you know," I said then, because pity had nothing to do with the reasons why I had come. I was there because of sleepless nights and desire, not sympathy.

"Coffee?" Finn said.

"With milk," I nodded.

"I haven't gone shopping." Finn smiled.

"Black is fine then," I told him.

While Finn was in the kitchen, I looked around—no paintings hung on the walls, no rugs covered the floor, cobwebs hung in every corner. I sat on the couch, across from a rocking chair. But the room was also Finn's bedroom, a single bed had been pushed against the far wall. When Finn returned, carrying two cups of watery instant coffee, that bed over in the corner was on my mind.

"Carter's away in New Hampshire," I told him.

"Carter's the one person I've met who wants me to be guilty," Finn said. "He wants me to make speeches for his organization. He talked to me about good and evil." Finn laughed. "Good and evil. I've never even thought about that."

"Don't judge him too harshly," I said. "He does have some good ideas."

"But they're only ideas," Finn said. "They have nothing to do with my life. The power plant was the closest thing to me— if I had been working on a hospital or a school, the explosion would have happened there. I was only thinking of myself, the times I was thinking at all."

"What do you want?" I asked. "How can you think about politics when you can't find any peace for yourself?"

"When am I going to find this inner peace?" Finn said, tiredly.

"You'll find it someday," I said.

"Oh really?" Finn said. "You seem to know a lot about me. I hope you get some good articles out of all this."

"There aren't going to be any articles," I said.

"But that's why you started with the whole thing. I'm an interesting case."

"That was before I knew you," I said.

"I'm no longer interesting?"

I shook my head. "I'm no longer objective about your case."

I scared myself when I said those words; it had been much easier to imagine talking to Finn than it was sitting across from him in his apartment. My feelings were so close to surfacing that when there was a knock on the front door, I jumped.

"Don't answer it," I said.

"It could be LeKnight," Finn said.

"But it could be anyone," I warned.

"That's why I have to answer it," Finn nodded.

When he went to the front door, I drew up my legs and sat huddled on the couch. The chain lock rattled and outside air rushed in from the hallway. There were no screams, no arguments; it was not Carter, returned from New Hampshire to find me in another man's apartment; there were no signs of the police or a posse. I heard Finn's voice and the voice of another man, and when Finn returned, an older man, dressed in work clothes and a heavy denim jacket lined with fleece, followed behind him.

Finn sat again in the rocking chair. He cracked his knuckles, one by one. "My father," he said.

Danny Finn was shorter than I had imagined, he didn't look like a man who beat his child, there wasn't a trace of glass left on his shoes.

"Where the hell have you been?" Danny Finn said to his son, ignoring me and not bothering to sit.

"I've been right here," Finn said.

"Your mother is worried," Danny Finn said. "She expected you to come to the house when they let you out."

"I'm fine."

"I don't care what you are. It's your mother who's worried."

"Well, then, tell her I'm fine."

"You're fine?" Danny Finn growled. "Every time I pick up a newspaper I see your name."

Michael Finn motioned to the couch. "Sit down, Pop."

Danny Finn didn't budge. "Are you guilty?" he asked. "Or just stupid?"

Finn reached for a cigarette; his knuckles were white. "Just stupid."

"That's no surprise," his father nodded. "That's nothing new."

There was no reason for me to be there, no reason for me

to see Finn cringe as his father spoke. If I could have, I would have sunk through the floor. I couldn't bear to look at either man.

"Aren't you wondering who she is?" Michael Finn asked with a nod toward me.

"I can guess who she is," Danny Finn said in an insulting tone.

"She was my therapist," Finn said.

I jerked my head up. "Nice to meet you," I said, too quickly.

Danny Finn frowned at me. "Therapist?" he said. "She's not a doctor."

"Social worker," I said, but Danny Finn had turned away from me.

"If she was a doctor she wouldn't be here. They don't make house calls any more. Not at night. Not for someone like you."

"Well"—Finn shrugged—"believe it or not, she was my therapist. Now I'll have to see a psychiatrist from the court."

"You're seeing everyone, aren't you?" Danny Finn said. "You're telling everyone all about yourself. Have you told her you've always been in trouble with the cops? Does she know that? Have you been telling her lies about me?" He now looked at me. "Don't believe anything he tells you."

"Why shouldn't I believe him?" I said. "He's not a liar."

"And I am, is that it?" Danny Finn said to me. "I don't have to listen to this. No social worker is going to call me a liar."

"That's not what I said," I told him.

"Calm down," Michael Finn said.

"I'm fucking calmer than you'll ever be," his father responded, but his temples pulsed and his hands were clenched.

"We'll see how calm you are when they throw you in jail. What the hell kind of welder blows up a power plant?"

"That's enough," Michael Finn told his father.

"Sure it's enough. It's enough to have you locked up for ten years."

Finn leaned his head against the back of the rocking chair and looked up at the ceiling.

"Maybe even fifteen or twenty years," Danny Finn went on. "That's how much time you could get for being so stupid."

It was still Finn's body in the rocking chair, but he was no more there than if he had gotten up and left the room; he was gone, far from the reach of any of his father's words.

"Are you listening to me?" Danny Finn walked over and peered into Michael's blank face.

"I think you should go," I told Danny Finn.

"You don't have to tell me to go, because that's exactly what I plan to do," Danny Finn said. "I don't have time to waste on him." He zipped up his jacket and headed for the door. Just before he left, he turned. "Don't forget," he called, "your mother wants to hear from you."

When the door slammed behind Danny Finn, I waited for his son to return, but Finn remained unmoved, he still watched the ceiling, not blinking an eye.

"Michael," I said.

"He's right," Finn said softly. "I'm going to jail."

"Stop it," I said.

"And even if I didn't," Finn went on, "what difference would it make? My whole life has been planned, it's been waiting for me, from the time I was born. I just follow in the footsteps ahead of me."

"Your father has had his life, and you have your own," I said.

"Really?" Finn laughed. "Oh, really?" Finn shook his head. "You don't know," he said. "That old man was once young, he was the same age I am now. And look at him, look at him. He wanted things once, he wanted things he could never have. Is that any different from me?"

Finn rocked faster in his chair, as if some demon moved him, back and forth, rocking him without mercy. Then he began to unwind the fragile thread of memories he had put away long ago.

FOUR

*D*ANNY FINN WAS TWENTY-
seven the first time he got really drunk. He thought he had
been drunk before, he had grown up with friends who carried
bottles of wine in their coat pockets, he had been drinking since
the year he turned thirteen. But this time was different. This
time he nearly forgot who he was. Danny had passed out in the
alleyway outside a bar east of Fishers Cove, and he didn't come
to, not even when a police officer found him in the snow and
shook him with a heavy foot. He didn't regain consciousness
until three days later. He opened his eyes to find himself in St.
Elmo's Hospital; tubes had been run into his arms and nose,
and a terrible sad feeling ran all through him. On that day,
when he opened his eyes to clean hospital walls, Danny Finn
no longer had a vague notion that he would die someday, now
he was certain that he would, and most probably the day would
come long before even one of his dreams had come true.

Before that time in the hospital, Danny Finn had been a
solitary man, a drinker, but he had never been mean. His wife,
Ada, who had picked him out at a church dance when they
were both nineteen, had nothing to complain about. Perhaps

the drinking, but Danny's father had been a drinker, and so had Ada's, and alcohol seemed natural to a man like Danny Finn. No, something had happened to him in that hospital, Ada would whisper years later to her friends, as the women sat together in their back yards with an eye on the children who played quietly on the sparse lawns. A part of him was missing when he came back; he drank even more, he slapped the boy, Michael, for the slightest misdeed, he didn't bother to shave, and he came home from work later and later each night.

Ada didn't tell those other women that Danny Finn had begun to beat her, and to demand sexual acts Ada would have never even thought possible, although Danny didn't seem to really expect to have his bizarre desires fulfilled, and Ada suspected his demands were only an excuse to shove her or slap her. Soon Ada wished that her husband would go on the road—to Arkansas or Florida—like some of the other construction workers. She wished he would just pick up and leave. But more than once, late at night, when Ada leaned far into her pillow and pretended to be asleep, Danny had whispered that he wasn't leaving; he wasn't going anywhere at all.

What Danny Finn lost, during his stay in the hospital, was his tunnel vision. He lost the belief that every man was fated to his life, he began to see that a glimmer of choice ran through each day. And after that, Danny Finn spent his whole life just trying to see straight, trying to see the way he did before his vision was all twisted around by a young woman he met on the third floor of St. Elmo's Hospital.

Though he would have to stay for days to have tests to check for damage to his liver and brain, the minute the tubes were out of him, Danny Finn got out of bed. He walked down the corridor to the patients' lounge, where he begged a cigarette from an orderly. When he had lit his cigarette and turned away from the orderly he saw her for the first time—a young girl so lovely she seemed to glow. She was dressed in a long, white hospital gown; she sat at a window so coated with dirt and film that she couldn't possibly be seeing anything on the other side. Danny Finn chose a seat near her. He took in her shining skin, the sweet face which looked as if it had never seen disease. He felt as if he had known her all his life. The girl was more beautiful than anyone Danny had ever seen, even more beautiful than his own mother, whose face he remembered only from photographs taken before she died in childbirth.

Danny was so enchanted that he watched the girl for nearly an hour, he even forgot to ask the orderly for another Pall Mall. Finally he leaned forward in his chair. "I'm here because I blacked out," he said.

He did not want to mention the drinking to a girl like her; he did not want to mention his wife or his child. He wanted to be born again, fresh, with no past history, no memory, and the power to do with his future whatever he wished. Because the girl hadn't seemed to have heard him, Danny leaned even closer. "Blackouts," he said. "That's my medical problem."

When the girl looked up at him her eyes were so deep Danny Finn and all his memories could sink down into them. Right then, Danny wanted to take back most of his life; it was a life that was too rough to ever explain to a girl like her; it was too bitter and too dry for her to have ever understood. Danny Finn smiled at her, and he wanted nothing more than for the girl to smile back, but instead she looked at him blankly and said, "My medical problem is death."

Danny Finn didn't move from his chair when the girl got up and walked out of the patients' lounge. He did not move until the orderly appeared in front of the windows and asked Danny Finn if he wanted another cigarette.

"That girl who was sitting here," Danny Finn said, pointing to the chair, still surrounded by an aura of youth and beauty. "What's wrong with her? What's she got?"

The orderly handed Danny Finn a cigarette and lit a match. "Leukemia," the orderly said. He bent down and blew out the match. "She's as good as dead," he told Danny Finn.

Danny Finn would never know that death, but he would imagine it over and over again for the rest of his life; it would hit him harder than the death of anyone he had ever known. Years later, Danny Finn would talk about the girl on nights when he was too drunk to drive and his young son drove him home from the Modern Times Bar. Danny Finn would lie on the back seat of his car and weep as if he had been at the girl's bedside right when she died, he would cry out as if she had breathed her last into his ear. On these nights, Danny Finn knew he hadn't had quite enough to drink, if he had he wouldn't have remembered the girl. He wouldn't have remembered that first time he wished that he could be a different man, the kind of man who could perform a miraculous rescue.

Before the girl, the only losses Danny Finn had faced were those of his parents. His mother had died before he had ever seen her face, before he had begun to breathe she had deserted him, she had closed her eyes and smiled, because after the birth of four sons, after a lifetime of crowded solitude, she really had not wished to go on. Danny's father, however, did not die until Danny was nineteen, but it had been wished for by all of his sons for quite a long time, and Danny Finn had wished especially hard.

Danny's father, John, treated his youngest son harshly, but none of his sons hadn't been beaten with a leather belt, none of them hadn't been knocked to the ground when they spoke back. Perhaps it was only that Danny Finn spoke back more than the others, particularly on the morning of his seventeenth birthday. That was the day John suggested, ordered really, that his son dress and accompany him to the union hall; it was time for the boy to begin his career. But Danny Finn shook his head and told his father his dream: he wanted to join the Navy, he wanted to travel, to sail across the seas.

"Not in my lifetime," John Finn told his youngest son. "What's good enough for me and your brothers is good enough for you."

"To hell with you," Danny Finn said, and he refused to get dressed in his one good blue suit and follow his father down to the union hall. "To hell with all of you," Danny crowed.

John Finn was the tallest man there had ever been in the family—he was six-foot-four and not one of his sons was more than five-eleven. And so even though Danny Finn was seventeen years old and stronger than he'd ever be again, when his father reached out and caught him on the jaw, Danny flew up into the air, and landed head first on a block of cement. Although he didn't lose consciousness, a stream of blood trickled through his hair, until his face was streaked red. John Finn knelt down and gently held his son around his shoulders.

"I just wanted you to come to your senses," John Finn explained to the boy. "You're not sailing any seas."

Later that day as they walked to the union hall, Danny Finn

wished over and over again that his father would drop dead in his tracks. But John Finn's strides grew no shorter, and he was still walking tall when they left the union hall after Danny's induction as an apprentice. But the resentment did not end; although it seemed to disappear by the time John Finn fell from a scaffolding and broke his neck. By that time, Danny Finn had forgotten all about the Navy, he had forgotten any dreams. He really believed he was telling the truth when he shook his head and whispered to his brothers at the funeral, "He was the one who brought me to my senses when I was a boy. Best thing that ever happened to me." As he stood beside the grave, Danny Finn really believed that all his old resentment was gone; but the curious thing was that he didn't feel a thing when they lowered the casket into the ground; when the first shovelful of dirt hit against the wood with a thud, he didn't even flinch. Still, he had convinced himself that his father had set him on the right road by forcing him to join the union. At nineteen, Danny Finn was a journeyman, he was earning a good salary, and soon there would be the benefits from John Finn's accident to share with his brothers. Danny Finn needed extra money: he had gotten a young woman pregnant, and the terrible thing was, she was the sort of woman that once you got into trouble you had to marry.

But somehow things never worked out. Danny Finn waited for his check, but after a while saw that his brothers meant to cut him out of his share. Danny Finn never saw a cent of his father's money; he learned to hate his three brothers. Dead, John Finn seemed to grow even taller; he became an invisible giant who would have guided Danny had he lived. The more Danny Finn thought about it, the more certain he was that his father would have approved of his marrying a woman like Ada; the old man, had he been alive, would surely have loved her as if she were the daughter he never had.

But after several years of marriage, after the birth of his only son, Michael, and the family's move into the new house in Harbor Heights, Danny Finn suddenly changed. He had seen the face of death; luminous eyes had drilled into his own, the breath of despair had touched him. Danny Finn was only twenty-seven when he left the hospital and walked across the parking lot where Ada and Michael Finn waited in the car, but he walked like an old man, he stumbled on the asphalt. He now knew, as he slid behind the wheel of his car and looked up toward the third-floor window where the girl had sat, where she might be sitting still, straining to see through the smudges and the mist, that his life was not ever going to be different. The only thing that would happen was that he would grow older. If he was lucky he would meet a quick death like his father, while he was still young. If not, he would spend his old age on a union pension, side by side with a woman who didn't even know him, who would not have guessed how he felt when he looked into a young girl's eyes.

That was when he began to grow meaner. He stayed out late every night drinking, hoping to erase all the terrors that had come together like a death knell when he saw that girl's face. He became terrified of life and of death, and of the years stretching out before him. Ada Finn never knew what he felt, she never knew any more than she saw: the young man she had married had disappeared, someone else had taken his place. She knew this could happen, she had seen the faces of women whose husbands it had happened to; she had never thought she would be one of them. But she was; just like the women she had heard whispered about by neighbors and friends, she became a woman who carried dinner out to her family without one word, just like them she was afraid that her husband might slap her for cooking the potatoes too long, or serving the meat undercooked. At night she was glad to sleep alone, and she shuddered when she heard the front door slam at 3 or 4 A.M., she wanted to weep when she heard Danny Finn's footsteps in the hall.

As the years went by, Ada Finn did not know that it was no longer her husband's footsteps she heard in the hall, but her son's. For years, Michael Finn had been illegally driving the family car. He was fourteen the first time he was dragged along to a bar. He sat at a rear table drinking Cokes until his father became too drunk to drive. Danny Finn threw the car keys over to his son that night. "Drive," he said. And Michael Finn did just that, although it took some time before he could shift the car into first gear. And from that time on, when Michael Finn awoke in the night to see that the car was not in the driveway, he got dressed, walked downtown to the Modern Times, and drove his father home. It was expected of the boy, it had become a habit, and in part he enjoyed it, because he was able to drive when no other boy he knew could even tell the brake pedal from the clutch. It was on these drives that Michael Finn first heard about the girl in the hospital. Danny Finn, lying in the back as Michael drove, would mutter about the girl, calling out to her, begging for her forgiveness, for her love.

For quite a long time Michael Finn thought that the girl had existed nowhere other than in his father's imagination; she seemed to be nameless and faceless, more like a spirit than anything else. But one night the boy discovered just how real that girl in the hospital was, just how much she meant to Danny Finn. When Michael arrived at the Modern Times, he found Danny Finn drunker than he had ever seen him before; several men had to lift Danny into the back seat of the car. It was winter, the roads were slick, and Michael drove slowly, hoping with each block that no policeman would stop him and demand the license he didn't have. From the back seat came a low moaning sound; Michael hoped that his father would not be sick; if he blacked out he'd be far too heavy for Michael to carry alone. When they turned onto Route 18, down by the harbor, Danny Finn cried out in pain. "There she is," Danny Finn cried. "I can see her face; she's like a Goddamn saint. Pull over."

Michael Finn kept driving, though he kept a careful eye on the rearview mirror. He was certain his father would fall asleep, but instead Danny Finn managed to sit up in the back seat.

"I said pull over," Danny Finn cried. He took hold of Michael Finn's shoulder and squeezed it so hard that Finn nearly lost control of the car. Finally, Michael pulled over, into the deserted parking lot of the old Fishers Cove Ferry. Danny Finn threw open the back door; he ran from the car as if chased by spirits. Michael Finn followed his father, who crouched close to the earth, a tired old wolf.

"I know her," Danny Finn said gravely. Saliva ran down his lips and his eyes were wide with liquor and memory.

"The girl in the hospital?" Michael Finn asked.

"I should have seen it before," Danny Finn cried. He looked up at his son, shivering in only a denim jacket. "I should have known who she was," Danny Finn went on. "My mother," he said, amazed and terrified. "It was a visitation, that's what it was," he cried. "A ghost."

The girl who had sat in the patients' lounge so long ago had probably died a quiet, bitter death not long after Danny Finn checked out of the hospital; she had surely never given the man in the lounge a second thought. But she had haunted Danny Finn for so long that he could not spend a night without her; she had become the most important person in his life.

"It was her," Danny Finn whispered. He held his hands over his face; tears dripped through his fingers. "My God. My God. It was her," Danny Finn shrieked.

Michael Finn crouched down next to his father; he bit his lip to keep his teeth from chattering; he wondered what he was supposed to do. Perhaps he was supposed to throw his arms around his father, perhaps he was supposed to carry Danny Finn back to the car and hold him until his father's outburst subsided. But after a lifetime of beatings and distrust, Michael Finn did none of the things he was supposed to do, none of the things he wished he could have done. Instead, he rocked back and forth on his heels. The harbor they faced was a phosphorescent green. He was so close to his father that he could smell the bourbon, he could feel his father's hot breath each time Danny Finn cried out loud, each time Danny remembered the man he used to be.

Michael Finn would have liked to run; he would have liked to kick up his heels and run far away from Danny Finn and his ghosts, but the boy couldn't take his eyes off his father, he couldn't see anything but the man he had despised for so long, weeping in an empty parking lot. Before Michael Finn knew it, before he had time to stop himself, he was weeping alongside his father. Michael Finn never knew if his father noticed his tears; he doubted if Danny Finn could have noticed anything but his own pain that night. Michael's tears were brief, he did not weep for long, still he had shocked himself. When his eyes were dry, Michael breathed deeply as he waited for his father to calm down. After a while, Daniel Finn did stop weeping; he lay down, exhausted and shaking.

Michael Finn helped his father back to the car. Danny Finn nodded off to sleep, and Michael Finn drove home slowly, all the time trying to forget all that he had seen and heard. When they reached the house, and Michael had pulled the car into the driveway, Danny Finn awoke suddenly; he looked at his son as if the boy was no one he knew.

"What the hell are you doing?"

"We're home," Michael said as he turned off the engine and the headlights. "I'm parking the car," he explained.

"All right then." Danny Finn nodded. "That's okay."

When they were inside the house and had closed the door behind them, Michael Finn felt a hand on his shoulder as he began to walk down the hall to his bedroom.

"Everybody makes mistakes," Danny Finn told him.

"Sure," Michael Finn said evenly, but the night had been too much for him; his voice was hoarse, and he wanted to escape to his room, where he would close the door and forget all that had happened in the deserted parking lot.

"Maybe I wasn't supposed to be a father," Danny Finn went on. "I should have been a Navy man." Then he looked over at his son, and for a minute it seemed as if he wasn't drunk at all, as if he'd never been drunk. "Maybe you wish that you had someone else for a father," he said.

Michael Finn wasn't a liar, but he didn't have the courage to tell the truth. Perhaps he thought a time like this would come again, a time when his father once more asked for forgiveness and love, when the two men would talk in the hallway while Ada Finn tossed and dreamed behind the bedroom door. But such a time would never come again, the two men would grow farther and farther apart, so far that when Danny Finn sent Michael off to the Stockley School, father and son really believed they were strangers. But that night when he might have said something, Michael Finn didn't answer and he lost the one chance he would ever have to talk to his father.

"Hell, maybe you would have liked a father who had money," Danny continued. "Somebody who didn't scream so much. But shit, the way I scream is nothing compared to my father. And if you think I leave my mark when I smack you, just remember that my father was six-foot-four and when he walloped you you didn't forget it. "No," Danny Finn shook his head, "you never forgot it."

Something was happening to Michael Finn—his throat was closing up, his lungs were heavy and full, he was afraid that when he breathed he might squeak, he might burst right open.

"My father," Danny Finn whispered, "was a real bastard. Forget everything I ever told you about him; he was a bastard and he killed my mother. That's right, he killed her with too much work and no love. That can kill a person." Danny Finn nodded.

"I have to go to school tomorrow," Michael Finn found himself saying. "I've got to get up early in the morning."

"Maybe he wasn't meant to be a father either," Danny Finn said. "Maybe he did the best he could."

"Maybe," Michael Finn said noncommittally.

"Maybe I did, too," Danny Finn said. He looked his son straight in the eye. "Think that could be a possibility?"

"Could be," Michael Finn said without conviction.

Danny Finn looked quickly away. "You better go to bed," he said. "I don't know what the hell you're doing up so late. You've got school tomorrow, and don't you forget it."

Michael Finn went to his room and shut the door. He tried to sleep, but each time he closed his eyes he saw Danny Finn's face, he saw his father's tears, he heard his father's choked pleadings. Michael Finn had always felt that he and his father would never know each other, they would never talk or be close; but now he felt a terrible sadness deep inside, one which threatened to explode. When he finally did fall asleep, Michael Finn dreamed that he was not a son, but a father. He and his son walked side by side across the snow; they followed a path on the other side of the harbor where the land was still wild with brambles and roots, and sea gulls nested in huge pines. Michael Finn and his son walked together, and they knew each other better with every step they took, as if their spirits floated above their bodies and conversed freely with words that were open and true. When Finn awoke he felt a terrible loss; he was as sad waking from his dream and having to face the day as he would have been had his dream son slipped through a hole in the frozen harbor, had the child's hands clutched the ice and finally disappeared before Michael Finn could do a thing to rescue him.

The next morning Michael went into the kitchen warily; he was afraid that he might no longer be able to tell reality from dreams, he was uncertain about the night, he now doubted that he had ever seen his father weep in the parking lot. And from

Danny Finn's behavior that morning at breakfast, where he gulped a cup of black coffee and complained of a hangover, no one would have guessed that anything had happened between the two just hours before. In fact, the tears cried in the parking lot and the explanation Danny Finn had offered for all the years of pain were never mentioned again. Danny Finn's plea for forgiveness was wiped away with years of anger and abuse, until Michael Finn himself nearly forgot the confidences in the hall-way with his father late one winter's night.

Even though Danny Finn had despised his father for forcing him to join the union, he did the same with his son as soon as the boy turned eighteen; perhaps because he did not know what else to do, perhaps because Danny Finn had been so terrified of his own father that he still trembled when he saw men over six-foot-three, that he was afraid to direct his son in a path that might displease his long-dead father. Everything Danny did he did for his father's approval, and in his father's image. And so he beat his son as he had been beaten, and when the boy broke the law, Danny Finn saw to it that the boy was sent away to the Stockley School, for the boy's own good or because he had no idea what else to do, or because he was afraid of his own father's ghost. Sometimes when he watched his son cringe as he beat him, or when he watched Michael driven away by a pro-bation officer to the Stockley School, Danny Finn was also a little afraid of the man he had become.

"I will never be like him," Danny Finn used to say to himself when he was young and his father was reaching for his leather strap. "Never. Never."

And now he had become so much like him, he walked so closely in John Finn's footsteps that Danny Finn could no longer remember saying these words to himself. And though there were times when Danny still wanted his life to be different, times when he wanted to throw a suitcase into the back of his car and take off to California, those times passed. And when there were moments when he wanted to hold his wife close instead of pushing her away, those moments, too, passed. And it was easier than anyone would have thought to look across the dining-room table and not notice how much Michael looked the way Danny had looked as a child. Danny Finn had become so much like his father that he did not even notice the hatred in his own son's eyes.

Danny Finn conveniently forgot the night he showed himself to his son, he refused to think about his own terror. And as his father forgot, so, too, did Michael Finn. Forgetting was easy. In time, Michael's memory of the two men kneeling in the parking lot, side by side but still too far away to touch, had totally faded; just as Danny Finn's memory of the young girl became hazier and hazier with every bottle of bourbon, until the girl was less than a dream. As far as both men were concerned, that long-ago night had never happened; and after a while, Michael Finn could even drive past that empty parking lot in winter without wanting to weep out loud.

FIVE

𝓘F HE HAD MORE FAITH IN himself, Michael Finn would have known that his father or grandfather would never have switched the valve at Angel Landing III. He alone had watched his past and the future he was always supposed to have rise up like a storm set loose. On the day of the explosion Finn had been fighting against the history which turned men into ghosts; he had been fighting it all his life.

"Listen to me," I said, "you won't turn out the way they did."

"I know what's waiting for me," Finn said. "I know my life will be the same."

I was now afraid that I might take the place of the girl who had drifted from the patients' lounge into Danny Finn's heart.

"Decisions can be made, lives can be altered," I said.

"You don't know anything about me," Finn went on. "You're only involved with my case."

"It's not your case I'm involved with, it's you," I blurted out.

"You'll get over it," Finn shrugged.

"I don't want to get over it."

Finn gripped the arms of the rocking chair. I was hit with the slow embarrassment of a confession which brings no response.

"Have you had dinner?" I asked when I couldn't stand the tension between us any longer. "Is there something here I can fix?"

Finn leaned forward in his chair. "You don't expect me to take you seriously, do you?" he asked.

"I could make scrambled eggs or spaghetti," I said.

"Do you know what it would mean to be mixed up with someone like me?" Finn asked.

"We could try."

"No."

I wondered if Danny Finn had been lucky to forget all that he wanted and never could have, instead of looking right into the center of heartbreak and despair as Michael Finn did now.

"All right," I said. "I'm not going to try and talk you into anything." I put on my coat then, even though I didn't want to go.

"I never asked you to care, did I?" Finn said.

"No," I agreed. "And if you want me to go, I will."

"And don't care about me," Finn called as I walked across the room.

"It's too late," I said. "I already do." But at the door I stopped. "Are you sure you don't want to talk about this?"

"I just told you," Finn said. "I never wanted this to happen, and you'd better stop wanting it, too."

"Then I'll leave," I said, but I didn't open the door. "I'm going," I said, though that was the last thing I wanted to do.

Finn got up; but instead of running to me and holding me

tight, he came to me slowly, a disinterested sleepwalker. "Thanks for stopping by," he said formally, as if I had been a guest invited for drinks.

"Will you think about what I've said?" I asked as Finn opened the door for me.

"Natalie," Finn said, "I've already told you. No."

By the time I ran down the stairs, Finn had probably returned to his rocking chair, and all the way home I could hear the slow, unfeeling creak of that chair. It mattered very little whether Finn asked me to leave because he didn't care or because caring was simply too dangerous—he had turned me down, and in the next few days I tried as best I could to deny everything I felt for him as well. Because of that I slept dreamlessly, I felt more separated from everyone else than ever before. But I wasn't angry with Finn for having begun it by asking me to meet him in the deserted high-school field, nor was I furious with the purple smoke which had so suddenly touched my life. In time I managed to feel nothing more than numb; I walked through each day, I met with clients, had dinner with Minnie; even Lark no longer annoyed me, and one day I found myself agreeing to meet her for lunch at Ruby's Café.

After we had ordered hamburgers, I gazed at the tabletop and tried to think of nothing but clean, empty space.

"What's wrong with you lately?" Lark asked.

"Not a thing," I said quickly.

"I'll bet. Well, whatever it is, I'm glad you met me for lunch. I've been wanting to talk to you for days."

"Talk," I said.

Lark waited until the platters of food were brought to us

and then she leaned forward and said, "It's about him. The bomber. Michael Finn."

That man who exposed every sorrow, each wound with a shiver, a brief rush of blood; Michael Finn who could look right through you? That bomber, that man? "The bomber?" I said casually as I reached for the salt.

"I want to know about him," Lark said.

"You know I can't discuss his case."

"I've already looked through his file," Lark announced.

"That was pretty unethical."

"I have to know about him," Lark said.

I sighed and listed some basic details: where he was born, where he now lived. Finally, Lark threw up her hands.

"I want to know what the core of his problem is."

"The core?" I said. "You're looking too deeply. He made a mistake, now he may go to jail, that's all there is to it."

"Is that the story you intend to give out during the trial when every reporter in the state finds out you were the bomber's therapist?"

"I wish you wouldn't call him the bomber," I said. "And yes, there's only one story."

"How boring," Lark said.

"I really can't believe you read through his file," I said, but Lark wasn't listening to me, she was thinking hard. She licked her lips. "I know. Send the reporters to me."

"You?" I said. "What do you know about Michael Finn?"

"Nothing," Lark said. "But I know other case histories that are ten times more interesting than his. EMOTE could really use the publicity. All I need is one or two interviews with the right people."

Weeks ago, days before, I would have laughed and walked out the door of the café. I was to be the one who stood on the courthouse steps with Finn's exclusive story, I was the one to write the articles, and then be patted and promoted at Outreach. But now I wanted nothing more than to quickly recite my testimony and then slink from the courtroom in secrecy. The more publicity, the more I had to think about Finn, the longer I would see his face, remember his history.

"All right," I agreed. "I'll send them all to you."

Lark reached for my hand. "You won't regret it," she said.

I counted the flecks of salt that had spilled near my plate; they looked like peculiar insects edging toward me.

"Natalie," Lark said now, "what's wrong?"

If I counted the brown spots on every french fry on my plate I might be able to forget the way Finn's voice dropped whenever he talked about the past.

Lark waved her hand in front of my face. "Are you still here?"

"If you really want to know," I said. "I'm miserable."

Lark slapped the tabletop. "This really makes me happy," she said. "You're finally opening up to me. You're beginning to trust me."

"I'll be all right," I said quickly.

"All right? You won't be all right unless you do something to help yourself. And what you can do to help yourself is to come to EMOTE."

"I don't think so," I said.

"Just give it a chance," Lark said. "What do you have to lose?"

"If I did come to an EMOTE meeting I wouldn't discuss my personal life. I would just be an observer."

"Fine," Lark said, as she reached for the check. "Just keep an open mind."

But an open mind was something I did not have on the evening when I followed Lark's instructions and arrived at her cottage on the grounds of a Shore Road estate. I was fairly certain that if there was anything that could chase away my doubts, it wasn't EMOTE. Still, I had promised to appear at the meeting, and so I borrowed Minnie's Mustang and parked at the end of a long line of cars. I walked up the driveway and knocked on Lark's front door.

As soon as Lark spotted me, she strode across the living room and took my hand.

"I'm so happy you're here," she said. "The trust that is growing between us is amazing."

I edged to the rear of the room.

"Friends," Lark said, and all eyes turned toward her. "It's time to begin our work," she said solemnly.

The participants obediently carried their coffee mugs, and then, grunting softly like a flock of sheep, they ranged themselves in a semicircle on the floor, sitting on pillows or on a pumpkin-colored oriental rug. In the center of the circle was a tall object hidden from view by a draped Indian bedspread. As Lark went to stand in front of the bedspread I crept farther into the background, hoping that the shadows in the corner would hide my skepticism. But a young man, dressed all in white, glared at me.

"I'd like to speak now," the young man called out. "Lark, I have something I'd like to say."

"You are talking to Lark," Lark intoned.

"You are talking to Sandy," the young man in white said as he stood.

"What would you like to say?" Lark asked pleasantly.

"I would like to know why we're being observed as if we were animals in a zoo."

"Now, Sandy," Lark smiled. "What are you really saying?"

"I'm talking about her." He pointed a finger at me. "Why is she creeping around in the corners of the room, why does she refuse to join the group? Does she think that she's better than we are?"

"Oh, not at all," I cried out apologetically.

"I'm sorry," Sandy shrugged. "I just can't get into somebody watching us. Either she's with us or she's not. She's in or she's out."

"Why don't you take a seat," Lark said to me.

I didn't have a seat because I wanted the option of bolting through the front door if I cared to. I didn't have a coffee mug in my hands because I wanted my fingers free to fight off any angry member of this cult who might suddenly decide to attack an outsider. Still, I didn't have the courage to stick out my tongue and slam the door behind me, and somewhere I had some hope, however tiny, that EMOTE might help me understand how my emotions had gone out of control. So I joined the circle, I sat on a blue and green striped pillow and smiled at the group around me.

"How do you feel now, Sandy?" Lark asked.

"I feel accepted," Sandy grinned as he sank back to his pillow. "I really do." He nodded at me.

"Well, now," Lark called out briskly. "Is everyone ready?"

"Readier than we've ever been," the members of EMOTE called.

I reached into my purse and took out the pack of cigarettes I had specially brought along.

"No smoking," the woman on the pillow next to me said. "We don't hate our bodies here."

I put away my cigarettes and looked up just as Lark reached to pull the Indian bedspread down. There, beneath the drape, was a six-foot mirror framed in oak. We, who sat on the floor, were now confronted by our reflections in the glass.

"Applaud yourself," Lark called out.

All around me people cheered; because I didn't wish to be accused of being an outside observer, I also began to clap.

"What are you clapping for?" the woman nearest to me hissed. "You haven't been through EMOTE. You don't know a thing about the technique."

"Who would like to begin?" Lark called out.

"I would," the woman to my left cried out. "You're talking to Denise," she said as she stood.

We all applauded as Denise walked to face the mirror. She smoothed down her long blond hair. "I'm ready." Denise nodded.

"All right then," Lark said softly, moving from the center of the circle. "What do we have to say to Denise?"

A man with closely cropped hair and a gold hoop through his left ear stood up. "You're a terrible mother. You should be punished. You should be sent away to an institution where you would never be allowed to see children again," he said evenly.

"I'm a good mother," Denise said into the mirror. "I can be whatever I want to be, and I want to be a good mother."

"How can a whore be a good mother?" Sandy called out.

Lark came to sit next to me on the floor. "The best method for ego building," she told me. "Force them to fight against criticism and take control of their own destinies."

"Interesting," I murmured as Denise spoke to her reflection. "Of course, there are always outside forces. Environment. The family."

Lark shook her head. "A strong ego can get through all of that."

As I watched Denise finish her ego-building exercises, I wondered what would have happened if Michael Finn had sat before that mirror. Would all of his pain and hostility have simply dissolved? And if I sat there now, would I be able to convince myself that I could be whatever I wanted to be—beloved or loner, it was all up to me. Denise had finished and the group applauded energetically; and when she returned to her pillow her cheeks glowed a faint rose color. As I thought about Denise, Sandy began to clap his hands rhythmically on the other side of the circle. "No observers," Sandy sang as he clapped. "No observers," he chanted. In no time at all, everyone else had taken up the song, and many of them turned toward me.

"Sandy has a point," Lark said. "An observer at EMOTE is an observer in life. Get involved," she urged me.

"I don't think so," I said.

"It can't hurt," Lark said. "Think of it as an experience."

"An experience," I repeated.

"It's really quite freeing," Lark said. "Your problems seem to disappear."

"Problems?" I said. "I wouldn't say I had problems."

"Never trust a person who claims to have no problems." Denise smiled. "Never believe it."

"You have nothing to lose," Lark said as she pushed me toward the full-length mirror.

As soon as I stood there I found myself wishing that EMOTE could work some wonderful spell on me, some voodoo which would allow me to slip back into the life I had led before the explosion.

"I can tell, I can see it in your eyes," Sandy called out to me. "You're a fool."

"Oh, I don't know about that," I said evenly, as if I were addressing a lunatic I didn't want to incite.

"Contradict him with a positive statement," Lark said.

"I'm fairly intelligent," I told Sandy.

"You're miserable," a young woman said. "You're so depressed you wish you could die."

"I may be a little depressed."

"What's good about your life?" Lark asked. "Tell them. Tell us all."

"I beg your pardon?" I said.

"Emote," Sandy said. "Just let it all out."

"Well," I said, "I really do care about other people."

"Other people?" Someone from the back of the room sneered. "We're not interested in other people. We want to know about you."

"I'm a hard worker," I said. "I make good fried chicken," I told my reflection. "I have nice eyes," I whispered. "I was always on the dean's list in college."

"Someone else's values," Lark said, shaking her head. "You're letting yourself be judged by someone else's values."

I studied myself; behind my own reflection Lark's living room and the members of EMOTE had begun to melt away.

"I'm in love with someone who doesn't want to get involved," I said.

"Why should this person care about you?" a voice asked. "What the hell is so good about you?"

I looked into the mirror as if there might be some answer etched onto the glass. "I don't know."

"You don't know," Denise echoed.

I stood quite still. In that room of crazy believers I felt alone; I bent my head and began to weep.

"Fantastic," Lark told me. "Let it out."

I shook my head and tried to speak, but my words came out in short gasps.

"Let all your defenses down. You've got to be nothing before you can be something," Lark told me.

Now all around me the group began the second stage of EMOTE; their voices bubbled with praise, they came to embrace me.

Sandy hugged me so tightly that my tears fell onto his white shirt. "You are an unusual person. A special person," he told me.

"Five minutes ago you told me I was horrible," I said.

"Five minutes ago you were horrible," Sandy smiled.

"Now that you've let your defenses down you're a different person," Lark said. "You're beautiful."

I looked at myself in the mirror; my eyes were red, my nose was running, strands of hair stuck out from my head in crazy, undisciplined wisps. There, in the glass, was the same sad woman who had been there before, only more tired, her nerves ran closer to the surface than ever before.

"I think I'd better be going," I said as I took a tissue from the box of Kleenex Denise held out to me.

"Running away is everyone's first reaction when they come to EMOTE," Lark said. "But you can't run away from your feelings. You can't escape."

"We can make you feel better," Sandy said earnestly. "We really can."

My feelings were not something I wished to be helped through, they weren't something I wanted to leave behind. "I've got to be going," I said. When I stopped at the door to pull on my coat the members of EMOTE rose to their feet and applauded me.

"Thank you," I said, just before I turned to run. "Thank you all so much."

I drove the Mustang out the driveway and headed toward town. I couldn't wait to get out of the neighborhood, away from the huge houses on Shore Road, away from the echo of that parting applause. I didn't slow down, not even when the Mustang skidded on the turns. I wouldn't feel safe again until I was back at Minnie's. There was no short cut, no way around: without Michael Finn I would be lonely for a long time; and if Carter had not been away in New Hampshire I would have driven to the Soft Skies office and let him know that we were through, that every Wednesday night in the world wouldn't help put the pieces back.

When I reached home I hoped to avoid Minnie; I went in through the back door only to find her at the kitchen table, polishing silverware and humming off-key.

"I'm glad you're finally home," she said.

I nodded and kept on walking, right out the kitchen door, and up the stairs. Sleep would be good for me, it would take away desire, and loneliness. When I heard Minnie's footsteps behind me on the stairs I didn't look back; I went straight to my room.

"I'm very tired," I said to Minnie, who continued to stand in my doorway. "I'm exhausted," I said. I felt so weak that I couldn't manage to undress properly. "Can you unzip me?"

My aunt took hold of the back of my dress, but she didn't touch the zipper. "You have a terrible memory," Minnie said.

"I wish I did," I said.

"Tomorrow is Thanksgiving," Minnie said.

"Very nice," I said. "I'm really happy about that."

Minnie looked at me more closely. "You look depressed," she said. "Have you been eating pork?"

"Do you mind? The zipper?"

"This is serious," Minnie said. "I'm too old to concoct an entire dinner for a horde of guests."

"What horde?" I asked.

"The old folks from Mercy."

How much could old people eat, how much could there be to cook? But perhaps Minnie would faint over a hot stove, perhaps an ambulance would be called, and I would be watching them drive her away as I stood at the back door holding a pumpkin pie in my wretched hands. "All right, all right," I said. "I'll help."

Minnie finally released me and unzipped my dress; I immediately sank into bed with a sigh.

"Tell me the truth," Minnie said. "Are you blue?"

"Blue?" I said. "An entire roomful of people just told me I was a beautiful person."

Minnie waved a hand impatiently. "What do they know?" she said. "Do they know you the way I do?"

"I'd like to be alone," I said.

"I've got something to pick you right up," Minnie said.

"Brewer's yeast," I guessed.

"Your bomber," Minnie smiled. "I invited him to Thanksgiving dinner."

I dropped the quilt and sat up. "What are you talking about?"

"He's listed in the phone book," Minnie said. "A party is very boring with only old people." She shrugged. "It has no juice."

"He said yes?" I asked.

"Why shouldn't he say yes?" Minnie said irritably. "You can think what you want, but there are plenty of people who think I'm a good cook, an excellent cook. I know my way around nutrition like a cat knows its way around a garbage can."

"Oh, Minnie," I said. "You shouldn't have invited him."

"He knows it's vegetarian," Minnie assured me. "Don't worry about that. I said: 'There will be no turkey in this house, let that be understood once and for all.'"

"How could you?" I said. "Finn is a client, nothing more."

"Well, he's coming to dinner and that's that," Minnie said. "I'm going to tell you something right now," Minnie went on, her voice softening, "and you'd better listen, because I'm old and I know. The road to love is rocky. I had quite a number of shocks when I fell in love with Alex. But the biggest shock of all," Minnie confided, "was that there were plenty of times when it was lonelier to be in love than it was to be on your own. Remember that," my aunt told me.

"I'm not going to be able to sleep," I said. "I just know it."

"What a sweet boy," Minnie said to herself. She got a familiar faraway look on her face, and I knew she was remembering Alex as he had been so many years ago, long before any Lansky had ever set foot in America.

Downstairs, Beaumont hammered on his raft in the cellar; outside, the temperature continued to drop. I would spend the night tossing and turning, worrying about meeting Finn, wondering if we had a chance.

"Go to sleep," Minnie told me.

"Now that you invited him, you've got me thinking again. I'll be awake for hours."

"Just try," Minnie advised. "Close your eyes."

Although I didn't think it would do any good I listened to Minnie. Instead of sheep I counted the number of times Beaumont's hammer struck wood two floors below. And because my aunt continued to watch over me, the night was filled with the faint odor of lavender, and I didn't toss or turn at all.

SIX

$\mathcal{I}$T WAS NEARLY NOON THE next day when I went downstairs, to discover the group from the Mercy Home settled into the parlor.

"Look who's here," Evie cried when I walked into the room. "You must have a glass of sherry right away. It's good luck."

"Too early for me," I said; but not too early to eye the front door, wondering if Michael Finn could already be just outside, hesitating on the front porch.

Arthur, the old gentleman, came over and took my hand. "Beaumont, that wonderful fellow, picked us up early this morning in the Mustang."

"If there's one thing I've always wanted to do in my life, it's ride in one of these modern sports cars," Yolanda said to me. "Of course, we couldn't go too fast, but I have a good imagination."

"Our father always had Fords," Evie added. "If someone even mentioned the word Chevrolet, he would spit on the floor."

"He wouldn't really spit," Yolanda said, annoyed at her sister. "He would just look nauseated."

When I left the parlor in search of coffee, all three were arguing about automobiles, though none of them had a driver's license any more, and none would ever drive a car again. In the kitchen, the coffee was on the back burner, and Minnie was carefully removing a sweet-potato pie from the oven.

"As soon as Finn sees those old folks he'll leave," I sighed as I poured coffee.

Minnie turned to me and placed a hand on her hip. "I wish you wouldn't call my friends the 'old folks.' Why don't you set the table? There's so much work to be done that if I hadn't been eating the proper diet for so many years I'd probably have a heart attack right now."

The large dining room off the hallway had not been used since the last group of Lanskys ate potato pancakes and applesauce there a decade ago. I set out the best china, the silver spoons, the linen napkins. While I was searching for a platter, Beaumont crept into the dining room like an old spy. He was dressed in his gray uniform and wearing his usual daytime sunglasses, which were strung together with wire across the back of his head to make certain his eyes were protected from the unaccustomed sunlight.

"There's someone at the door," Beaumont said as I pulled a platter from the drawer. "Lord knows what he wants, but he looks pretty damn familiar."

We peered out of the dining room to the front door, which Beaumont had left slightly ajar. Michael Finn stood out on the porch.

"Oh, Beaumont," I said, dropping the crystal platter into the old boarder's hands. "You know him. The bomber."

Michael Finn's hair was combed back; he wore a black sports

jacket and new blue jeans, and he carried a bunch of yellow chrysanthemums.

"I thought I would never see you again," I said softly when I met Finn at the door.

"Your aunt invited me to dinner," Finn said, but he didn't make a move to walk through the door. I went outside to stand with him on the porch.

"Don't feel that you have to be polite," I said. "Don't feel that you must accept my aunt's invitation."

Finn's eyes were ringed with circles and his face was drawn. "The trial date has been set for next week," he said. "LeKnight called me yesterday."

"Then you should prepare for it." I was afraid to look at Finn for too long, and just as afraid that he would turn and run. "Maybe you'd rather go home."

"I want to talk to you," Finn said, shifting his weight from foot to foot.

But instead of talking, we merely stood on that porch trying to ignore the wind that rose off the harbor. We might have stood there for a very long time if Arthur had not come to investigate the open door.

"Get inside on the double," Arthur said; he reached for my arm and handed Finn a glass of sherry to combat the weather. "Young people never understand the consequences of pneumonia," Arthur said, leading us into the parlor. "Too much cold air and your lungs just give up, they can't handle the strain."

When Minnie saw that Finn had arrived, she rushed over to him. "I'm so glad you could make it," she said as she took his hand. And then, by way of introduction, she called out to Arthur and the sisters, "Michael's the fellow who's been accused of causing the power plant explosion."

"Minnie," I cried, but Finn looked relieved. He didn't seem to mind if everyone in the room knew his true identity, he even smiled as he handed Minnie the yellow chrysanthemums.

"You must be extremely busy," Arthur said admiringly to Finn. And from that moment, until dinner was served, Arthur followed on Finn's heels, using every bit of his sparse legal vocabulary. When Minnie announced that dinner was ready and waiting, it was Arthur who led Finn into the dining room. I followed behind the sisters, while behind us Beaumont slunk along in the shadows, carefully avoiding each unshaded window. If Minnie had not sent us to our seats, Finn and I might have sat on the opposite sides of the table, nodded goodbye after the meal, and never have spoken. But Minnie firmly directed us to chairs next to each other, where we stood until she carried the main dish of eggplant stuffed with black mushrooms.

"Ah!" Arthur said when Minnie appeared, and he sniffed appreciatively.

Beaumont pushed his sunglasses down on his nose and sighed. "No turkey," he said sadly.

"Who needs turkey?" Minnie said gaily. "We have a totally carcinogen-free meal."

We circulated Minnie's specialties: banana bread, sweet-potato pie, and deviled tofu. I passed each dish to Finn without looking at him, because I could feel him next to me. I grew confused and handed him more and more food until Finn's plate was piled high with seconds when everyone else was just taking a first bite.

"The best food I've ever tasted," Arthur said, raising a fork-ful of sweet potatoes to salute Minnie.

"Not one additive," Yolanda said admiringly.

Beneath the table, Finn suddenly reached for my hand. My breath grew shallow, my pulse was so loud that I was afraid everyone could hear its wild beat. But no one turned to look at me, no one pointed a finger; Beaumont continued to munch banana bread, and Evie poured cider for herself and her sister.

"I've thought about what you said," Finn told me. "I think I was wrong to ask you to leave my place."

"Oh, I don't know about that," I shrugged, not wanting to draw the others' attention to us. "You seemed pretty certain of what you wanted. And didn't want."

"I wanted you to stay that day," Finn said. He lifted my hand to his mouth and kissed my palm so quickly, so lightly, I might easily have imagined it, but Evie noticed and clapped her hands.

"Oh, my! How European," she cried happily.

Minnie had also seen that tentative kiss. "My husband Alex," she said, "was the sort of man who would kiss a woman's hand. He had an appreciation for beauty."

"You understand I'm not saying I'm in love," Finn told me. "Nothing like that."

"When I was very young," Evie said, "I was in love. He had red hair. Red as blood. But he wasn't what anyone would call a gentleman. He was a fellow who couldn't stop at a woman's hand—he went straight to the mouth. All women, women he had just met, he would kiss them right in front of me just as easy as eating an apple."

"That's true," Yolanda said. "I remember him."

"James," Evie nodded. "I canceled our engagement. I had to. The man couldn't control himself. He wasn't exactly a gentleman."

"No," Minnie agreed. "He sounds like a lady-killer."

"But his red hair was beautiful," Evie said. "I can still remember how people would turn and look at him in the street."

"But the truth is," Finn went on, "I wanted to be with you then, and I want to be with you now."

"Red hair always goes with a fiery personality," Arthur pointed out to Evie. "What folks call myth is often based on reality. You'd better believe it."

"But you don't feel anything for me?" I said.

"I wouldn't say that," Finn smiled. "I told you I wanted you."

Arthur poked my arm. "Lucky for you this boy's not a redhead." He smiled. "Then you would surely have trouble."

Maybe I only imagined myself in love with Finn. After all, how much did I really know about him? Perhaps I had even picked him because I knew a man with his past could never have a future that included me. All my thought of romance might have been only to disguise pure desire.

"You're talking about sex," I said.

"If I had ever seen your ex-fiancé kissing another woman, I would have given him a piece of my mind," Arthur told Evie.

"You," Minnie shrugged. "You're from the old school."

"A gentleman is a gentleman," Yolanda said. "Those rules never change."

"Well yes," Finn said. "But I want you to understand I can't make a commitment to you. I may disappear tomorrow."

"Watch," Arthur said. "Those two are made for each other."

"Love," Minnie said, and we all turned toward her and she sat stiffly at the head of the table, pursing her lips as if to begin a psalm or a prayer. "You sure can't ignore it."

The sisters and Arthur nodded their agreement, and Beaumont slipped his sunglasses down to take a look at Michael Finn and me.

"I want to spend the night with you," I whispered to Finn.

"Only if you understand there won't ever be anything more," he said.

But I knew I would want more. One night with Michael Finn in my bed could only pull me closer to him; already, before there had been one kiss, I was ready to wait for Finn on the courthouse stairs, and without one promise to sustain me I was ready to stand outside high prison walls.

"No romance," I agreed.

"Romance," Yolanda said dreamily.

"Dessert." Minnie signaled me with a nod of her head to join her in the kitchen.

"Do you think I'm making a mistake?" I asked as we scraped the dishes into the barrel of biodegradable trash. "Do you think I should ask him to spend the night?"

"Who am I to tell you what to do?" Minnie asked.

"You're right," I said, gathering dessert plates and the pumpkin pie onto a silver serving tray. "I have to make my own decisions. If I get hurt, at least I was honest, at least I gave it a chance."

"If I were you I would get a commitment." Minnie pointed to the gold wedding band she still wore. "It never hurts."

"You call that a commitment?" I laughed. "Do you know

how many marriages end in divorce? A commitment nowadays has to be a commitment of the soul."

"All right," Minnie nodded as she picked up the serving tray and headed for the kitchen door. "Then I'd get one of those."

But if I tried for that, Michael Finn would shrug ruefully and walk right out the door. It was my decision to accept Finn as he was. No one forced me up the stairs with him late that night. I had plenty of time during dessert to recant; the end of dinner was so quiet that I could hear the rustling of the lace tablecloth each time Finn moved, and the faint whistling sound in Evie's lungs every time she inhaled, no doubt remembering the man with the red hair. When dinner was over and Minnie's friends retired to the parlor before returning to the Mercy House, Finn and I found ourselves alone in the kitchen.

"You understand my situation," Finn said as he dried the dishes. "I'm not very stable. I may soon be going to jail."

"Oh, jail," I said with a wave of my hand.

"Not only that," Finn confided as he put down his dish towel, "I can't take any risks."

"And there may be an earthquake, a tornado, a plague." I smiled as I put away the last silver spoon. "I'll take a chance," I said.

But when Beaumont had left to drive Arthur and the sisters back to Mercy, and Minnie had curled up in the parlor to write to Congressman Bruner, taking a chance seemed like a crazy thing to do. Natural disasters were one thing, the losses of earthquakes and floods were unavoidable. But the unnatural losses I would face if Finn left me could still be avoided. I simply had to send him home. I thought of this as Michael Finn and I walked up the stairs to the second floor, but every step made turning back more and more impossible.

In my room, the curtains waved. I looked around as if the room belonged to someone else, as if I had never been there before. The metal bedframe stood in its place and the mattress was covered with the same goosedown quilt. When I took off my shoes and socks, the wooden floor was the same one I walked across every night, but when I closed the bedroom door I felt as anxious as if I had stepped into a lonely motel.

Finn turned away while I undressed. I could not remember a night so cold; even when I was in bed, between the sheets, I could not get warm. Finn crossed the room to undress in privacy. Every move took forever, every move echoed; his boots fell with a thud onto the floor, the clothes he set on the chair sighed as if they had a will of their own. When Finn pulled back the quilt, the chill was piercing, but once he was in bed, there was suddenly a line of heat between us etched into the mattress.

Finn leaned his head against the wall and looked up at the ceiling for such a long time that he might have been meditating, and not even the shrill whistle of the train as it traveled toward the last stop pulled him back. Though he looked like marble, his hands had begun to shake, tension drifted beneath his skin. I reached over and touched him.

"I don't think I can," Finn said, moving my hand away.

I went back to my side of the bed and sighed.

"It's not that I don't want to," Finn said. "That's what I came here for."

"Are you certain?"

"It's your aunt," Finn told me. "We're not really alone."

"Minnie has gone to sleep by now," I said, wondering if Finn had forgotten just who had invited him to dinner in the first place.

"I'm too nervous," Finn said.

I got out of bed and slipped on my robe. "I'll check to see if she's asleep," I told Finn. I was sure I would find Minnie in her room, exhausted from the day's work, but when I opened her door the bed was empty. I went down the stairs in search of my aunt, nearly forgetting that Michael Finn waited in my bed. I worried about heart attacks and angina; I might find Minnie sprawled on the bottom step. I walked stealthily, as if the Lanskys who had spent summers in the second-floor bedrooms might try to follow me down the stairs, watching and pointing as my robe flapped around my legs.

By the time I reached the parlor I was out of breath and convinced that some disease of old age had come upon my aunt. But though the parlor was freezing and Minnie's fingers were white as stones, when I bent over the easy chair where she had fallen asleep, I could hear her slow, regular breath.

"Go upstairs to bed," I whispered.

Minnie sighed and buried her head in the pillows of the easy chair. I did not want to frighten her or interrupt any dreams. So instead of waking her, I added some logs to the fire in the stove. Then I went to the linen closet to get an afghan which had been knitted by a Lansky who came all the way from San Diego one summer. When I had covered Minnie and checked the fire in the stove, I poured myself a glass of Scotch and sat on the couch.

"I suppose everybody makes mistakes," I said to my sleeping

aunt. "I guess everyone has to take a risk now and then," I told her.

Minnie turned and pulled the afghan closer to her chin.

"Falling in love is like falling asleep," I said to Minnie. "It just happens," I nodded as I sipped the Scotch. "For all you knew, Alex might have made your life miserable. Poets have that tendency; it happens all the time. You just took a chance. Well, who can fault you for that, who can say you didn't have any courage?"

I sat on the couch even after I had finished my drink; I watched Minnie sleep as if I might learn something from her dreams, although I would never be able to know more than I could guess. But when I left the parlor and walked back up the stairs, I felt as though I had been held by Minnie and then given a gentle shove, although the only move she had made was to turn in her sleep. When I returned to my room Finn was sitting on the edge of the bed. I slipped off my robe and got back into bed, wondering if Alex had helped Minnie sew the quilt; together they might have sat up late at night and counted stitches and feathers till dawn. "She's asleep," I said to Finn.

"She could wake up," Finn said. "Anything could happen," he said. "Anything."

"You can leave if you want to," I said.

He got up and began to pace, but carefully so that the creaking floorboards would not wake the old woman downstairs in the parlor. "I'm going to be honest with you," Finn said when he returned to the bed, and I slipped out to sit next to him. "This is it. Just this one night."

"All right," I agreed. "I already know that."

"I'm serious," Finn warned. "No long affair, not even a relationship. After tonight I might see you on the street sometime and turn to walk in the other direction, as if we never knew each other. Just tonight," Finn said. "Only tonight."

I reached out to touch him, and when I did, Finn placed his hands on my shoulders as if he might suddenly push me away, but instead he pulled me toward him and we lay together on top of the handmade quilt. We held onto each other like people who were afraid of drowning, people who might never see each other again. And I was drowning, over and over again; when he moved his tongue over my skin nothing else mattered, and when he came inside me I didn't think about the future, I didn't care about the risks. With every shudder, time dropped farther and farther away, the seconds stood still, held motionless with desire, caught by kisses and white heat.

"If I want to," Finn whispered to me, "I can pretend that we never met. I can pretend that none of this ever happened."

I didn't care, I refused to take his warning to heart. Instead I lay back in the bed which had always reminded me of summer; beneath the Russian quilt, in front of every Lansky ghost, I had to admit I never wanted the night to end.

In the morning, when Beaumont had finally quit his nighttime hammering, Finn and I made love again. When we moved together I was certain that we could forget the future and the past, we could keep clocks from ticking. The sun rose over the harbor that day, but neither of us saw it; beneath us the floorboards creaked, the bed swayed on its metal legs, and there was no place outside of those bedroom walls either of us wanted to be.

DEAD OF WINTER

ONE

$\mathcal{I}$N DECEMBER, THE TRIAL began. If Carter hadn't returned from New Hampshire and insisted that I attend the trial from the start, I might not have gone to court at all until I was subpoenaed.

The morning after Thanksgiving, Finn had simply walked out the front door, out of my life. He had never promised anything—no phone calls, no letters; and in return he had asked for nothing except the one promise I now knew I would break: that I attend the trial only to testify.

"Carter's convinced me to go to the trial," I told Minnie.

"I could never understand why you ever said you weren't going," my aunt said. "It isn't everybody whose lover goes on trial."

"That's an unsubstantiated conclusion."

"Wait a minute," Minnie said. "Do you think I'm dead? Do you think I'm blind?"

"All that is over with," I said.

I reached for my coat and went out to warm up the car. There was a tap at my window; Minnie was standing there, bundled up in scarves. I rolled down the window.

"What is it?" I asked.

"Move over," Minnie said. She opened the driver's door. "You're too nervous to drive."

I slid over into the passenger's seat. "I'm not nervous at all," I said.

"Really?" Minnie said. "What's the capital of South Dakota?"

"I don't know," I said.

"Aha," Minnie said, shifting into reverse. "I'll drive."

"We'll have to hurry," I said. "I'm supposed to meet Carter inside the courtroom."

I hadn't seen Carter since he had gone to New Hampshire; I dreaded our meeting, I was afraid of arguments and careless words, I was afraid I wouldn't have the courage to tell him goodbye.

Minnie drove well above the speed limit, but when we reached the courthouse, there was already a crowd and we couldn't find a space to park.

"Damn," Minnie said. "We should have walked."

Outside, the courthouse camera crews had set up; a line of reporters and Fishers Cove residents wound along Main Street. Minnie and I circled the block looking for a parking space. On our second time around I spotted Reno LeKnight's car.

"Stop," I said to Minnie. "Is that Finn?"

Even though the spotlight in front of us was green, Minnie slammed on the brakes. We strained our necks to see, but a crowd gathered around LeKnight's car and we couldn't tell if Finn was a passenger.

"Just park anywhere," I said to Minnie. "Park illegally."

We left the Mustang in a space marked DELIVERIES ONLY, then hurried to the court.

"We'll never get in," I said when we reached the courthouse.

A group of local residents had already been turned away from the courthouse, but the group lingered, buying chestnuts and pretzels from a vendor who had set up near the courthouse stairs. Two police officers watched over the street; unused to crowds, the officers patted their nightsticks and waited for signs of a riot.

"We'll get in," Minnie said, and I followed as she pushed her way through. The courthouse was filled. Minnie spotted Congressman Bruner, but there was no one I recognized except Carter, who was sitting close to where we stood in the aisle. I had expected to see Danny Finn, but he wasn't there.

"Natalie," Carter called. "Come on, I've saved you a seat."

Minnie and I both inched through the crowd and sat in the space Carter had saved.

"How was New Hampshire?" I asked Carter.

"Terrific," he said. "I didn't know you were bringing her with you," he whispered.

"Would you like me to sit somewhere else?" Minnie said. "Is that what you'd like?"

"Minnie, please," I said.

"I have as much right to be here as anyone," Minnie told Carter. "I consider myself a friend of the defendant, how about you?"

"I'm a friend of the people," Carter said.

"Well, well, well," Minnie said. "Isn't that nice."

"Will you two stop it?" I said.

A door in the front of the room opened and Finn and Reno

LeKnight walked out and went to the defendant's bench. Away from the streets, away from all the places I had seen him, Finn looked more helpless than ever before, he looked as he must have when he slept in the parked car above Montauk Point, when he stood alone on the wide lawn of the Stockley School. LeKnight spoke to him, and although Finn nodded calmly, his profile was tight, as if his skin were too small, as if he might suddenly explode right there in the courthouse.

"He looks terrible," Minnie said. "Just look at what tension can do to a man."

While we waited for the judge to enter, Carter and Minnie talked about Reno.

"I just don't like him," Minnie said. "He looks too slick. He's not my type."

"Minnie, he just happens to be the best lawyer around," Carter said.

"I don't care," my aunt shrugged. "What kind of lawyer wears a suede sport coat?"

"With Reno LeKnight here, you don't have to worry about Finn going to jail."

"Well, I am worried," I said.

Carter removed his glasses and cleaned the lenses. "You sound upset," he said.

When the judge entered and we all stood, I watched Finn: his long hair fell over the collar of his black sports jacket, his shoulders fluttered nervously, like wings.

After we sat again, Carter turned to Minnie. "What kind of judge can he be? A judge in Fishers Cove is used to traffic fines. I'd like to know the last time he tried a criminal case."

"Just because we're a small town, don't think we don't have

crime," Minnie said. "We've got everything here. You name it, we've got it."

"Murder," Carter said. "Have you ever had that?"

"In nineteen sixty-seven," Minnie said. "A dentist murdered his entire family. Including his children."

Reno LeKnight stood and faced the judge. "My client would like to offer a plea of not guilty," he said. "Although Michael Finn did install the faulty valve in the second unit at Angel Landing Three, he was unaware of his error until after the explosion."

The district attorney looked puzzled. When he was recognized, he turned to LeKnight. "You admit your client installed the valve?"

"Of course," LeKnight said.

"He installed it with the intent of destroying the power plant?" the district attorney asked.

"Absolutely not," LeKnight said. "Absolutely ridiculous."

"How does it look?" I said to Carter. "Do you think Finn has a chance?"

"The trial's just begun," Carter said. "Who can tell?"

We spent the rest of the day listening to the opening arguments. The district attorney announced that Michael Finn had been an accomplished welder for more than ten years. A sudden accident? The D.A. smiled. An error? he said. Later, Reno LeKnight insisted that Finn had been plagued by insomnia and headaches, he had been suffering from dizziness and loneliness and viruses of every sort in the weeks before the explosion; he had been touched by all of the things which would lead a welder into the realm of human error. By the end of that day, both sides had argued with passion, and without facts.

Carter said he was annoyed; he had expected a better performance from Reno LeKnight, he had paid for it, and now he announced he was driving out to the attorney's house in West Hampton to question LeKnight's tactics.

"I'll drive out there with you," I said to Carter.

"You?" Carter said. "Why do you want to do that?"

"You're not the only one who cares about this trial," I said.

I watched as Finn followed LeKnight from the courtroom. He looked at no one, he never even noticed I was there in the room. My presence in the courtroom that day could have been kept secret, all our promises would look as if they had never been broken, unless I went out to the beach with Carter, unless I gave myself away.

"I want to go," I said to Carter. "That's all there is to it."

We walked out of the courthouse together, but Minnie stopped on the stairs when Congressman Bruner walked by. "Congressman," Minnie called. "It's me, Minnie Lansky."

The congressman came over and embraced Minnie like a long-lost relative. Minnie looked up at him, surprised. "Mrs. Lansky," the congressman said. "How is your work at the nursing home?" He turned then to a reporter at his side. "Seventy-two, and Mrs. Lansky still finds the strength to volunteer in the Mercy Home. She would make a good human-interest story, don't you think?"

"Seventy-four," Minnie said. "And to tell you the truth, things aren't going so great at the home."

"Seventy-two, seventy-four." The congressman smiled.

"Not good at all," Minnie went on. "The food is still terrible, and too many people are there who don't belong. In fact, I'm thinking of getting some of those senior citizens out of Mercy, I'm thinking of starting a halfway house of my own."

"Halfway house," the congressman said. "Halfway between this world and the next," he said to the reporter at his side. "Tell me, Mrs. Lansky, when are things ever good enough? Can a nursing home become a palace overnight?"

"Maybe, maybe not," Minnie said. "But we'll certainly give it a try, won't we? And if an elected official like you can't take care of it, tell me who can?"

"I'll do my best," the congressman said. "I always have the people in mind," he stated hurriedly as he led the reporter away.

Carter and I walked Minnie to her car, and then went on to the lot where Carter's MG was parked. Before he turned the key in the ignition, he crossed his fingers; luckily for us the old sports car decided to start in spite of its damp wires and old alternator. We drove to the Long Island Expressway, and then went east. It was dangerous for the MG to go faster than forty-five miles an hour, the engine block might explode, and so we drove slowly toward West Hampton, slower still when it began to sleet. I had fallen in love with the MG almost faster than I had with Carter; five years ago the car had been old enough to be a classic, but had not yet begun falling apart. Carter and I would drive for hours, listening to the radio, wearing sweaters, insisting on keeping the top down even on cool nights. Now the radio no longer worked, rust and salt had eaten away the floorboards so that I could look through to the highway as we drove.

"Is there something wrong?" Carter asked as he switched on the windshield wipers.

"No," I said.

"We used to talk to each other," Carter said sadly.

"Look, I just told you nothing is wrong."

He turned off the expressway at the West Hampton exit.

"All right," I said. "I'm upset about the trial."

"Of course you are," Carter said when we stopped for gas at a station in the town of West Hampton. "You've never been through it before. You're beginning to understand how unfair the legal system is."

"It's not that," I said.

When Carter rolled down his window to pay the gas station attendant I wondered how I could tell him what a traitor I was. Even if Finn refused to see me when we got to West Hampton, I would still continue to betray Carter every time I sat calmly beside him and pretended that my feelings for him were the same as before. When we rode over the wooden drawbridge which led to Dune Road I was racked with nerves and remorse.

"Maybe I should have stayed home," I said.

But we had already crossed the bridge.

"I'm glad you're with me," Carter said.

Dune Road was deserted, the summer people would not return for months, huge houses had been boarded up and forgotten; alone with the winter sea, they rose up before us like giants. The closer we came to LeKnight's house the more afraid I was of forcing Finn into a corner.

"It's Finn." There was a lump in my throat. "I think about him a lot," I said, watching Carter carefully.

"So do I," Carter said.

"No, I don't think you know what I mean," I said.

"Yes, I do," Carter told me as he turned into a long driveway which led to the wooden beach house. "The guy's a mystery, he's a real unusual case."

I wished then that Carter would have guessed; it would have been so much easier if he could have taken my pulse whenever Finn's name was mentioned, if only he could have seen photographs of us together in bed, there wouldn't be a need for explanations or sorrow; Carter would have simply turned and said goodbye. Instead he kept going up the long driveway, avoiding the deep ruts in the sand. He parked by the garage near a grove of gray reeds which grew taller than our heads.

When I got out and closed the car door behind me, I was afraid I might be lost in the reeds; they towered above me, they moved and sighed.

"This way," Carter called, and I followed the footprints he made in the sand. I could have turned back, I could have run back down the driveway and hidden in the feathery reeds, I might even have hitchhiked down Dune Road; if I waited long enough a car would certainly come, no matter how desolate the road looked. But I wanted to see Finn, so I followed Carter's steps and stood beside him at the door. And when Reno Le-Knight answered the bell I walked inside. Through the doors to a wooden deck we could see the white stretch of foam the waves left along the sand.

"What the hell are you doing here?" Reno LeKnight said irritably.

"I want to make certain Finn's entirely satisfied with his legal representative," Carter said.

"Of course he's satisfied," LeKnight said.

"I don't know," Carter shrugged. "I wasn't too pleased with what I saw in court today."

"I thought you told me you had experience in court?" LeKnight said to Carter. "But it seems to me you're an amateur. The first day is nothing, you should know that."

It occurred to me that Michael Finn might not even be in the house; Reno might have hidden him away, protected from people who cared too much. "Are you sure he's even here?" I asked Carter.

"And I'd like to know what she's doing here?" LeKnight asked Carter. "She's supposed to be an objective witness and you're supposed to have nothing at all to do with the trial. Do you know how a judge would react if he knew Finn was consorting with some radical fringe?"

"We're a grass-roots movement, not a fringe."

"To be perfectly frank," LeKnight said, "I don't give a damn about your organization."

"I was sure you didn't," Carter nodded.

"But all of us are interested in Finn's winning," Reno went on. "So take my suggestion. Stay away."

It was then I saw Finn; he was out on the deck, standing by the railing watching the slow, dark Atlantic.

"Why don't I get you both a drink and then you can go," LeKnight said. And when he left the room I turned to Carter.

"He's out there," I said. "On the deck."

"You're not going to try and stop us from seeing him, are you?" Carter asked the attorney when he returned with our drinks.

"I can't," Reno LeKnight said. "But let me just warn you, the man is depressed and depression doesn't go over well in court. Contrition is fine, humility is even better, but once a district attorney smells depression, it's all over."

Carter walked over and slid the doors open.

"Five minutes," LeKnight called to us. "Don't stay a minute longer," he said as Carter closed the doors behind us.

Finn stood out there without a coat, he held onto the railing tightly, his hair was tangled with salt. Carter went over and tapped Finn's shoulder, and I was glad that he did; if I had been the first person Finn had turned to see, he might have bolted and run over the sand dunes like a horse crazy with moonlight.

"Here you go," Carter said as he handed Finn his own whiskey. "I came to find out what you think of LeKnight. I want to make certain you have faith in him."

"Oh, he's great," Finn said bitterly, "considering he has no case to present." He took a sip of whiskey and then saw me in the shadows. "What are you doing here?"

"She came with me for the ride," Carter explained. "Listen, LeKnight just said you were depressed. Is that true?"

Finn was looking at me. "What?" he said to Carter.

"Because I know a cure for your depression," Carter went on. "Come work for Soft Skies, think about a cause larger than yourself."

"Please," Finn said. "Leave me alone."

"Are you certain that's what you want?" Carter asked.

"I'm certain that's exactly what I want."

"Then I'll go," Carter said. "But if you want to change your mind, if you decide to come and work for our office when the trial is over, call me."

"Please," Finn said. He moved away from us. "I just want to be alone. Can't you understand that?"

"I want to stay for a few minutes," I told Carter.

"What?" Carter said.

"Just give me some time. I'll meet you in the driveway. Please."

Carter eyed me suspiciously, but he nodded and then walked down the deck stairs to the sand.

"I'm not here to pressure you," I said quickly. "I'm not here because of that one night. I'm here because I wanted to make sure you were all right. I just want to stand here for a few minutes with you. We don't even have to talk."

Finn still faced away from me. The sleet had ended, yet there was a hard, salty wind. I had on a heavy winter coat, but Michael Finn wore only jeans and a white shirt.

"What is he going to think?" Finn nodded toward Carter, who was slowly walking back to the driveway.

"He'll think I care about you," I said. "After all, it's true."

"You shouldn't have come out here," Finn said. "I didn't want anyone to get hurt. This way, sooner or later someone will."

"You don't know that," I said.

"I know what happened before," Finn said.

He looked frozen, and beneath all my heavy winter clothes, I shivered, too.

"I left someone," Finn said absently. "I just took off." He turned to face me. "I'm not to be trusted."

"It could be different this time," I said.

"Could it be?" Finn shook his head. "I'll be damned if I ever give anyone the chance to do to me what I did to her. And I couldn't do it to someone else again."

Finn's face was set in anger, and I realized how little I knew him, and how possible it was that he could be cruel. Maybe I was lucky that he wanted to turn away from me; I might have been saved from some terrible mean streak I never even imagined if I now walked past the soft gray reeds, and left him alone with his memories.

"Who was she?" I asked.

"Does it matter?" Finn asked.

Gulls circled the beach house in the dark, sleet had coated the deck like a second skin.

"I think it might," I said.

"It was a long time ago," Finn said carefully. "There was a woman."

Already I could see her; she walked barefoot in summer, she smiled slowly, easily; she put her arm through Finn's and called him darling. I didn't want to hear about her, I wanted to hear every word. I waited for Finn to go on, hoping that once she was before us, standing on the deck of the beach house, we would be rid of her once and for all.

TWO

WHEN HE WAS TWENTY-
one, Michael Finn drove down to Buckley, West Virginia, during a summer when there were record heat waves and the hills
he drove through had turned a parched gold color, like a
woman's hair that had been too long in the sun. It was the start
of things going dry in New York, and many of the men in
Finn's union had found jobs in faraway places, places as promising as San Jose and Santa Fe, and as poor and desolate as
Buckley, West Virginia.

If Finn hadn't known his destination he might have felt free,
he might have enjoyed speeding down the New Jersey Turn-
pike in his battered Ford Falcon, he might have noticed owls
in the trees when he passed over the Pennsylvania state line at
dusk. But Finn knew that he was not driving on to New Mexico
or California; he was headed toward a small mining town hidden in the hills, a town full of construction workers building a
new coal-processing plant, and Finn didn't smile once the whole
drive down.

When he first saw Buckley, from high atop the Interstate,
Finn's heart dropped, it sank down low; not in his worst dreams

had Finn imagined the thick halo of smoke that surrounded the town, he could not have guessed that a long stretch of clothesline strung from tree to tree in front of an old farmhouse could have made him so sad. He pulled into town and rented a room in a boarding house right away. That first night he lay on a small metal-framed bed with all his clothes on; he left the bedside lamp on. Even though he didn't move a muscle as he lay there, Finn felt as though he were still driving, the white highway line seemed to be right in front of him.

When Finn reported to the half-built power plant for work, he tried to pretend that he was a drifter, a man just passing through town, instead of another construction worker trapped in Buckley by the overtime that would send his paycheck over five hundred dollars each week. Like all the other workers, Michael Finn took on as much overtime as he could get, even if that meant staying for twelve hours or more in the broiling hot rooms of the plant, metal rooms that did not cool down even after the sun had set and the night birds flew from tree to tree. When he finally returned to the boarding house each night, his room was a furnace; if Finn touched the iron bedpost he burned his fingertips. The toilet was down the hall, and Finn's landlady had announced that boarders were allowed only one shower a day, and she was none too pleased if they all took one, for water wasn't free. Nothing in Buckley was free; it was a town so poor that when it finally saw money, in the high paychecks of the out-of-state construction workers, the entire town whistled, winked, and raised prices by nearly double. Because there was so little to spend money on in town, workers bought whatever there was, and mostly there was alcohol. Even Finn, who had never been a drinker, found himself spending every evening until closing time in the Iron Horse, a bar crowded with arguments, and money, and hot, unmoving summer air.

It was there, at the bar of the Iron Horse, that Michael Finn met Marlene. He had ordered a gin and tonic, which was bitter and warm, when Marlene first saw him, and immediately she knew something was about to happen. Marlene was twenty-seven, six years older than Finn, and she hadn't been to the Iron Horse for months. The mother of a six-year-old girl called Sunny, she was on welfare—and if her brother, Ben, didn't take her out for a drink and spring for the price of a babysitter, Marlene wouldn't have gone anywhere at all. When she noticed Finn sipping his drink, Marlene knew that she would take him home with her when she left. She wasn't afraid: Marlene had lived in Buckley all her life, and once someone else lived there, too—even for a day or a week—he was no longer an outsider as far as Marlene was concerned.

"I like his looks," Marlene murmured to her brother. She nodded toward Finn.

"You've got to watch out for construction workers," Ben, a miner, said. "They move around so much, they're in another state before you blink your eyes or pull your zipper up, and they all have wives back home."

"They can't all be married," Marlene said.

"Well, most of them are," Ben said grudgingly, straining to see if there was a wedding band on Finn's finger. Ben was younger than Marlene, and he was convinced that nothing was too good for her. Although he tried to persuade Marlene to forget about the man at the other end of the bar, she hadn't been out for months and was determined not to go home alone.

As for Finn, he was so lonely that evening that he found himself smiling when Marlene walked over to him.

"Drinking gin?" Marlene asked. When Finn nodded, she smiled. "They make the best gin and tonics in the world here," Marlene confided, which should have let Finn know, right away, that he was about to become involved with a West Virginia woman who believed in absolutes.

They left the Iron Horse together an hour later, although Finn hadn't uttered more than a dozen sentences. But his reserve didn't bother Marlene one bit—she always said she had a thing for strong, silent types. She slid into the front seat of Michael Finn's Falcon as if Finn were an old trusted friend; and, leaving young Ben behind to worry and order another beer, they drove to the edge of town, where Marlene and her daughter lived in a trailer park surrounded by tall, green pines.

Marlene went in alone to dismiss the babysitter, who lived only a few trailers away; but she was back for Finn before he had time to change his mind and drive out of the trailer camp at full speed, leaving a cloud behind him as he fled over the dirt road. Instead of running away, he allowed Marlene to lead him across the pine needles. Once inside the trailer, she held a finger to her lips. They tiptoed by the cot in the living room where Sunny slept, covered up to her neck by a cotton quilt, even though it was nearly eighty outside, and the midnight temperature inside the trailer was surely higher. Marlene's bedroom was so small that there was room for only her double bed, carefully made up with pink flowered sheets, and a wooden dressing table loaded with bottles of cologne. After they had undressed, Finn was surprised that Marlene was nearly beautiful; he was even more surprised when she dropped to her knees and took his penis into her mouth and actually seemed to like doing so. Michael Finn could hardly protest, he had been lonely for a very long time, for as long as he could remember; he closed his eyes and tried to pretend that he was no longer alone.

After that first time, Finn saw Marlene more and more often. Soon it was every night. She had begun to assume that he would come around to her trailer as soon as he had gone back to the boarding house after work to shower and get rid of his work clothes; and to Finn, anything would have been better than the still heat of his rented room. The truth was, Finn was intoxicated by Marlene's beauty, by the easiness of their relationship, and by Marlene's low expectations—if he didn't say a word for hours, Marlene didn't seem to care. If there was anything in that trailer that could disrupt the comfortable routine Finn had settled into, it was Marlene's daughter, Sunny.

How she had gotten her name Finn never knew. Certainly it was not because she was tall and fair like her mother; Sunny was small for six, and her hair was cut in rough bangs which nearly hid her eyes. And it was not because of the girl's disposition; she was often glum, she read books in the corner of the trailer, and went outside in the summer heat only when bribed with ice cream or the promise of a swim. Marlene had admitted that she was not certain who Sunny's father was—she had been seeing two men around that time—a local boy who had later been killed in Vietnam, and a marijuana dealer who drove a Corvette and left town several months before Sunny was born. At first Sunny did not like Finn and refused to talk to him, but by the time he moved his suitcase out of the boarding house and into the trailer, she no longer cried each time he came through the door. Three months had passed since the day of Finn's arrival in Buckley, and although dinner was waiting for him every night when he came home to the trailer, Michael Finn still felt like an outsider; he was still driving down that white-lined highway.

What really changed things, what let Finn know that he was no longer a stranger in Buckley, but a man who might actually get stuck in a small West Virginia town, happened one morning when he drove Sunny to school. Now and then Finn would drop her off—the elementary school was on the way to the coal plant, and Marlene was convinced that the early morning drives would bring the two closer together. And, after a few trips together, Sunny and Finn were able to hold polite conversations; they discussed what was eaten for breakfast, and how hot it was for mid-September. It was Finn who did most of the talking; even though he was a man most comfortable without words, he could not bear to see Sunny sit so quietly in the front seat of the Falcon. Sometimes, when the two of them were riding to-gether, Finn had the impulse to stop the car and drop Sunny off on a deserted stretch of road. But he was never quite certain how he would feel if the girl disappeared; he might be thankful for one less interference in his life, or he might just as possibly grieve.

One morning, when the heat blew through the open window in waves, Finn felt he simply couldn't go on. Life was too hot, too lonely, and much too long.

"Jesus Christ," Finn muttered. He lit a cigarette and inhaled. He could barely tell the difference between the heat of the cig-arette smoke and the heavy morning air. "I'd give anything not to go to work today," Finn said to himself.

"Anything?" Sunny said, wrinkling her face and biting her lower lip. "I'll give you a quarter."

Finn looked at her, surprised. "Where would you get a quarter?" he asked.

"From you," Sunny shrugged. "I don't have any money of my own," she said with none of the sweetness Finn despised in children.

They made a deal that day: they would take off and go swimming, and not tell Marlene a thing about it. Finn parked in front of the Buckley Five-and-Ten and handed Sunny a five-dollar bill, which she used to buy a cheap yellow bathing suit. After they had driven out of town, Finn parked and then rolled up his jeans while Sunny changed into her new suit behind a grove of pines which stood beside the nearly deserted pond. There were no swimmers, only a troupe of old-timers, fishermen who dipped their bait into the pond without any real hope of a bite.

They didn't talk much that day, they barely looked at each other. Despite Sunny's love of the water, she was not a great swimmer; she stayed close to the shore and spent most of the afternoon collecting stones. But Finn swam as though he would never grow tired; he raced across the width of the pond dozens of times, he swam so fast that the old-timers took time away from their fishing to cheer him on. Finn smiled, and shook the water out of his ears; he waved to the group of old men. It was almost as if he was free, as if that coal plant in Buckley didn't exist; it was almost as if there wasn't a woman waiting for him, counting the hours until he came home, ready to throw her arms around him, as if he weren't a man who still felt alone.

They waited for Finn's jeans to dry; then Sunny disappeared and changed back into her school clothes.

"Are you going to marry my mother?" Sunny asked casually when they walked back to the parked car.

"I don't know," Finn admitted. He had never thought about marriage.

"I was just curious," she said. She was more than that; she felt differently about Finn now, she had decided that he was not so horrible after all, she had begun to want him to stay.

"Do you think I should marry your mother?" Finn smiled.

Because he had to ask that question, Sunny knew Finn had no plans to marry Marlene, he had no real plans at all.

"Yes," Sunny said quietly.

"Well, we'll see about that," Finn said, suddenly nervous. He realized for the first time that he was actually touching people's lives in a way an outsider never could have. They threw the yellow bathing suit in the trunk of the Ford, and Finn hid it beneath the spare tire he knew Marlene would never touch. "For next time," he told Sunny. But the girl didn't answer, she looked at Finn gravely, knowing full well that there would not be a next time. The day had been a freak; the weather would not be this good until next spring, and even if Finn didn't know it yet, Sunny at least was fairly certain that Finn wouldn't be around when the pond grew warm again and dragonflies flew over the surface of the water like tiny blue dancers.

Though Sunny trusted her instincts and tried to prepare herself for the day when Finn would leave, she still wanted to keep Michael Finn in Buckley; she may have even wanted it more than Marlene. When Finn and Marlene argued about money, and Finn disappeared for a few days—sleeping in the back seat of the Falcon and drinking six-packs of beer, even though he couldn't stand the taste of the stuff—Sunny stopped talking. After Finn returned, and Marlene explained that Finn was now back for good, Sunny still refused to look up. She wouldn't say a word, she refused to be bathed or to comb her own hair. Marlene, who had very little patience, and even less patience with things psychological, took Sunny to the local hospital when spankings and threats did no good. There, Sunny was diagnosed as having autistic tendencies. Marlene was now more satisfied— at least Sunny's behavior had a name, and all her troubles would go away as quickly and mysteriously as they had come. But Michael Finn knew better. He knew it each time he caught Sunny staring up at him from beneath her dark hair. Sunny was letting Finn know just how much responsibility he had. Still, Finn felt like a transient after eight months in Buckley and the West Virginia accent still grated on his nerves, but the postman and the milkman both knew his name. Michael Finn was suddenly a man with a family.

When Finn phoned his parents in New York at Christmas, Danny Finn lowered his voice at the end of the conversation and said, "I hope you're getting it down there in West Virginia. Those hill girls open their legs for anyone, but believe me, they want a ring like any other woman." Finn began to imagine that he was living someone else's life. He felt as though everything he did—every word he spoke, every kiss, had all been done before. There were terrifying times when Finn imagined that he was living his father's life, repeating it with slight variations. Yet, when Marlene suggested that they get married, Finn found himself agreeing. He sat Sunny down and told her of their plans, but Sunny watched him suspiciously.

"When are you going to get married?" Sunny asked.

"I don't know," Finn said. He saw the girl's eyes drop to study the floor. "February fifteenth," Finn said, picking the date arbitrarily and wanting to make Sunny believe that the marriage would truly happen. Finn was rewarded for naming a date; Sunny threw her arms around him and touched her face against his. But as quickly as she had embraced him, she moved away, waiting, perhaps until February 15th, to allow her emotions to surface. Finn began to save his paycheck; banking all that he could in the hope of buying property out in the hills, far from the trailer park, far from the coal plant. But when he told Marlene his plan, she wrinkled her nose.

"The hills?" she said. "Too far away."

"Far away from what?" Finn asked. They were sitting on the metal porch of the trailer, bundled up in sweaters, watching the bare trees.

"From everything," Marlene said firmly. "From town."

For Marlene, going back to the hills would be a terrible fate. Her own mother had worked on a farm before moving to Buckley; the sorrows of that life had been told to Marlene every day throughout her childhood, so that even talk of moving back to the hills made her shudder. Soon, Finn gave up the idea of owning land, but he continued to bank his paycheck, although he no longer knew what he was saving for. Marlene seemed perfectly happy to stay on in the trailer park forever, and her satisfaction annoyed Finn, and more; it made him keenly aware of how much more he wanted from life. Michael Finn began to go to the Iron Horse again; he imagined that what made him spend hours over a single beer was what had made his own father spend more and more time away from home. An emptiness followed Finn wherever he went, an emptiness Marlene seemed not to notice; she had her younger brother to talk to, and girlfriends she had known all her life. Marlene did not believe in moods; she could get herself out of a rut with one drink or a new blouse or a bouquet of wild flowers that wouldn't have sold for more than a dollar in the florist's shop.

The snow began in late January, and there were times when Finn would be sent home from work, without pay, because the weather wouldn't allow for outside welding at the plant. Most often Finn went straight to the Iron Horse, but some days he drove home and lay down on the bed in the small bedroom. There he would turn his face to the window and watch snowflakes hit against the panes. On these days he was surprised to discover that Sunny was almost always home too; she rarely went to school and spent most of her time following Marlene around, learning how to set the table and do the wash in the trailer park laundromat, or simply reading in her corner while Marlene watched TV or cooked the hamburgers or macaroni they would eat for dinner.

"Is she sick or something?" Finn finally asked when he returned home in midmorning and found Sunny sorting socks on the living room floor and listening to a portable radio which belted out rock-and-roll hits.

"Not one bit," Marlene said, kissing Finn on the neck. "She's a very healthy kid. Never gets sick."

Finn moved away from Marlene and watched Sunny, her head bobbing in time to the song on the radio. "Why is she home from school? She's always home."

"School," Marlene frowned. "She can learn a lot from me. Right here. She can learn everything she needs to know."

"She's six years old," Finn said. "She's supposed to be in school."

"I went to school even less than Sunny does," Marlene said. "I had more important things to do. I had to help my mother. And I don't think it hurt me one bit."

Finn sat down at the kitchen table and closed his eyes. He tried to picture Sunny all grown up; he saw the same image, over and over again: an older Sunny, a woman, sitting in another trailer, sorting a man's socks and listening to the radio.

"Don't you want her life to be different?" Finn said softly to Marlene.

"Why?" Marlene said, confused and a little angry. "What's wrong with the way things are?"

"Come on," Finn said, "do you want her to end up in a trailer camp without an education, even a high-school diploma?"

"What's wrong with that? Are you saying there's something the matter with my life?" Marlene said, wishing that Finn would keep quiet the way he usually did.

"Well, I want things to be different," Finn said. He tried as hard as he could to picture another grown-up Sunny, one who wouldn't bother with radios and laundry, one who would go off to college, but all he could see was the little girl sorting socks. "I don't want any more of this," Finn said to Sunny. "I want you to go to school every day. I want to see you doing some homework." He had wanted to say I love you, he had wanted to tell her to move far away from Buckley, to major in physics or engineering, but instead he had merely talked about homework. And he had shouted so loud that the little girl on the floor jumped.

"You can't tell me what to do," Sunny said to him from her seat on the floor. "You can't because you're not really my father."

"Stop that," Marlene warned.

"He's not," Sunny insisted. "My father died in the war."

"That's what I told her," Marlene said to Finn. "And that might have been him. The boy who died in Vietnam had the same kind of hair as Sunny."

"You can't tell me what to do," Sunny said. She had raised her chin and her bangs fell into her angry eyes.

Something was happening to Finn, something inside. His head felt like a firecracker, and when he stood up, his pulse was so loud it deafened him. If he didn't do something he would explode, he would break in two. Michael Finn threw the kitchen table on the floor; a toaster and a crystal vase which had been a present to Marlene from her brother, Ben, fell with a crash, and an open package of Sugar Crisps scattered all over the floor like bits of shrapnel. The crash of the table was so loud that it echoed through the metal trailer like gunfire; it echoed in Finn's own head. Finn then looked down at Sunny, who sat very quietly on the floor, her eyes wide and her mouth open in surprise. He knew that if she had been a boy, his son, Finn would have ignored the table he had sent crashing down. Instead, he would have walked across the room and slapped the boy so hard that the child would have risen up like a puppet, like old trash paper, like Michael Finn himself used to do when his own father had hit him in a rage that Finn had never understood before.

It was then that Michael Finn began to cry. He put his hands over his eyes, and sobs began to escape in a low-pitched wail.

Marlene backed up against the stove, her shoulders were stiff. She had been waiting for the punch she was certain she'd receive before Finn started crying. But now she was more shocked than she would have been had Finn blackened both her eyes. The man she was to marry in less than a month was weeping, like a baby; and for the first time Marlene studied Finn as if he truly was a stranger. She did not dare to go near him. Instead, Sunny stood up, left her pile of sorted socks, and walked toward Finn, stepping carefully over the spilled Sugar Crisps. She did not touch him, but she stood so close that Finn could feel her breath, and smell her odor, a soft combination of laundry detergent and spearmint gum.

"You can be my father," Sunny said nonchalantly.

Finn shook his head, tears streaked through his fingers, he couldn't speak.

"Sure," Sunny nodded. "You can. I want you to be."

"No," Finn said finally when he had wiped his eyes. He could not look at the child who stood so close to him. "I can't be." Finn shook his head. "I don't want to be," he whispered.

A few days later, Finn withdrew all his savings and bought a brand new Camaro with wire-spoked wheels, and he left Buckley, West Virginia, taking with him even less than he had brought when he first arrived, nearly a year before. He left at dawn, without bothering to say goodbye to Marlene. Since the day Finn had allowed her to see him cry, without even trying to run out the trailer door before the first tear fell, Marlene could no longer look at him. Although now and then Finn had caught her eyeing him when she thought he could not see, as if he was an impersonator, an impostor who had invaded her trailer and her life.

Finn did not say goodbye to Sunny either, he made it a point not to; he had been avoiding her, and the child seemed not to notice—she had taken to humming to herself as she sat in her corner of the trailer, she sang a soft, private melody which pierced Michael Finn's heart. The morning he left, as he followed the white highway line which would lead him back to New York, Finn tried to convince himself that Sunny had never really expected him to stay. And although he was certain that if he tried for the rest of his natural-born days he still would never have belonged, Finn could think of nothing but the child who sat sorting socks on the floor.

Later that day, when he crossed the West Virginia state line, Finn imagined that Sunny was with him; she was following him over the hills, she was floating somewhere near his left ear beating a small pair of wings that filled his head with a low whirring noise. In time, the strange noise died away, but even on the second day of his trip, Finn was still looking in his rearview mirror. All the distance in the world couldn't separate Finn from the steep West Virginia hills he had left far behind, and no matter how fast he drove his new Camaro, he couldn't ever outrace the incredible speed of sadness and regret.

THREE

H ERE ON THE BEACH, THAT small despairing angel of guilt who had sprung from Finn's imagination still buzzed around us.

"That all happened a long time ago," I said.

"Oh, come on," Finn said. "Don't you see? I'm the same person I was then."

"You're wrong," I said. "You've changed."

Finn shook his head. "I would still leave when things got tough. I'd do it again. Even though I wouldn't want to hurt anyone, I'd still do it."

"But you were smart to leave West Virginia," I said. "Everyone was drowning, and if you stayed you couldn't have rescued anyone; you would only have gone down, too."

"The risks are too high," Michael Finn said. "Don't you see that? Can't you tell?"

Down the driveway, Carter flashed the headlights of the MG.

"He's calling me," I said to Finn.

Inside the house, Reno LeKnight had poured himself another drink and was watching the deck carefully, just to make certain there was no foul play and that Finn would not suddenly disappear into the wild night.

"I think you should go," Finn said. "You shouldn't have come here."

Carter flashed his headlights once more; I wished the MG would disappear.

"Are you saying you don't want to see me?" I asked.

Finn looked down the driveway. "He's calling you."

I wished I could shoot down all Finn's memories; one by one they would fall into the sand.

"Go home," Finn told me. "There's nothing else to talk about."

Finn's shirt was as white as a hand raised in treacherous water, his skin was as pale as a man who had never known daylight, but I was too tired to fight, I didn't even know where to begin, or how to combat bodiless enemies, stronger in spirit than they could ever have been in the flesh.

"Go home," Finn whispered.

I walked down the icy deck stairs; behind me the double door opened and Reno LeKnight came onto the deck to scold Finn for standing outside without a winter coat. I didn't hear whether Finn answered the attorney; for all I knew Finn might have been staring after me with tears on his face, for all I knew his feet had been frozen to the wooden deck so that each time he was about to run after me he pulled back, rooted to the spot where he stood. I walked over the sand, through the faded reeds, until I reached the car. When I climbed inside, I slammed the door so hard that the window crank fell off.

"Oh," I said, picking it up. "I'm sorry."

"Never mind," Carter said softly.

He started the engine, drove out the driveway, and then made a slow U-turn on the wide empty road.

"I'm sorry to have kept you waiting," I said once we were over the bridge and the beach house was behind us.

"I never mind waiting for you," Carter said with a smile.

"I might as well tell you the truth," I said as we pulled onto the expressway. "I'm in love with Michael Finn."

"Ah," Carter said.

I leaned my head against the window, afraid to look at Carter.

"For someone in love, you don't seem very happy," Carter said gently.

"I'm not," I said. "I'm not."

I lit a cigarette. "Are you angry?" I asked.

"I'm confused," Carter said. "I don't understand."

"Neither do I," I confessed.

We drove the rest of the way back to Fishers Cove without talking. When we reached Minnie's house, I asked Carter inside for tea, hoping he would refuse the invitation.

"I think I should come in," Carter told me.

We sat in the kitchen, and I made the tea which neither of us would drink. The house was quiet, Minnie and Beaumont were both out.

"It's like a freezer in here," Carter said, pulling his sweater down over his hands like mittens, and then warming his fingers on the cup of tea I set down in front of him. "I knew something was wrong," he said now. "I knew you were unhappy."

"I'm sorry," I said.

"I thought you were unhappy with your job," Carter went on. "I thought you needed a challenge." He reached inside his coat pocket and brought out several pamphlets. "I got these for you."

"What are they?" I asked.

"Lists of jobs," Carter told me. "Political action, solar energy groups. They need social workers, too, you know."

When I looked through the pamphlets I couldn't help thinking of Minnie's letters. If all those letters she wrote over the years had been collected and stored, they would have filled the kitchen from ceiling to floor. Some of them had been written on summer evenings when all the visiting Lanskys wanted to do was drink lemonade and watch the sunset. But Minnie would always appear with white paper and sharpened pencils, along with the addresses of state and county officials. I had refused to write even one of those letters, instead I had gone off to the beach and watched sea gulls drop clamshells on the rocks while up on the porch all of the other Lanskys folded their messages into clean envelopes.

As I leafed through Carter's pamphlets, I was not so certain as I had once been that all those letters were worthless. Perhaps Minnie had been right when she called down to the beach for me, waiting on the porch with envelopes and paper.

"There's a possibility I may be fired from Outreach," I said. "And you're right, I've been unhappy at work."

"That's all I thought it was," Carter said. "I never thought it was anything like love."

"This doesn't mean I don't care for you," I said. "And it certainly doesn't mean I'll ever see Finn again."

"If you aren't going to see him, we can still go on as before," Carter said. "We can try."

"You know we can't," I sighed. "Everything between us is gone."

"Not everything," Carter said.

I walked Carter to the door and we kissed good night in the hallway.

"Let's not do anything right away, Nat," Carter said. "Take some time. Think about it."

When I closed the door behind Carter I went to the parlor, and then sat down to read the pamphlets. There were jobs in California and Florida, offers that would take me far away from both Carter and Finn. Some of them even seemed important: a court advocate in San Luis Obispo, an organizer for workers who had left a working power plant in western Florida to form a grievance committee. It seemed to me now that Minnie was quite the opposite of Finn. Her Russian village had been more of a trap than anything Finn had ever faced, the odds against her more heavily weighed. Still, she had managed to survive. And if she hadn't begun an explosion that would shatter steel, she also hadn't allowed an implosion that would crack her own heart and rupture every vein. She had taken one step at a time, refusing to accept a fate that was centuries old. Minnie had gotten herself across the Atlantic and stood up to her life with a barrage of letters, and with hope.

By the time Minnie got home I was ready to throw my arms around her and forget all our past differences. I would live without Carter, if I had to I could live without Finn, all of this seemed trivial compared with the destiny that Minnie had had to face. But when I went to greet my aunt and let her know how wrong I had been all those years, I found that she wasn't alone.

Minnie kicked open the front door with the heel of her boot. "Help," she called to me. "We need some help here."

My aunt was struggling with an old brown suitcase. Behind her stood the sisters, Evie and Yolanda, each carrying a box full of clothing and memories.

"They're moving in tonight?" I asked.

"There's a TV and a dehumidifier out on the porch," Minnie told me. "Beaumont's taken the Mustang and gone back for Arthur. There are times when a compact car isn't practical, no matter how much fuel it saves."

I went out to the porch and carried in the TV and dehumidifier.

"Careful," Evie called to me. "I don't know what I'd do without my TV. I don't know how I'd face the morning without the 'Today' show."

"Put everything right there." Minnie waved her hand toward the parlor. "We'll sort it out tomorrow."

"I was thinking about all the summers I spent here," I said wistfully, but Minnie was studying the boxes and appliances with a scowl.

"Garbage, garbage, garbage," Minnie said. "What human beings don't collect in a lifetime."

"I used to get so angry at all the letters you had the Lanskys write," I went on.

"You were angry?" Minnie said. "I never noticed."

"Oh my," Evie was saying as she stood in the hallway. "Oh my," she said as she watched her belongings pile up in the parlor.

"Let's get the show on the road," Minnie advised. "Let's get your rooms straightened out."

But the sisters refused to move from the hallway; they stood clutching each other's arms, two old women terrified by the freedom they had just been granted.

"I don't know if we can," Yolanda said shyly. "I don't know if we can do anything at all."

Minnie eyed her friends carefully. "What we all need," my aunt said, as she removed her coat and her gloves, "is a cup of tea."

Minnie and I walked the sisters into the parlor; the old women held each other so close that they seemed to be one being. Minnie seated them on the loveseat, and then we went into the kitchen.

"I hope they don't both have breakdowns," I said.

"They need a good night's sleep," Minnie said.

"I keep thinking about the past," I said to Minnie.

"The past?"

"I've been mistaken about a lot of things," I admitted.

"Of course you have," Minnie agreed, as she collected cups and saucers. "But take my advice," my aunt said, while she loaded the tea tray, "don't think about the past too much. Don't dwell on mistakes. What's done is done."

And so I followed Minnie back into the parlor without ever letting her know how much I regretted feelings I had never let her know about in the first place. As far as Minnie was concerned, there was too much of the present to be concerned with to look back to the past. I decided to follow her advice, and have tea with the sisters; Evie and Yolanda had now calmed down enough to remove their coats and spoon honey into their tea.

"I never thought I'd feel like this," Yolanda said, apologizing for the way her teacup shook in her trembling hands.

"Why shouldn't you be nervous?" Minnie said. "Even I'm nervous. This communal living is a big step for all of us. It's a new start, and if you were perfectly calm, you'd be dead. Believe me, it's better to be nervous than dead."

When the front door opened and then slammed shut, the three old women smiled at each other.

"That will be Arthur," Evie said.

"If anyone can cheer a person up, it's Arthur," Minnie confided to me.

Beaumont and Arthur came into the parlor, each carrying a suitcase. "Freedom," Arthur called out to us in greeting.

"This place is getting too crowded," Beaumont said as he shifted a suitcase from hand to hand.

"Nonsense," Minnie said. "The more the merrier."

Beaumont declined to have tea with us; instead he carried suitcases up to the second floor, and then retreated to his quiet basement. I sat and watched the fire. I could have easily fallen asleep, lulled by the old-timers' voices. But Minnie suddenly stood; she remembered that she had been saving something for me.

"It can wait till morning," I said, but Minnie had already jumped up and begun to rummage through a bureau drawer in the hallway. When she returned to the parlor she held out a crumpled envelope.

"Maybe I should have given this to you before," Minnie said. "But what good would that have done? You would have been upset, it would have been terrible for your blood pressure."

I looked from my aunt's sympathetic face to the envelope

she held. Even before I opened it, I knew it was my subpoena, since LeKnight had warned me I would soon be called; but I had had no idea the court date was to be the very next day.

The conversations in the parlor seemed terribly far away, I could no longer hear them. Minnie had to ask me three times if I was all right before I could understand her; every word sounded like broken English. And even when I had deciphered my aunt's question, I found I could not answer; I didn't yet trust myself to speak.

FOUR

By SEVEN O'CLOCK THE next morning, every bit of clothing I owned was strewn over the unmade bed. I started out the day unable to decide what to wear; and before the sun had risen I, too, sat on that bed, wondering how I would make it through the day.

When Minnie knocked on my door, I pretended to be asleep.

"I know you're in there," Minnie called through the door. "I heard your closet door slamming."

I let her into my room. "But don't talk," I warned her. "It's too early to talk."

"Anxiety shows itself in mysterious ways," Minnie said as she surveyed the mess in my room. "Come downstairs. We can have tea and rehearse your testimony. And if you ask me," she said as she walked out the door, "you should wear the tweed."

A little while later I came down to the kitchen, wearing the tweed suit Minnie had suggested.

"Ask me whatever questions you want, but promise me you won't come to the trial today. I don't want anyone I know to be there."

"Carter will be there," Minnie said. "He wouldn't miss your testimony for the world."

"But not you," I said. "A relative."

"That's fine with me," Minnie agreed. "I've got better things to do with my time. Now sit down," she said after I poured myself a cup of tea. "How long have you been acquainted with the defendant?" She paused to sip her apple juice. "You can bet they'll ask you that one."

"Two and a half months," I said.

"Really? That's not so long," Minnie said. "All right then," she continued, waving a slice of wholewheat toast in the air, "what is your relationship with the defendant?"

"Mr. Finn was my client since early November."

"Are you sure you know him long enough to be in love?" Minnie asked. "One month, two months, this is a very short time."

"How long did you know Alex before you were in love with him?" I asked.

"We were cousins. I knew him all my life," Minnie said, before going on with her next question. "At the time Mr. Finn was your client, did you know that he was the bomber, pardon me, the accused bomber?"

"No," I said. "I did not."

"Not too bad," Minnie said admiringly. "No one would guess that you were lying."

"He had told me but I had no proof," I said. "For all I knew he could have been crazy, a psychopath. How can you say I'm lying?"

"Natalie," Minnie said. "You're lying."

"All right," I said.

"It's okay," Minnie said, "as long as you know what you're doing."

The quizzing continued until Evie and Yolanda came down from their rooms. The sisters were both dressed in chenille robes; they seemed much more relaxed than the evening before.

"What a pleasure not to have to face seventy-five other residents in the morning." Evie sighed.

"How wonderful to wear a bathrobe to breakfast," Yolanda added.

I was too distracted to speak to the sisters; I had begun to talk to myself, repeating my testimony in a jittery voice.

"She doesn't always act like this," Minnie explained to Evie and Yolanda. "But today she takes the stand in the bombing trial."

"Oh my," Evie said with real sympathy.

"Break a leg," Yolanda called gaily as I slipped on my coat and left through the back door. Minnie stood behind the screen and waved solemnly, as if I were a soldier off to war. I went straight to Outreach before the office opened so I could pick up my files on Michael Finn without having to face any co-workers. I used my passkey and opened Emily's filing cabinets. I sat at Emily's desk and began to leaf through Finn's file. Then I heard a key click in the door. It was too early for the workday to begin; there was no watchman. The door opened and a shadow fell over the floorboards. I wondered if some masked marauder was about to hush my testimony forever. I dropped Finn's file, picked up a vase which stood on Emily's desk, and waited behind the door, ready to defend myself, or at least to try. The door opened wider, a head came into view: it was Lark. She blinked and looked up at the vase I held over her.

"Do you intend to give me a concussion?" Lark said, when she realized it was I who held the vase. "What are you doing here?"

"I'm here to pick up Finn's files, in case the court requests them," I told her. "I take the stand today. Why are you sneaking around here so early in the morning?"

"Sneaking?" Lark said. "You have to watch that paranoia of yours," she advised as she headed toward the filing cabinets. "I have a friend at the court who told me you'd be on the stand today, and I wanted to be ready. I need my best case studies." Lark looked at me sharply. "You do remember promising to send the reporters to me?"

"Of course I remember," I said.

"I thought you might have changed your mind," Lark said as she stacked her most interesting files into a brown leather bag. "I thought you might have been upset by the EMOTE meeting you came to."

"Upset?" I said.

"Come on. Admit it. The meeting got to you."

"I don't know about that," I said.

"I do get some results, you know," Lark said. "I'm getting results with Susan Wolf."

As hard as I tried, I could not imagine the anorectic at an EMOTE meeting. But perhaps when Susan tried to keep the rest of the group away with her evasions, they would have forced her right up to the front of the room. And when she stood in front of the mirror and saw who she was—a terrified, skinny girl—Susan might have broken down and cried.

"Is Susan doing well?" I asked.

"Is she doing well?" Lark smiled. "She's gained four pounds already."

Four pounds with Lark, and if she had stayed with me Susan might have turned into a skeleton. During one of our sessions I might have had to call an ambulance to take her away.

"Maybe EMOTE can work for some people," I said.

"It worked for me," Lark said.

"You?" I said.

"I used to steal," Lark said. "I used to steal a lot."

"When was this?" I asked.

"Up until last year," Lark said. "Until I began EMOTE."

"You were stealing while you were working here as a therapist?"

"Don't sound so shocked," Lark said. "It had nothing to do with money. Do you see this coat? Bloomingdale's," she said. "I wear it to remind me of what I used to be."

"It is beautiful," I had to admit.

"Sometimes the reasons why you do something don't matter; the important thing is to get control of your life. I was so out of control I was afraid to go to the market; I would slip cans of Alaska king crab into my purse, I would steal Dutch chocolate I knew I would never eat."

"I would never have guessed," I said.

"Last year, about this time, I sat down in front of a mirror and listed every horrible thing I had ever done. I did it every day for a week, and by the end of the week I was so depressed I couldn't move, I couldn't get out of my chair. But on the eighth day in front of the mirror something happened—I began to list my good qualities. I had broken through, and only then could I build. And I knew I had found more than a way to stop stealing, I had found a technique."

"EMOTE," I said.

"EMOTE," Lark nodded.

"Amazing," I said.

"I know you think I'm an opportunist," Lark said to me. "You don't even think I'm a good therapist."

"I never said that."

"You didn't have to," Lark smiled.

"I'll never be behind EMOTE," I said. "I'll never really trust it, but you"—I shrugged—"I think I could trust you."

"Do you want me to go with you to the courthouse?" Lark asked. "I could give you a ride, my car's right outside."

"I'm going to walk," I said. "Thanks anyway."

"I didn't make that offer because I thought we'd run into a reporter from the *Herald*," Lark said. "I just thought you might want someone with you. For courage," she added. "For company."

I shook my head. "I need to walk," I said. "To go alone."

We walked outside together, and I waited as Lark locked the door to Outreach.

"Remember," she said as we stood on the sidewalk. "I'll be right outside the courthouse."

"Don't worry," I smiled. "I'll send the reporters to you."

"But also if you need me," Lark said.

Standing on the sidewalk, I felt so lonely I almost accepted Lark's offer of a ride; but my head seemed too hot, it spun slightly, and I was afraid I wouldn't be able to take the rocking of Lark's car as she drove down Main Street.

The day was dreary, the sky threatened to turn into a terrible storm. When I reached the already crowded courthouse steps, Reno LeKnight's Lincoln was just pulling up. The attorney bounded out of the car, ready to do battle; behind him came Michael Finn, dressed in a blue serge suit which might have belonged to Reno, for it was much too big, and Finn looked frail beneath the yards of material. Flashbulbs hissed and the crowd came together to encircle Finn and his attorney; but it was Reno LeKnight who smiled for the photographers and drew the eyes of the crowd; Michael Finn seemed little more than a shadow. I saw Carter across the crowd, and waved, and when Reno had led Finn into the courthouse, Carter came over to me.

"You're going to be great today," he told me. "I'll be rooting for you all the way."

Carter offered to walk me into the courthouse and sit by my side. I thanked him but I had to refuse. An objective professional, I figured, I couldn't risk being associated with Soft Skies. But there was more: I couldn't risk the urge to hold Carter's hand and take advantage of a kindness I would never repay. I walked into the courthouse alone and sat in the front row, on the district attorney's side of the room so that I could see Finn more clearly: when he moved his head, when he coughed or turned to consult Reno LeKnight, I could get a glimpse of his frown, I could see the shadow of the scar across his cheek. There was nothing unusual about that morning; I would be called to the stand just after the testimony of a welding instructor, who would admit under Reno's careful questioning that although it was unlikely for an experienced welder to make an error such as the one Reno claimed Finn had made, it was, all the same, quite possible. In fact, mistakes such as Finn's happened all the time.

I wordlessly rehearsed my testimony as the welding instructor spoke, so I did not hear the beginning of Carter's outburst. I looked up just as Carter stood and began to walk down the aisle of the courtroom.

"Are you idiots?" Carter called. "Are you fools?" Carter's face was flushed, his eyes glowed with dedication. "Don't you understand what this welding instructor has just admitted? He's admitted that errors can exist in every nuclear power plant in this country."

The judge nodded, the district attorney wiped his brow with a linen handkerchief, Reno LeKnight shuddered beneath his fine silk shirt. Two bailiffs walked briskly down the aisle, their handcuffs chiming with every step. I had no idea that Carter intended to disrupt the trial; it was the first time he hadn't told me his plans.

"Are you going to wait until a working power plant explodes?" Carter called out to the courtroom. "Is that what you're waiting for? Michael Finn shouldn't be on trial," Carter went on, even though the bailiffs were so close that their breath fogged up his glasses. "The oil companies should be on trial," Carter cried as the first bailiff grabbed his arm. "The utilities companies should be on the stand," he screamed as the second bailiff held his shoulders in a tight embrace.

The court was quiet as Carter was dragged from the room, still calling out accusations. Minutes after he was removed from the courthouse, the welding instructor was excused from the stand and my name was called out. It was a bad beginning. Carter's screams echoed, they stayed with me; and when I took that long walk down the aisle, past Michael Finn, who did not even bother to turn and look at me, I knew that my testimony would not go as easily as I had planned.

As soon as Reno LeKnight asked his first question about my professional relationship with Finn, I began to feel that I was stuck in molasses; both Reno's voice and my own seemed too slow, the judge eased into the distance, like some faraway eagle, and the spectators in the front rows of the court seemed hidden in slow-moving spectrums of color. I concentrated as hard as I could, I gave the answers I had given Minnie earlier that day: I had seen Michael Finn on twelve occasions, I had seen progress during these therapy sessions. It was true that the defendant was a moody character, and that he often felt guilty, but quite often he felt guilty when he was not at fault. Most certainly, I had known nothing about Mr. Finn's association with the bombing until his official statement to the authorities. Most definitely Mr. Finn was insightful and responsible; he had never mentioned any hostility toward the power plant for nuclear energy.

When Reno LeKnight was quite satisfied, he thanked me with a brisk nod, and I knew that I had done well, no matter how odd I felt. My voice had had the correct professional inflection, my tweed suit was not too fashionable, and I had presented Finn as a man who certainly wasn't angry enough or bright enough to blow up a power plant, or even imagine such a thing.

The real trouble began during the cross-examination. What happened was not brought about by the art of the district attorney, a man in his sixties who was used to dealing with tax evasion and petty larceny. When I confessed, it was not because

I was badgered or tricked, for the district attorney stuttered noticeably, and he seemed more surprised than anyone that he was prosecuting a case as important as Finn's.

"So you say that you saw Mr. Finn twelve times," the district attorney began, as much to refresh his own memory, it seemed, as to question mine.

I felt quite dizzy; when I looked over at the defendant's table there were two Michael Finns. "Perhaps a few more times," I now told him.

"A few more times," the district attorney said pleasantly.

"All right, all right," I said, pinching my tweed skirt between my fingers. "Several more times."

"I see. But just what do you mean by 'several'?" The district attorney smiled. "Exactly *how many* times did you see the defendant?" The courtroom was much too hot, my head was spinning, and I imagined that the district attorney could see Finn and me that first night in the field, he could see us beneath Minnie's goosedown quilt.

"All right," I said. My own voice sounded as if it belonged to someone else, the words I spoke echoed off the mahogany that paneled the courthouse ceiling and walls. "I admit it," I cried. "We were lovers."

Reno LeKnight sat up so fast that he nearly shot out of his seat. The district attorney eyed me carefully. "Would you please repeat that," he asked.

"What?" I said, hoping that I had not actually spoken. Perhaps my guilt was so strong that the words I thought inside my head had begun to echo. "Repeat what?"

"I believe you just said that you and Mr. Finn were lovers?" the district attorney said tentatively.

Reno LeKnight jumped up. "The witness has stated all the information she has. I suggest that she be excused from the stand."

But the judge denied the motion, and the district attorney certainly didn't plan to let me go now. Reno LeKnight did manage to win a twenty-minute recess; and when the court was adjourned, Reno took my arm and led me from the witness stand to a corner in the outside hallway.

"Are you crazy?" he asked. "Are you mad?"

I shook my head, though I myself was not certain just what it was that had possessed me on the witness stand.

"Listen to me, just listen to me," LeKnight said. He spoke slowly, as if I might no longer be capable of understanding the language. "Do not give out any more information. The damage has been done. Not only is your credibility as a witness worthless but you've also cast doubt on the entire defense. Don't make it worse than it already is." LeKnight went on, shaking my shoulders for emphasis. "Answer all the D.A.'s questions as briefly as you can."

Reno turned and walked away, clearly disgusted with me. I walked outside. If I didn't have fresh air I would sink to the floor in a faint; but out on the courthouse stairs, immediately encircled by reporters, I still had trouble breathing. I ran over to Lark, who was waiting for me and the reporters I would bring her.

"Come with me for a minute," I said, tugging on Lark's coat sleeve.

"Introduce me," Lark said, nodding toward the reporters who had followed me. Lark smiled broadly and reached into her bag of case histories, but I kept walking to Lark's parked station wagon, where I sat in the driver's seat, rolled up all the windows, and locked all the doors. If I had had the key, I might have turned on the ignition and driven away from the courthouse, and Michael Finn. But instead I sat without moving until Lark came up to tap at the window; then I unlocked the passenger door.

"What's wrong with you?" Lark asked.

"Lock the door."

"We had an agreement, didn't we? You told me that you weren't interested in publicity, though Lord knows those media people seem to be interested in you." Lark eyed the photographers who leaned on the hood of the car.

"We were lovers," I said to Lark.

"Who?" Lark asked.

"Michael Finn and I."

"Jesus Christ."

"I confessed on the stand."

"Confessed to what?" Lark asked. "Oh, no," she said when I didn't answer. "You didn't?"

I nodded.

"You see what comes from keeping your emotions bottled up inside," Lark said sadly. "You wind up doing something tremendously stupid."

"I go back on the stand in a few minutes."

"Do you love him?" Lark asked suddenly.

"Well, yes."

"And he refuses to get involved," Lark guessed.

"That's what he says."

"Well, if your testimony does one thing, it will certainly force the man to admit he's involved with someone; he'll have to when he reads about it in the newspapers." Lark smiled.

"Will he ever be able to forgive me?" I asked her.

"Certainly he will." Lark opened her door, and persuaded me to leave the station wagon and return to the court. "But if he doesn't," Lark said as we neared the courthouse stairs, "you'll just have to forgive yourself."

I sent all the reporters, with their questions about my relationship with Finn, right over to Lark. By the time I had returned to the courthouse, Lark was surrounded; she dodged questions about me and set about convincing the crowd that EMOTE was far more interesting than a brief affair between a social worker and an accused bomber.

My testimony was over in less than twenty minutes. At first, the people in the courtroom craned their necks and leaned forward in their hard wooden chairs. No one coughed, or fluttered or moved. But when the district attorney failed to ask for intimate sexual details, the crowd quickly grew bored. Only Reno LeKnight sat on the edge of his seat until I was dismissed. In the end, I confessed to little more than not being quite as objective as I had once been presented; and my relationship with Michael Finn caused a smile or two instead of a sensation. When asked if he wished to question me further on redirect, Reno LeKnight shook his head and turned to the crowd.

"I think she's already told us more than enough," LeKnight said.

As I walked away from the witness stand the courtroom had already turned its attention to Reno. The attorney tossed his head like a peacock as he prepared to call his next witness: the court psychiatrist who had met with Michael Finn for less than half an hour the day before. It seemed the only one who watched me get up and leave the witness stand was Michael Finn. When I stopped at the doors, before leaving the room, Finn was straining to see me; one of his arms was thrown across the back of his chair, his forehead was wrinkled, his eyes were as careful and narrow as if he had been stalking a deer.

For a minute I saw the confusion in his face, the pain beneath the borrowed blue suit and the white shirt which was buttoned up high. If we never saw each other again, he would still be easy to remember. He would be wearing the same borrowed clothing each time I imagined him, he wouldn't change any more than a photograph, and I would carry him with me just as if he had been trapped on paper. For me he would remain as he was when he watched me cross the room just before I closed the courtroom door and hurried away as fast as I could.

FIVE

*M*Y ANNOUNCEMENT AT
the trial might have done some terrible damage, Reno Le-
Knight's carefully planned tactics might have been thoroughly
shattered, and I might have spent the rest of my nights tossing
and turning, if it hadn't been for a welder in Elizabeth, New
Jersey, a man none of us in Fishers Cove had ever met.

If I had known what was to happen, I might not have been
so depressed when I returned to Minnie's after the trial. I sat
in the kitchen with my head in my hands, refusing to look my
aunt in the eye.

"So you screwed up," Minnie told me when I finally confessed that I had broken down on the witness stand. "So what?"
my aunt demanded. "When you let yourself get down in the
dumps, you're heading right down the road to high blood pressure."

"Finn will go to jail and I'll be fired for unprofessional activities," I said.

"Are you breathing? Can you walk? Do you have food and
a roof over your head? Consider yourself lucky."

"Minnie," I said, "I'm not lucky."

"You can't get yourself worked up over every mistake," Minnie told me. "Relax. Stretch out. Chalk it up to experience."

"There's something wrong with my life," I said.

"Please," Minnie said as I got up from the table and grabbed my coat, "don't be hasty. Let me mix a little brewer's yeast into a glass of tomato juice for you."

But tomato juice wasn't what I wanted, and I found myself walking toward the Modern Times. At the bar, I slipped off my coat and ordered a whiskey and water. I was prepared to spend the evening alone, until finally, fortified by whiskey, I would walk home. But before I had taken my first sip, the barstool next to me was pulled out, and I was joined by Carter Sugarland.

"What are you doing here?" I cried. "You're in jail."

"Correction." Carter smiled, ordering a beer and stomping his Frye boots on the wooden floor to clean the heels of ice. "I was in jail. I am now out on bail. This was my eighteenth arrest. Disturbing the courtroom was worth a couple of hours behind bars."

"Really?" I said, thinking of Michael Finn standing on the wide green lawn of the Stockley School.

"Minnie told me you were here. I came to cheer you up. I heard about what happened in court." Carter took my hands in his. "The first time on a witness stand everybody makes mistakes."

"A catastrophe, not a mistake," I corrected.

"Have another drink. It'll seem less like a catastrophe."

We sat at the far end of the bar, but all the same, we seemed to attract attention. The construction workers who eyed us might have only been looking at Carter Sugarland's long hair, and his rimless glasses. They might not have known that I had been Michael Finn's lover, they might not have recognized Carter from the photo on the front page of the *Fishers Cove Herald* that very same day. But all the same, I avoided their eyes, and looked upward, at the color TV which sat on a platform high above the cash register.

"Self-pity," warned Carter, "is a dangerous thing."

"Yup," I said, "it certainly is."

"I'm glad you agree." Carter took off his glasses and cleaned them with a cocktail napkin. "Now what do you plan to do about it?"

"Do?" I said.

"Well, you'll have to find another job."

"I suppose so," I agreed. Eventually I would be called into Claude Wilder's office, eventually the board of directors would hear of my confession. "And there's nothing to keep me in this town."

"Nothing?" Carter asked.

"Are you serious?" I said. "Look what I did to him in court."

"If you did anything like that to me, I'd forgive you," Carter said. "I'd forgive you in a minute."

"There were some jobs in the pamphlets you gave me," I said. "In Florida."

"The one working with radiation victims?" Carter smiled. "I never thought you'd really be interested."

There would be palm trees and no winter; sleet would never touch the Florida streets I would walk. After my radiation group had filled out their grievance forms, we would all walk down to a local diner and order home fries and eggs. Instead of therapy, I would be in charge of finding a lawyer, dealing only with facts.

"Florida," Carter said thoughtfully.

It was then that I happened to look up at the soundless TV hanging above us. In color, on a twenty-four-inch screen, was a power plant exploding. Iron and steel flew higher than birds, the sky was a deep orange color.

"Look," I said to Carter.

"Angel Landing," Carter said when he saw the screen.

But there was no harbor bordering the power plant, no sea gulls flew in the orange sky; the landscape that surrounded this explosion was not the one I had known for so many summers.

"It's someplace else," I said. "It's another explosion."

Carter sat up. "Jesus Christ," he cried, and he grabbed the bartender's shoulder. "Make that louder," he demanded. "Turn the sound up."

All around the jukebox there were groans when the sound on the TV was turned up. But Carter and I didn't listen to any complaints; we watched the screen above the bar, the falling iron and steel. We were transfixed, we saw nothing but the orange sky. Even after a TV reporter wearing a hard hat appeared on the scene, it took some time for me to realize that another explosion, just like the one at Angel Landing, had occurred in Elizabeth, New Jersey.

"It's another accident." Carter shook his head. "Another fucking accident."

The reporter avoided the falling flames; he tried his best to interview the welder responsible for the accident. But the welder, who lay in the New Jersey dirt, had fallen from high atop a scaffolding when a faulty valve he had installed accidentally some days ago caused a weld to explode during today's testing. Both his legs were broken, and he now waited for two ambulance attendants to lift him out of the mud and carry him away.

Several construction workers had left their tables to join us at the bar and watch the TV.

"Look at that," one of them said, pointing to the welder on the TV screen. "Why the hell do they have to show him laying in the mud? Jesus Christ."

The reporter's tone grew even more serious as he mentioned Michael Finn's name and the TV screen above the bar flashed to the landscape I knew so well: the heavy purple clouds hanging above the gray harbor, the sea gulls flying in crazy circles.

"This may make quite a difference to the ongoing trial of welder Michael Finn," the reporter told us solemnly. "The question is: Just how common are accidents in nuclear power plants?"

"Pretty fucking common," Carter snapped. "That's what I've been trying to tell everyone."

"Just how important is the human-error factor in the construction of these plants?" the reporter went on.

"Pretty fucking important," Carter cried.

"And what will this new explosion mean to the case of Michael Finn, already on trial for his error in installing a valve?"

"What will it mean?" I asked, but the reporter had finished his story, and I turned to Carter for the answer.

"It will mean that people may begin to realize how dangerous these plants are," Carter said.

"Everything is dangerous," the construction worker to our

right said. "Everything gives you cancer," he went on. "The only way to avoid danger is to be dead."

"I disagree," Carter said. "I for one am going to try and stop the danger."

"Good luck," the man said, and he turned back to his friends.

"What about Michael Finn?" I said to Carter. "What will it mean to him?"

"I'm talking about a technology that could destroy the planet, and you're concerned with Finn?"

I hung my head.

"I'm talking about millions of people," Carter told me. "Billions."

He searched in his pockets for change, and then walked to the rear of the bar, to the telephone booths. He was calling the members of Soft Skies to mobilize a demonstration in Elizabeth, New Jersey. I drank the rest of my whiskey and glanced around the Modern Times. There were men in the room who probably knew Finn, who had worked with him; it was such a small town some of them might have even gone to Fishers Cove High School with him, or sat by his side in first grade at the old elementary school. Over by the jukebox, a young man sang along with an old song about loneliness. When he sang he closed his eyes; his face was pained, as if he meant every word. I pushed my glass away and followed Carter to the telephone booths. He was so filled with energy that the phone booth couldn't contain him; he stretched the cord out into the hallway and gestured with his arms as he spoke with the New Jersey chapter of Soft Skies.

"Can you lend me a dime?" I asked.

Still talking, Carter reached into his pocket for change, and handed me a fistful of quarters and dimes. I sat down in the second booth, closed the doors, put in a dime, and dialed. I could still hear the song about loneliness, I could hear Carter talking about raising bail for the welder from New Jersey if he should be criminally charged. I waited, listening for the phone to be answered until, finally, on the fourth ring, Reno LeKnight picked it up.

"I'd like to talk to Michael Finn," I told the attorney.

"Aren't you too embarrassed to be calling here?" Reno LeKnight said when he recognized my voice. "Aren't you even going to apologize for fucking up my entire defense?"

"Will you let me talk to him?" I asked.

"I certainly will not," Reno LeKnight said.

I had not really expected that he would, I was not even certain I wanted to talk to Finn, I only wanted to share the news that might free him. "Did you watch the evening news tonight?"

"Listen, I'm not about to make polite conversation with you," LeKnight told me. "I'm not going to make any conversation at all."

"There's been another explosion." I spoke slowly, flatly, for I was afraid that LeKnight might not believe a word I said.

"What?"

I could hear Reno LeKnight's breath come through the receiver like soft expectant waves. "An explosion," I repeated.

"Where?" he asked.

"Elizabeth, New Jersey."

"What's the situation?" Papers rustled as Reno must have been reaching for a pad and a pen.

"A lot like Finn's," I said. "A valve was installed wrong.

Actually the welder fell and broke both his legs. Right now they're calling it a mistake."

"My God," Reno LeKnight said. "My God," he crowed.

"You don't think he might want to talk to me?" I asked.

"Do you know what this means?" LeKnight said. "I've got to get that other welder. I've got to subpoena him."

"He's broken both his legs," I reminded Reno LeKnight.

"They may even drop the charges," the attorney went on. "Of course, the dramatic impact of Finn's case will be minimal if that happens. For all I know this case could set a precedent; it may end up in the lawbooks."

"Of course, if he doesn't want to talk to me, I'll understand," I said. "I just wondered if he might."

"Finn won't talk to you," Reno LeKnight said. "Don't take it personally; he's not talking to anyone, he's not even talking to me."

I sat in the phone booth after Reno LeKnight had hung up. I stayed there until Carter had finished making plans with the New Jersey group. When he hung up the phone in the other booth and banged on the doors, I went out into the hallway.

"I've got to get to New Jersey tonight," Carter told me. "The gas line in the MG is frozen, and I need a ride to the bus station."

"I'll borrow Minnie's car," I said.

"If you want," Carter said slowly, "you could drive me to New Jersey. I'll be back for the rest of the trial. We could stay at a Holiday Inn."

"I don't think so," I said. "I think it's too late for that."

We walked out of the Modern Times to go pick up Minnie's Mustang. At the house, I went to tell Minnie and to open the garage door. Carter stood in a snowdrift at the side of the driveway. He stomped his feet and blew on his ungloved hands; he counted his change for the bus to New Jersey. I wondered if there was a minute, one second when Carter was not threatened by the dangers he saw all around him; even when he rode the Greyhound bus, when he checked into the Holiday Inn in New Jersey and prepared his speech for the Elizabeth demonstration, he would be shivering. When I pulled the Mustang out of the garage and Carter came to sit in the passenger seat, I threw my arms around him so suddenly that he lifted his hands up to protect himself.

"What's this all about?" Carter asked when I had moved away from him and had begun to back the car out of the driveway.

Until I had seen him shivering in the snow, counting his change, I had not realized how serious Carter was about the danger he spoke of, the danger he fought as if radiation and terror could be weighed on a scale as easily as a dragon. I had not realized I would miss him until I imagined him riding off on that bus to New Jersey and never returning.

"I'll miss you," I said.

"You will?" Carter said as we drove through Fishers Cove toward the bus station at the edge of town. When we got there, we sat in the car, with the engine turned on, waiting for the bus.

"I hope everything turns out the way you want it to with Michael Finn," Carter Sugarland said.

"Oh, there's no chance of that," I said quickly. "But thank you."

We watched as the headlights of the bus appeared on the

hill above Fishers Cove. Carter checked once more to make certain he had his notes, his pamphlets, his money, and a list of telephone numbers to dial in case of emergencies.

"Good luck," I said when he was ready to go. "I hope you close down the plant."

Carter got out, but he leaned in the open door. "Don't do anything rash."

"I'm not jumping out of any windows." I smiled.

"No," Carter said. "I suppose you won't."

Still, he looked at me carefully as the engines of the Greyhound strained.

"Honestly," I said to Carter. "Don't worry about me. I'm going home right now and mailing my résumé to Florida."

Carter nodded slowly, shut the car door, and walked to the bus. I watched as he got on; he moved to the rear, where he sat by a window that was coated with a film of frost. Carter couldn't possibly see out that window, but I waited in the idling Mustang until the bus had shifted gears and rolled out of the parking lot, and then I drove slowly home. I would start a new life, I decided, deep in the sands of western Florida. I would drive home to Minnie's, and later that night I would sit in the parlor and address a blue envelope to the agency in Florida. I passed through the familiar streets of Fishers Cove on the trip home, imagining that I was on my way to Finn. Any minute now I would see Finn's white shirt sway in the wind and the long scar across his cheek. There he stood in the shelter of the already bleached piece of time that had unmistakably become the past.

THE NEW YEAR

ONE

$\mathcal{T}$HE ONLY MENTION OF
our affair was a small article in the *Herald* entitled "Beyond the
Call of Duty." Photographs of Reno LeKnight were published
in *Newsweek*, and a long article about EMOTE was printed in
Psychology Today. But in our town only the *Herald* was read,
and it was about me and Michael Finn that everyone was talking.

Even those who didn't care at all whether Angel Landing
stood or fell understood the seductiveness of stolen kisses. Wait-
resses at Ruby's Café wondered if Finn and I had made love
right across the street in the Outreach office; taxi drivers waiting
at the railroad station for the next train wondered about the
secrets Finn and I had traded with our tongues. Because Fishers
Cove was so small, it wasn't long before everyone knew that
Michael Finn and I had once been lovers, and that certainly
included the staff at Outreach.

I stayed home from work and persuaded Minnie to tell
Claude Wilder I was out each time he called. Yet, sooner or
later I would have to face Outreach's board of directors, and so
a few days after my appearance in court, during the trial recess

that Reno LeKnight had requested in order to secure a surprise witness, I went to the Outreach office. I opened the door slowly, afraid that Claude Wilder was lurking behind the wood, but only Emily sat in the waiting room.

"Hello," I called softly.

Emily dropped the pencils she was sharpening and ran to embrace me. "I think it's wonderful," she said. "I knew it all along. I knew it the first time I saw you and Michael Finn walk out of that office together. I just knew it." She lowered her voice. "They're waiting for you," she nodded toward Claude's office. "They've been waiting all morning."

There was no putting it off; I walked into the office to face the eyes of the tribunal.

"Ah ha," Johnson said when I entered and closed the door behind me.

"Good morning," I said, choosing the chair nearest the door.

"Let's not play games," Gerkin the fund raiser said. "Someone tell her she's fired."

"How could you?" Sally Wallace said to me. "How could you have betrayed our trust?"

"I don't think I actually did," I said.

"You don't?" Claude said. He held a copy of the *Fishers Cove Herald* in the air. "Have you seen this?" He opened the paper to "Beyond the Call of Duty."

"I've seen it. I haven't read it, but I've seen it."

"Christ," Johnson shook his head. "How could you?"

"Just one question," Claude said, "because we don't want any rash accusations made." He waved the newspaper in front of me. "Is this article factual?"

"Does it say that Finn and I were lovers?" I asked. Claude nodded solemnly. "Well, then, I suppose it's factual."

"Ah," Johnson said.

"That's it then," Sally Wallace agreed.

"It's all in your contract," Claude told me. "It's in the Outreach guidelines. No personal contact with clients outside of working hours. Those were the rules that you were legally bound to."

"I understand," I said. I was prepared to give up my job; I would sign any documents they asked me to.

"It's nothing personal," Claude went on. "But let's face it— you broke the rules. And when you do that, you have to expect to pay the price."

The door of the office swung open and Lark appeared in the doorway dressed in cashmere and pearls. "I heard you," she said, shaking a finger at Claude. "But who here hasn't broken the rules?"

"I beg your pardon?" Claude Wilder said.

"You've never taken fees for private consultations?" Lark asked Claude.

"I don't know what she's talking about," Claude said to the board of directors.

Lark threw a copy of the Outreach guidelines onto Claude's desk. "We're not allowed to accept payment for private consultations, and yet I know of at least eight times when you did exactly that."

"Ridiculous," Claude Wilder said.

"You deny accepting money from private clients?" Lark said.

"These young women are overly sensitive," Claude said to the board of directors.

"Have you accepted fees?" Sally Wallace asked.

"That's not the point," Claude said. "The point is the publicity that surrounded Michael Finn's trial. Rules were broken in the public eye."

"All right," Lark said to Claude, "you may be unwilling to admit that you've broken the rules, but I'm not, and I'm afraid I'll have to hand in my resignation."

"Just a minute," I said to Lark, "this isn't necessary."

"I've broken the rules continually," Lark went on, ignoring me. "I've had contact with my clients outside of the office. I've had clients to my home, to dinner, I've given most of them my home phone number, I've even let one or two of them sleep on my couch."

"This has nothing to do with you," Gerkin said. Without Lark, Outreach would lose a great deal of funding: the parents of some EMOTE members donated generously to both agencies.

"But I've broken the rules," Lark said. "Quite a number of them."

"Lark," I said. "Don't."

"This is ridiculous," said Johnson. "There's no parallel between your situations."

"There's no comparison," I added.

"Of course there is," Lark said. "If they fire you, they'll have to fire us both." Lark smiled as she twisted the gold and ruby ring on her finger.

"This is impossible," Claude said to Lark. "You can't leave."

"I'm afraid I'll have to," she said.

"This means a lot to me," I said to Lark. "I never thought we could be friends."

"Quiet," Lark said, for the directors seemed to have compromise in their eyes.

"I never thought you would run this sort of risk for me," I went on.

"Ssh," Lark hissed. She turned to Claude. "You've got to make a decision. Do we both stay on, or do we leave?"

"But I've applied for another job. In Florida," I told Lark.

"You don't need another job," Lark insisted. "You could stay. They're about to give in."

"There's no therapy involved in this new job, and I think I really have a chance for it; the salary is so low that no one else may even apply."

"In Florida?" Lark said. Her eyes were wide, imagining hundreds of potential EMOTE members meeting beneath a bright yellow tent under the Florida sun.

"You could visit me," I suggested.

"It's so difficult for me to get away," Lark said. "EMOTE is so focused in on me as a leader. And if you leave, I'll have to help train a new therapist here."

"But you could get away for a couple of days, couldn't you?" I asked.

"Maybe," Lark agreed. "A few days."

"Thank you all," I said to the board of directors, who had begun to relax the moment they heard me whisper the word Florida. "But I'm afraid that I have to resign."

Later, as I was sitting in the parlor, wondering what I would do if I didn't get the job in Florida, the telephone rang. It was Carter, calling from a Holiday Inn in New Jersey.

"How was the demonstration?" I asked, glad to turn my attention to some fate other than my own.

"Ten thousand people in the snow in New Jersey," Carter said. "I would say that was pretty good."

"I would say so," I agreed.

"But the real news," he went on, "is about Finn's trial."

I felt weak in the knees. "Yes?"

"The welder here, the guy who broke both his legs . . ."

"What about him?"

"I went to see him to make certain that he could raise bail, but he didn't need any help from Soft Skies. Because he's not even being charged," Carter said. "There's not one criminal complaint out against him. The D.A. here and the electric company both agree that the explosion was an accident. He's a free man. Of course, he won't be walking for quite a while—but he's free."

"That's fantastic," I breathed.

"Yes and no," Carter said. "It might have been better in the long run if he had been tried. The more accidents that are brought into the public eye, the more the danger will be seen."

"Still," I said.

"Still," Carter agreed, "it helps Finn's case."

What, I wondered, would Finn do if he, too, were a free man? Would he ride out of town on the next train, or would he walk right back to the life he had once led, slipping into his work clothes again and into another job he hated.

"I'll be back tonight," Carter told me. "I'm taking the next bus out of here. The welder from New Jersey has already left."

"Left?" I said, wondering where a man with two broken legs would go.

"Reno LeKnight's already picked him up. I'm certain that welder will be driven right to Fishers Cove; he'll be the first witness to testify when court reconvenes tomorrow. I would bet all I own on that."

Carter's bus didn't arrive in Fishers Cove until after two in the morning; I waited in the parking lot of the bus station with the car heater turned on high. From the minute I had hung up the phone I knew I would not sleep, and insomnia was easier to face in a bus station than at home in a quiet bed. When I had driven Carter home with me to Minnie's, and made up the couch with pillows and sheets, I sat in the easy chair and watched him sink into the bed I had made.

"Exhausted," Carter said. "The bus ride."

I didn't mind that Carter fell asleep almost immediately; his soft breathing made me feel less alone, and when he turned in his sleep, my own sleeplessness was easier to take. I was still sitting in the easy chair watching Carter sleep when, hours later, at sunrise, my aunt came into the parlor, looked at me with raised eyebrows, and then stood over the couch.

"Which one is this?" she whispered.

"Carter," I said.

"Very nice," Minnie said. "He sleeps with his boots on."

"He was exhausted, he just came back from New Jersey because Finn's trial is resuming."

Minnie crossed her arms. "You don't look good," she told me. "You look tired."

Minnie was right; when Carter and I walked to the court-house, I wanted to lean against a lamppost and rest. The court-room itself was stuffy and hot; I leaned my head on Carter's shoulder and closed my eyes. But when the court was called to order there was so much excitement in the room that I found myself sitting on the edge of my seat. Reno LeKnight walked in smiling like a cat; the district attorney eyed the defense bench uneasily. And while everyone carefully watched Reno Le-Knight, who was dressed that day in a blue velvet suit, the doors behind us opened; a wheelchair rolled down the aisle.

"It's him," Carter whispered. "The welder from New Jersey."

Reno LeKnight turned and pointed dramatically to the welder in the wheelchair. "Will Harris," Reno LeKnight cried. "Our next witness."

Will Harris wheeled himself up to the witness stand. Both of his legs were in heavy white casts, and several of his front teeth were missing, knocked out by the impact of his fall from the scaffolding. Reno LeKnight bent down and helped Harris from his chair, dragging the welder from New Jersey up to the stand like an offering. When Harris had been sworn and had stated his address and occupation, the welder looked at the defense table and nodded gravely to Finn.

Harris was questioned for over an hour; after that time, everyone in the courtroom knew how easy it was to reach for the wrong valve when a man was working twenty feet off the ground, when his eyes teared and he was surrounded by a haze of burning metal. Harris was astonished when the valve he installed shot out as soon as steam was let into the pipes by the testing crew. Harris had never expected to fly off the ladder and land twenty feet down, flat on his back on the cold hard cement. Even the judge and the district attorney winced in sympathy when Harris explained how he had felt when he flew off the scaffolding.

"I felt like I was looking God right in the face," the welder said. "I felt like my time had most definitely come."

"In summation," Reno LeKnight asked when it was clear to everyone how similar the welder's experience was to Finn's, "what would you say, based on your expertise in welding and your personal experience of twenty years, was the primary factor which led to the tragedy of the Elizabeth explosion?"

Will Harris chewed his lip. Then he looked Reno LeKnight in the eye. "Human error." He nodded thoughtfully. "Fucking human error is what blew up that plant," the welder announced as he tapped the cast on his left leg.

The judge raised both his arms in the air, he pleaded for the wisdom of Moses or Job; but because he had neither, he called a conference, in his chambers, with the district attorney and Reno LeKnight.

"What do you think?" I asked Carter when we had gone into the corridor during the recess.

"I think the case will be dismissed," Carter answered. "Unfortunately."

"Unfortunately for your cause," I said.

"My cause?" Carter sighed. "Jesus. Did you ever think that Finn himself might be better off if he had a cause? He might fight harder to survive if he were fighting for something more important than himself."

"Oh, Carter," I said, "I don't want to argue with you anymore."

"As soon as the trial is over I'm leaving to work out of the New Hampshire office. I've asked Finn to come with me, I've offered him a job."

"Thanks a lot," I said.

"But you said it was over between you. Don't forget I'll have to pay Finn's salary out of my own pocket."

"You can afford it."

"Don't be angry," Carter said. "Try to understand, Soft Skies may be what Finn's been searching for all of his life."

When we went back into the courtroom, I still could not believe that a political organization was what Finn had been seeking for so long. I was convinced that what he had been looking for, what had been missing from his life, could be found within, planted in his memory like a row of perfect roses.

Reno was the first to come out of the conference. He ran to whisper in his client's ear.

As Carter had expected, the judge announced that the state thought it best to drop the charges against Michael Finn because of the related circumstances in the New Jersey case. Both the prosecuting attorney and the defense attorney had decided that the case could be taken no further.

"We apologize to everyone whose time was wasted by this trial," the judge said. "And I would like to thank you all"—he nodded to Michael Finn—"for your patience and your time."

Carter and I stayed in our seats as the courtroom cleared; the crowd left quickly, having witnessed a trial that never should have taken place. No one ran to embrace Michael Finn, although both the district attorney and the judge walked over to congratulate Reno LeKnight. By the time Carter and I walked up to the bench, the courtroom was as deserted as the harbor at dawn; the only sound was the soft whirring of the radiators and the shuffling of paper as Reno LeKnight packed up his briefcase.

"It's all over," Reno said as he clicked his briefcase shut. "Come on, I'll buy you a drink," he said to Finn. "Because now you are a free man."

I watched for the beating of Finn's heart beneath the linen shirt, the borrowed blue suit. Even when Carter went up and embraced Finn as if they had been brothers, Finn's breath came in short, shallow gulps, not at all the crazy sighs of a free man.

When Reno invited Carter and me to join in a celebration at the Modern Times, I thought first of saying no. And although I tried to shake off any hopes for a reunion, the hope was still there, floating just below the courthouse ceiling which had been carved out of mahogany in the time when whaling boats still set out from the harbor, and women selling scallops and clams called out as they walked down Main Street.

When the four of us walked on to celebrate Finn's victory, Finn hung back; he walked carefully, as if he was afraid that if he went too fast he would slip. All of us were quiet as we walked, no one's feet lifted off the pavement in a soft and desperate dance of victory, no backs were slapped, no lips touched. Fishers Cove had never seemed quite so lonely. It was as deserted as it must have been years before, when ships still sailed, and a man like Finn was likely to be on board, perhaps tasting salt on his lips for the first time, a sailor who left the protection of the harbor to know he was free the moment he saw what constellations rose above the waves.

TWO

$\mathcal{W}$ E CELEBRATED WITH GIN
and whiskey—except Finn, who wouldn't touch his drink. He
had barely said a word, but Reno LeKnight was ready to talk
for all of us.

"Tomorrow I leave for Westchester," the attorney told us.
"Two kidnappers. A fabulous case. Not that you weren't interesting," he said to Finn, "but these two guys are guilty as sin."

"I was guilty," Finn said.

"Yes, but no one believed you were," LeKnight said.
"There's no doubt when it comes to these kidnappers. The vic-
tim was found in the trunk of their car. With you, there was
always some doubt, whether or not you were guilty was all up
to what was inside your head when the valve was installed."

"Sorry," Finn said.

"Hey, don't worry about it," Reno said. "We won, didn't
we?"

After Reno had paid our bill, he turned to Carter. "I think
you got your money's worth."

"Money's worth," Carter muttered after the attorney had

gone. "The second unit is being rebuilt, so what did I get? I'll be here until the day all of Angel Landing is closed down."

Finn still looked as gloomy as if he'd been sentenced to a life term, but he had begun to drink, and once he had started he ordered a second gin and tonic and then a third.

"This is some celebration," Carter said.

"Sorry." Finn shrugged.

"Have you made up your mind yet?" Carter now asked Finn.

"About what?" Finn cracked the ice cubes between his teeth.

"I'm going to New Hampshire for a meeting, and I think you should go up there with me. You know, you can't be tried on the same charges twice. You can come out with the truth now, you can let people know what really happened."

"Well, I just need some time," Finn said.

"I've got news for you," Carter told Finn. "There isn't any time. We're racing against the clock, and talking about survival. Tell him, Nat."

"Survival." I nodded, though I couldn't imagine Carter and Finn working side by side in New Hampshire.

"Well, I'm not going anywhere right now," Finn said. "I'm not going anywhere at all, understand?"

"All right," Carter said. "At least I tried." He stood up. "If you decide you want to help me close down Angel Landing Three," he said, "I'll be back from New Hampshire next week. That goes for you, too," he said to me. "And if you feel you have other things to do which are more important," Carter said as he kissed me goodbye, "I'll understand that, too."

Without either Carter or Reno, there was no way around it:

Finn and I were the only two people at the bar, although no one would have guessed we were together.

"Congratulations," I said to Finn.

"Isn't it wonderful?" Finn said.

"What do you do now?" I asked him.

"I have a drink," Finn said. "Alone. What the fuck do you think I do?"

"Forget it," I said, turning quickly away and reaching for my drink.

"What the hell kind of question is that?" Finn said. "What do you do now?" he mimicked. "Shit."

"Let's not talk about it anymore," I suggested, my back to him.

"You think I should give lectures with Sugarland about nuclear power?" Finn went on. "Maybe a corporation would like to hire me as a consultant. Maybe I'll write the story of my life."

"Forget it," I said.

"Everyone asks me what I'm going to do," Finn said. "What the hell is different? My life is still the same. The only difference is now I'll be asked to leave the union. I'll have even lousier jobs, lousier pay."

"You don't have to do that," I said.

"You don't know anything about it, nothing at all, so keep quiet," Finn said.

"Fine," I said. "Fine."

"You people who think everyone has control of his own life don't know anything," Finn said.

"Let's not talk about it anymore," I said.

Finn's hands were shaking, and he finished his third gin in one gulp. "I've told you before," he said, as he signaled the bartender for another drink, "I only want things I know I can't have."

"You're so wrong," I said.

"You say that now. But I know what would happen. I've seen it happen before. Men start wishing for things, wanting things, and they start going crazy, it gets into their blood. Better not to," Finn said. "Much better."

I ordered another whiskey and soda and turned to watch the men in the barroom who were reaching for their drinks, men who were long past middle age, long past wishing for a different sort of life. They ordered whiskey and beer and remembered when they were still young enough to believe their day would come: then they would quit the jobs they hated, the lives that took away everything they had. One of those men got up from a table at the rear of the room, left his drink, walked up to the bar, and stood behind his son.

When Finn felt someone behind him, he turned. "Pop," he said.

"I couldn't make it to the trial," Danny Finn said. "I've been working at the power plant ever since it reopened."

"It was all just a stupid mistake," Michael Finn said.

"Hey, what did you think?" Danny Finn said. "Did you think you were too good to make a mistake? Shit, everybody makes a mistake."

The two men did not look at each other as they spoke.

"Would you like a drink?" I asked Danny Finn.

"I've got one," Danny Finn responded. "Back at my table." He turned to Michael, who was reaching for his glass. "When are you going to start working again?" Danny Finn asked him.

"I don't know if I'm still a member of the union," Michael Finn said.

"You'd Goddamn better believe you are," Danny Finn said. "I saw to it."

"I'll probably have to take nonunion jobs."

"I told you don't worry about it," Danny Finn said. "We had a vote, and I saw to it that you were voted in. I stood up and told them I would know who voted against you, and I would remember that fucker, and I would be watching him, because somebody makes a mistake every day at the job, and even if they didn't get caught or have something blow up on them, I would know. I'd be watching."

"What did they say?" Finn asked.

"They didn't say anything," Danny Finn said. "They just voted you in."

Finn turned to face his father. "You did that?"

"And I would have known who voted against you," Danny Finn went on. "Nick Albert, who counts the ballots, was going to let me see every one marked with an X if you were voted out."

If Finn had held his glass any tighter it would have burst in his hands; gin would have fallen in between his fingers and into the hollows of his palms. "You said all that?" he asked.

"Sure," Danny Finn said. "So when do you think you're coming back to work?"

Michael Finn didn't answer.

"You can't find better money," Danny Finn said.

"I've gotten a couple of other offers," Michael Finn said.

"Oh, yeah?"

"I've got an offer up in Massachusetts. I may even be offered something in California," Finn went on.

"California," Danny Finn said. "I'm impressed."

"I've got to weigh the pros and cons," Michael Finn said so softly I could barely hear him. "You understand," he said to his father.

"This offer union work?" Danny Finn asked.

"No, no," Michael Finn said. "But there's a lot of money in the deal."

There were no offers from California, no big money, I knew; but Finn was trying to give his father something in return for standing up at the union meeting. He was giving out hope, a story to tell the other welders, a son to be proud of.

"You let us know what happens about California," Danny Finn said. "Your mother will want to know." He reached out and touched Finn's shoulder. There was a flutter; it seemed that a nerve had been touched right through the suit jacket and the clean white shirt. "And, son, if things don't work out, I'll see you at the plant next week," Danny Finn said.

"Sure," Michael Finn said. "Next week."

Michael Finn didn't move or speak until Danny Finn had left us and returned to his table, where his beer had grown flat. Though they were on different sides of the room, the two men were closer than they had ever been before. Danny Finn was proudly announcing to a table full of construction workers that his son had just beaten a trumped-up rap and now had an offer in California for big money. His son, Danny Finn smiled, was too smart for cops and district attorneys; someday the boy would be rolling in cash, and Danny Finn always knew it, or at least had always hoped for it; he had dreamed of his son's success in his private hours when no one could even guess that he ever had dreams.

And at the bar, where he had just begun another gin and tonic, Michael Finn's eyes were damp. "Son. He never called me that before. Not to my face."

"Let's go outside," I suggested, reaching for Finn's coat and my own and paying for our drinks. I expected an argument. I thought Finn would refuse to walk outside with me, but instead he nodded and followed me out the door. We walked with no destination, with no purpose other than a need for darkness and clean air. We walked west on Route 18. Even without looking, I knew Finn was crying. Up on Main Street some stray dogs bayed, and the howl shook the night as if it had come from Finn's own throat.

We found ourselves down at the harbor; in only a few months the parking lot where we stood would be crowded with cars: in the morning vans carrying groups of swimmers, in the evenings the Chevys and Fords of lovers who had nowhere else to go. But now, ice covered the parking lot, as it had years before when Michael Finn and his father crouched and hid their heads from the shadows they were most afraid of. The wind from Connecticut hit against us; sleeping gulls, frightened by our presence, flapped their wings and took off, flying unevenly. Michael Finn looked as if he wished he could throw back his head and howl along with the chorus of strays on Main Street.

Suddenly Finn spoke. "I always wanted him to say it."

It would never be enough to make up for years of sadness, the hours of wasted rage, but Danny Finn had reached across the years, he had called Michael son, their terrible bond was now a fragile rope.

"I'm not even like him," Finn said, taking my hand for a moment and then letting it fall. "I'm really not," he said. "Not at all."

He looked at his hands: the blisters, the blue veins, the nails topped by half-moons; they were nobody else's hands, no palms of ancestors, they were his alone.

We stayed in the parking lot until Finn was finished; and although there were times when I thought he would never be done crying, when he faced into the wind and closed his eyes and let all the pain free, running down his face, finally he did turn away.

"Are you sure you're ready to leave?" I asked.

Finn wiped his eyes with his palms. "Yeah, I'm ready," he said.

I hesitated; ready to go where, ready to do what? When we walked away from the parking lot, would we walk in opposite directions, would we wave to each other from a street corner?

"Come on," Finn said. "I'll walk you home."

We walked toward town, I put my hands in my pockets so I wouldn't be tempted to take Finn's hand. Every step I took hurt, I walked on daggers, on hot blue fire. Not holding him was like not breathing, not being quite alive.

As we walked, Finn's tears continued to fall, but he ignored them, he brushed them away as if crying in the night was the most natural thing a man could do.

"It's crazy," Finn grinned. "The tightness in my chest is gone. It's disappeared."

"I knew it would happen," I said to Finn.

"You did, didn't you?" Finn smiled.

It had been happening since the first time I met Finn; the

past had been unwinding inside him, and with it all the terror and pain he had tried to ignore for so long.

"I can breathe," Finn said, taking in air. "I can breathe," he told me, delighted.

I tried to walk as slowly as I could, I tried to make it last forever. But when Minnie's house came into view, I knew I would soon be standing outside her front door, and Finn would nod, and grin, and disappear forever.

I stopped on a street corner. "Do you mind," I asked Finn, "if I ask you now what you plan to do?"

"Do?" Finn said. He leaned against a lamppost and reached into his pocket for a cigarette. "I don't really think that matters." He cupped the match in his hand and bent down. "Anything," Finn said. "As long as it's new. As long as it keeps the past in its place."

I was part of that past, I was probably fading right before his eyes.

"I'm leaving town," I said. If I stayed there would be too many things to remind me of Finn; every coffee shop, every street in town. I would take a room until I found an apartment. On summer nights I would swim in the ocean, or in a town pool ringed by lifeguards. And after swimming, when my hair was still wet, I would walk home. Sand would stick to my bare feet. The roses and the jasmine would smell so strong that when I opened the window in my room I would nearly grow dizzy from their scent. I would sit by the window, fanning myself with a Miami newspaper that was long out of date, and later I would write a letter to Minnie and one of my local congressmen. And when the winter came I wouldn't even notice; the jasmine might give way to zinnias, but there would be no ice, no cold stars, no harbor to remind me of Finn. No one would haunt my dreams when I fell asleep on clean white sheets beneath a tier of mosquito netting. "I think I may be going to Florida," I told Finn. "I've applied for a job there. Therapy doesn't seem to be what I'm best at."

"You were good for me," Finn said.

"I was never your therapist," I said.

"What do you mean?" Finn said. "Of course you were."

"We just talked," I said. "That's all."

"I don't care," Finn said. "I'm glad you hadn't already gone to Florida that day I walked into Outreach." I looked up at him. "I am, you know." He smiled.

We stayed on that street corner until Finn had finished his cigarette.

"Thank you," Finn said to me. He took my hand in his as if we were about to shake hands, but instead he held my fingers entwined with his own, he pressed hard, and then let go. I left then, I turned and ran, I couldn't bear for him to walk away from me. And when I had crossed the street and stood in front of Minnie's house, I turned, but he was gone.

Finn had left. From now on he might only appear on an occasional night when the temperature rose over ninety and the past was like a fever which refused to be still. I went home then to a house that was so quiet I could almost hear the breathing of the sleepers on the second floor: Minnie, the two sisters beneath matching blankets, Arthur with his head on a clean linen pillowcase. I left my coat on and went into the parlor; when I heard Beaumont hammering in the basement I was relieved, calmed by the steadiness, and the sound of wood and nails. I picked up a goblet and then wondered if Minnie and Alex had both drunk from the crystal glass I now used, one of a set presented by a Lansky from Detroit. Or perhaps Minnie had never drunk sherry before Alex's death; maybe one night, when Alex had already been dead for some time, Minnie was unable to sleep. She may have come into the parlor dressed in a flannel nightdress mailed to her from one of the Manhattan Lanskys who worked in the 34th Street Macy's. Then Minnie may have sat in the easy chair and wondered how many more days she would have to live, how many more nights she would sleep alone.

She may have even tried to conjure up Alex right there in the parlor; even if she didn't believe in spirits. But that night in winter, Minnie may have found that she wasn't able to recall what Alex had looked like as a man, she could only remember him as a very young boy, as he was when she first met him.

It was then that Minnie would reach for the bottle of sherry she kept in the parlor in case a guest should be accustomed to drinking. She would pour the liquor into a small crystal glass and then raise a toast to that invisible boy she had once known, the boy who had slowly replaced the memory of the man she had been married to for so many years. It was as if, so many years after his death, the two of them were starting all over again; only this time there would be no ending, no sadness to forget; Alex would be a young boy forever—all other memories had been slowly washed away. I, too, poured myself a drink; and I also raised my glass, in memory of Finn, and then I sat down in the easy chair and proceeded to try to forget.

THREE

A LETTER CAME FROM THE
agency in Florida sooner than I expected. I would receive six
thousand dollars a year and the use of a three-speed bicycle the
previous worker had left behind. Already, reservations had been
made in my name at the Blue Parrot Motel; the bicycle could
be found around the back, waiting for me behind the soda
machine. It was much more difficult than I had ever dreamed
to tell Minnie that I was leaving.

"Florida?" Minnie said. "There are alligators there. The temperature goes over a hundred, people eat nothing but grits and
Coca-Cola."

"I'll be working for a grievance committee of workers from
a nuclear power plant," I said.

"You?" Minnie said, cocking her head. She leaned back in
her chair and folded her arms. "A political job?"

"I know I haven't done anything like it in the past."

"I'll say," Minnie agreed.

"I thought you'd be pleased," I said, disappointed by such a
cool reaction.

"Don't run off to Florida to please me," Minnie said. "If I

had wanted that sort of relationship with someone, I could have had a child."

"Well, I've agreed to take the job," I said.

"Why Florida?" Minnie said. "What's wrong with Angel Landing? We have our own power plant right here."

"You always told me to try something new."

"That's true," Minnie said. "But you'll have to stay a while. I'm having a party. You'll leave after that."

"All right," I said.

My aunt looked at me. "What about Michael Finn?"

"The past," I said. "All in the past."

"I certainly hope you're not running off to do good works just because of the lousy state of your personal life," Minnie warned. "That sort of thing never works out."

"It's nothing like that," I said.

Minnie left the table abruptly and went to the stove, where she put up water; she stood there until steam began to rise. Finally she turned back and faced me. "You're going to Florida," she said.

"That's right," I said, accepting the cup of peppermint tea placed before me.

"I'm going to miss you," Minnie said.

"Oh, Minnie," I said. I would never have believed I would be so sad to leave my aunt's house.

"Naturally, I have my own life to lead," Minnie went on. "And I'm pretty damn busy. In fact there's someone at Mercy who could use your room, there's no reason for her to be in a home, she's as strong as an ox. One day one of her earrings fell off and rolled onto the floor. She picked up the bed to find it. But all the same," Minnie said, "I'm going to miss you."

"You can visit."

"I wouldn't step a foot into Florida," Minnie told me. "Old people live to be a hundred in Russia and Maine, never in Florida. It's a place for young people," she said. "Young people and mosquitoes."

"Then I'll visit you," I said.

Minnie waved her hand in the air. "We'll see."

While we had our tea our sadness circled the kitchen as if a jar full of blue moths had been let out to spin across the room.

"We'll think about the party," Minnie suggested. "That will keep us busy for the next week."

"Yes," I agreed softly. "That's what we'll do."

We spent the next few days cleaning house, burning off our anxiety with vacuum cleaners and brooms. After we had made whole-wheat dough for pastries or scrubbed the windows till they shone like crystal, I would go upstairs and pack. Suitcases lined my bedroom, everything I owned was slowly, carefully catalogued and put away. The night of the party came much too quickly, it came just as I was clicking the last suitcase shut. Soon, Beaumont would be driving carloads of old folks out to the house; soon I would be on a southbound bus. But Minnie refused to allow me time to sit down and weep; even when the house was spotless and all the food was set out on china platters, she thought of errands to keep me busy. When she could think of nothing else, Minnie sent me out to the health food store to pick up some last-minute extras we really didn't need.

I walked down Main Street for the last time; in the morning, before sunrise, before anyone else in the house was awake, Beaumont would drive me to the bus station. I would ride for hours, for days, watching the ice melt, waiting for the palm trees, looking for the white flowers that grew along the highway like weeds.

I stood on the pavement outside the window of the Green-wood Natural Foods Store. When I walked inside it took a while before my eyes adjusted; it took some time before I realized that the cashier, who was recommending golden seal tea to a young woman who complained of frequent headaches and colds, was Jack, the truant.

I picked out the herbs and honey candies Minnie wanted, and when the other shopper had left, I went up to the register. "Jack," I said, "I never expected to see you here."

Jack smiled. "Hey this is terrific," he said. "I didn't know you were into natural foods." He looked down at the packages of candy I put on the counter. "This stuff is all natural, sure, no sugar, but you can't live on sweets alone," Jack advised.

"This is all for a party," I explained. "What about you?" I asked. "You're involved with natural foods?"

"Your aunt was the first to turn me on to it," Jack confided as he rang up my purchases and packed them in a recycled brown bag. "No more cafeteria lunches of sugar and starch for me," he smiled. "I turned sixteen and dropped out of school. Though now I'm trying to get a program of natural lunches started in the public school system. What about you?"

"Me?" I said. "I'm going to Florida."

"Fantastic," Jack beamed, handing me my change. "I can just imagine the kind of produce you can get down there."

After I left the store, Jack stood by the window; he smiled and waved like the sunny twin of the boy who had once sat so dejectedly in the Outreach office. I thought about Jack and my other clients all the way home. Even after I had gone upstairs to dress for the party I couldn't help thinking how well they were all doing without me. Lark reported that Susan was cheerfully attending EMOTE meetings, carrying with her a list of her daily calorie intake. Jack had smiled more at the mention of Florida oranges and lemons than I had seen him smile in all our months together at Outreach.

"You know," I said to Minnie when we had begun to set out the crystal wine goblets in the dining room. "I'm certain I made the right decision. Leaving Outreach wasn't a mistake."

"We never know about these things, do we?" Minnie said.

"Well, tell me what you think," I insisted, because after this night there would be no going back; the bus would move down the highway right on schedule.

Minnie sat in a dining-room chair and sighed. "What can I tell you?" she said. "How do I know what's right or wrong? I don't even know if starting this home for old people is a good idea—I may become so rejuvenated that I live past ninety-five. Who can tell?"

I reached into the bureau drawer where the silverware had been stored since Minnie and Alex first came to Fishers Cove. "I wish I could know what will happen," I said.

"Not me," Minnie said. "I don't want to know. If a fortuneteller came to my door right now, I'd kick her off the porch, I'd toss her back into the snow, I'd throw out her tea leaves and her tarot cards. It's much better not to know. Otherwise it would be like reading the last page of a novel. Why would you ever bother reading the whole book?"

"You never read novels at all," I reminded Minnie.

"True," Minnie said. "I never do. But all the same, I would get rid of that fortuneteller as soon as I saw her at the door."

If it was I who heard the knocking at the door, if I saw some fortuneteller out on the ice with a blue turban wrapped around her skull and a pack of tarot cards tucked into the sleeve of her Persian lamb coat, I would not be so certain what to do. I would stand at the door, undecided; by the time I sent her away, snow would have blown into the hallway and I would be shivering.

"We don't have to read tea leaves to know we'll see each other again," Minnie said.

"Of course," I said.

I watched as Minnie laid out the natural candies I had bought. She did it slowly, carefully, as if the design of each candy dish would be terribly important to Arthur and the sisters and the others Beaumont was now bringing over from Mercy. After she had finished and each almond and honeyed bit of pineapple was in just the right place, Minnie went upstairs to dress. When she had left the dining room, and Arthur and the sisters had begun to set up card tables in the parlor, I sneaked downstairs to the basement.

I was certain that Beaumont would not return for some time; still, I did not switch the lights on. I walked down the wooden steps like a nighttime creature afraid of seeing too much. Each step creaked so loudly I was certain that Minnie would hear me invading her tenant's privacy when she returned to the parlor. But soon the phonograph was turned on, and no one seemed to notice I was missing. I crouched to avoid the pipes which hung from the ceiling, pipes which had forced Beaumont to walk with a permanent stoop. But I didn't have the boarder's night sense, and I tripped over my own feet and fell into Beaumont's lifelong project—his raft. I twisted my ankle and landed inside the raft, sprawled out on my back. I reached into my pocket for a match; then I was able to see, to my surprise, that the raft itself was not made of wood. It was a huge inflated rubber raft, and built right in the middle was a small, perfect house made of redwood and oak. There were two oval windows, a handmade door with a brass doorknob, and dark shingles on the roof. I found a candle on the floor. I lit it and it released the odor of jasmine.

Certainly, in all the years Beaumont had lived in the house, Minnie must have seen the raft. She must have realized that it was much too large ever to be removed from the house—it could have never been lifted up the steps, out the basement door, or squeezed through the one small window. It was, quite obviously, a raft which was never meant to go anywhere at all.

I sat on the side of the raft, my hand out, resting on concrete rather than salt water. In a corner of the basement was a small pot-bellied stove which Beaumont must have planned to add to his raft house, and scattered around with bits of wood and nails, tools that would lead to more work, to perfection. This was a project that would take forever, a project never meant to be finished. If a tornado lifted Minnie's house right off its foundations, and the raft was finally set free, Beaumont probably would have chosen not to move an inch; he would have raised a tent to protect the redwood from the dangers of snow or rain, and chosen to remain on land.

I sat on the deck like a sailor, then leaned back like a passenger on a lazy cruise. Even when I heard the Mustang pull into the driveway, I didn't budge; Beaumont and the others would be joining the party upstairs; none of them would guess I was here in the raft which would never sail, never be sighted in the Florida waters, not if I watched from my window at the Blue Parrot Motel for a hundred years.

When I decided to blow out the candle, the scent of jasmine was even stronger. The longer I stayed in the raft the more it seemed to move, just as if it traveled in a China blue sea; I expected my fingers to touch the cresting waves. The raft moved faster all the time, with such enormous speed I wouldn't have thought of hiding when the basement door opened, even though I had not been invited on board. When the door opened wider and light from upstairs filtered down I didn't move an inch. I watched for a shadow on the wall as if I were charting stars; I listened for boot heels hitting the wooden basement steps as if I were a sailor expecting lightning.

I was on the raft, dipping through crazy blue waters, guided by silvery fish swimming just above the waves. I saw now that shadow moving down the wall didn't have Beaumont's stoop. It wasn't the old boarder; it was Michael Finn.

"I'm going with you," Finn said to me.

He reached out his hand and helped me from the raft; I held tight, but there wasn't any reason to hurry. Soon enough I would be coming home to him through the hot Florida night. After dinner I would write Carter a letter, asking him for news of Angel Landing and letting him know how difficult the struggle was against a power plant that was already functioning, already claiming victims with slow poison.

But at night, in climates as hot as ours, there was no sense in struggling. As soon as darkness fell we felt calm; evenings lasted forever, evenings were ours. And so we would wave mosquitoes away with our hands and walk down the road that led to the Gulf. Finn and I would stare out to sea, thankful that the night had brought cool air from deep inside Mexico; then we would bend to wash our hands in the slow southern current. Later, as we walked back, the stars would be low in the sky, and the song of crickets and frogs would urge us on.